PRAISE FOR MOLLY MOLLOY & THE ANGEL OF DEATH

"A quiet masterpiece...intimate & strange & real all at once. One read isn't enough."

— ADRIANA ANDERS, AWARD-WINNING AUTHOR
OF *WHITEOUT*

"Heartbreaking & humorous...unexpected as it is gorgeous. I adore this book."

— JOSEPHINE ANGELINI, BESTSELLING AUTHOR
OF *STARCROSSED*

"One of the loveliest, most unique, most thoughtful, and ultimately best books I have ever read. I loved every second of it."

— JESS HARDY, BESTSELLING AUTHOR OF *COME
AS YOU ARE*

MOLLY MOLLOY AND THE ANGEL OF DEATH

MARIA VALE

SUNGRAZER
PUBLISHING

Published by Sungrazer Publishing.
ISBN: 979-8-9878321-3-4

Names: Vale, Maria, author
Title: Molly Molloy & the Angel of Death
Subjects: LCSH: Fantasy fiction, American| Speculative fiction |GSAFD: Love
stories.| Occult fiction.

Cover design and illustration
by Victoria Heath Silk

*Content warning: This book contains depictions of suicide, physical abuse, and sexual
assault.*

For M, H & G
Life is the day to day living of it.
With you.

PART I
THE BOOK OF
ADMONISHMENTS

CHAPTER 1

$\mathcal{N}$eil Steinhauer occasionally thought about Janine. She'd been very sweet and liked him, possibly loved him. Well, probably not loved, but she would have married him, if he'd asked. He hadn't asked because he thought he could get someone prettier. Someone who showed better at office parties and reunions.

It hadn't happened that way and now in his sixties, Steinhauer was ten years past giving up. The skin of his hands had thickened and dried and he had one (borrowed) kidney and nine toes. Everyone who saw him at the Donut Hole in Harrow watched disapprovingly when he bought three jelly-filled.

Then he shuffled painfully past the censorious line waiting for Chillattas and died.

At which point Neil Steinhauer's part in the salvation of the world was done and taken up by a raspberry jelly-filled that Death took from Mr. Steinhauer's bag, because he was always hungry and because he knew any food in the immediate vicinity of the First World dead would be discarded.

Death's next appointments were in places that are typically called war-torn, as though war had only ripped them once, rather than shredding them time and time again like a Weed-whacker through bluegrass. So when Death entered the room in Mount Sinai, he pulled on the elbow-length rubber gloves he got by the gross from a restaurant supply shop on the Bowery and checked the first mirror he'd seen since eating Mr. Steinhauer's donut. There was powdered sugar on the lapel of his greatcoat. He shoved his list into one big outer pocket and flicked at the pale dusting.

Between the pocketing and the flicking, he rather lost track.

In the room, an ancient woman lay in her bed, her eyes closed, her mouth open. Although she was covered by a gown and sheet, Death knew that underneath, her body had shriveled and bruised around the places where tubes had been pushed in to extract some fluids and to insert others.

He missed the days when the whole family gathered at home and the old people would give away the teapot to this one and the cow to that one and when he touched them, the old men and older women would smile at him, because they knew that he wasn't a problem to be solved by intubation.

At least this one wasn't alone. There was a young woman next to her wolfing something down. Her head was bent low over the box, her lips smeared bright orange.

Chicken wings, by the looks of it.

Slow down, Death thought, patting her absently on the back.

She coughed once, then wiped her mouth on a stained napkin.

After looking at him for a disconcertingly long moment during which Death dusted his lapel again, she said, "You're here for my grandmother?"

Death craned his neck around to see who she was talking to.

"You. I'm talking to you."

"Me?" he said, alarm making his voice sound squeaky.

"You've come for my grandmother, right?"

Death looked toward the shriveled pile of blankets and nodded dumbly.

"Just a minute. I really gotta wash my hands," she said, wiggling her fingers in the air in between them.

"What?"

"The doctor said you could be coming at any time. But they've been saying that for years, so I wasn't quite sure I believed him. Can you give me a minute?"

"Yes?" Death squeaked again, then cleared his throat.

The girl headed to the sink and washed her face and hands in the pink antibacterial soap. She wiped her mouth on her sleeve. "Mind passing me a couple of paper towels?"

"Thanks," she said after he had. Then she held out the Styrofoam container filled with bright orange wings. "Want some? They're good but I'm kind of done."

Death had been called the Devourer of Worlds but that didn't mean he was above a meaty chicken wing, so he took one.

"Sorry," the girl said, pouring iced water from the mustard-yellow pitcher into a plastic glass, while Death flapped his hands in front of him, desperately gulping air that was doing nothing to cool his seared tongue. "I suppose I should have told you they're Atomic."

While he flapped and gulped, the girl leaned over her unconscious grandmother as though meaning to say something but an awkward moment later seemed to think better of it.

"I guess we're ready," she said, holding her grandmother's limp hand and looking at him expectantly.

Using the gloved hand that wasn't stained orange by Atomic sauce, Death pushed his fingers to the old woman's sunken abdomen just at her omphalos, the spot that whatever other tragedy hit in the womb, was always there. It was the place that tied the baby to its mother and through her to the whole long disastrous chain of humanity. It was the doorway of the soul. The entrance and the exit. The beginning and the end.

Most of the time the souls in failing bodies came easily, recognizing an escape from pain, from fear, from despair, or simply from having been around too long.

This one did not. He had to push in deeper, digging around until he found the stubborn old woman. He pulled hard, but she held on even harder. He buttressed one thick-soled black boot against the side rail and pulled with both hands.

Death felt more than a little embarrassed at making a muddle of things in front of his first audience ever in the history of this whole sordid adventure. To speed things up, he took out the sharp shard of obsidian he kept in his outer pocket and drew a line across the old woman's forehead. It didn't pierce the skin, but her soul zipped up like a roller blind in an old cartoon.

Then with one more mighty tug, a length of velvety black emerged from the weakened body accompanied by a final breath.

"Do you always have trouble like that?" the young woman asked.

"N-no. Not usually," he said. He held the old woman's Rag high and swirled it expertly into his curved palm. Opening the oversized gray greatcoat that he'd been wearing ever since his well-worn cassock had gotten caught on a bayonet at Passchendaele, he slipped grandma's soul into a red flannel pocket, one of the multitude of tiny patches he'd sewn and resewn over the years.

"So," she said, "we done here?"

"I guess?" he said.

"Alrighty, then."

Then the young woman started to squeeze past him toward the door. He touched the warmth of her and took in the faint mossy scent beneath the smell of antibacterial soap and Betadine and habanero.

It made him feel uncomfortable and like he ought to say something to pretend he wasn't. "Until next time?" he offered.

She paused for a moment, one eyebrow slightly raised.

"You know what? Don't rush."

Yuh-oh, he thought. *This is going to be trouble.*

CHAPTER 2

*A*s soon as he got home, Death cleared out his overstuffed mailbox and headed upstairs to his apartment. Once there, he dropped the mail on his kitchen table and emptied his big outer pockets into the upside-down lime-green Cake Taker that sat on top of the chest he'd been schlepping around since the Second Babylonian Captivity.

Gently laying his coat across the futon, he retrieved the orange plastic laundry basket from the defunct fireplace. He'd fitted the basket with a liner sewed from a flannel blanket, so that even if it was full, none of the souls would slip through the cutouts that served as handles.

He carefully unloaded each of the little inner pockets of his coat, pausing for a moment with the struggling Rag he had collected with such difficulty at Mt. Sinai, before dropping it among all the other writhing splotches of charcoal and black.

As soon as he was done, the basket disappeared with a hushed whoosh.

Death retrieved a new box of Peanut Butter Crunch from a shelf filled with them and pulling either side of the waxy bag, opened it with no tears, an act that always gave him inordinate satisfaction.

Hunched over his large bowl, he looked through the pile of letters and free magazines. He set aside an Intimate Male catalog addressed to Resident for later and started reading the cards addressed to Dear Friend or Valued Neighbor. Their congenial concern for his well-being always made him feel appreciated, which was no small thing in his line of work.

He didn't bother to look when his laundry basket—empty now—fell back to the floor with a loud thunk.

Death'd been doing this job for 197,856 years, ever since that woman in that cave held her babies close and thought, *I am going to die.* Not in the specific, *I am being eaten by this larger, hungrier creature* or *I am sinking into this smelly, inescapable bog,* but in the more existential, *I am alive now and I will not always be and I am afraid.*

At that moment, the stinking, lice-ridden, combative, sex-mad, perpetually decaying, fearful animals became human and, it had been decided, they needed a psychopomp, someone to guide them through the transition from the existence they were now aware they had.

That someone would have to live among the stinking, lice-ridden, combative, sex-mad, perpetually decaying, fearful humans. There was a lot of nervous shuffling among the Custodes Rectorum, the Keepers of Righteousness. Quick side-long glances were followed by the holding of hands smelling faintly of frankincense to delicate upturned noses. Then someone—Death always suspected it was that jerk Salaphiel—called out, "How about Azrael?"

A murmur swept through the Custodes. They all agreed it made sense: Azrael had failed Righteousness four times, was always the last chosen for any game of Obedience, a complete botch-up at Venerating (Are you sure you know what you're doing? Sanctus, Sanctus) and sang all the time even though he couldn't carry a tune.

More to the point, it would keep him busy, keep him out of trouble because, well, they all remembered what happened last time.

Plus nobody else wanted the job.

Azrael had some reservations but then he'd looked at the prissy Hosanna singers to the right of him and the prissy Hosanna singers to the left at which point he said, "Oh, what the hey."

A sigh of relief blew across the heavens like a jasmine-scented wind on an evening in Sorrento.

We'll visit, they'd promised, patting him wanly on the back.

"Don't bother," he'd responded and leaned backward, letting himself fall through the ether. When he landed, he was no longer Azrael. He was Death, the Gray Walker, the Pale Rider, the Dark Companion and many other descriptive turns of phrase, though in fact the only time any human had seen him was at the exact millisecond they snuffed it, which went some way toward explaining the diversity of opinion as to his appearance.

Death wiped out his bowl and set it on the grooved, enameled drainboard.

One thing was sure: that girl had seen him, not only seen him, but recognized him, talked to him. Bossed him around. Offered him a chicken wing then poured him a glass of water. Watched him struggle.

Then she'd made it clear that she didn't want to see him any more than he wanted to see her.

To distract himself, Death sat on his futon with the Intimate Male catalog in one hand and his obsidian blade in the other.

He'd started out like every other Custodes, with—"Eyes to Gaze, Lips to Praise, Hands to Raise and a Nose to Smell Out Corruption"—but then he'd started making changes. At first, he'd lengthened his nose and enlarged his eyes, explaining to anyone who asked that it was necessary because the stench was strong and the light was weak.

Other changes, he hid. He didn't want to have to explain, as he knew he would, that his body looked so bland, so empty by comparison to the variety of muscle, fat, color, hair, scars, moles, bone and all the other baroque embellishments of mortality.

Here, for example. He looked at the picture on the cover of the Intimate Male Big Blowout Sale catalog. This man walked through the surf wearing nothing but white beach pants that were on sale for $35. There was so much complexity: the graceful broad ridge at the top of his chest. Two big bulgy bits with teeny-tiny, dark bulgy bits on top. Like muffin tops with a chocolate chip plunked down in the middle of each. A series of lumps divided down the middle that looked like a big cicada shell. Dark hair scattered all over.

He'd been working on ribs for the better part of a century. So far, they were just a few shallow runnels, palpable, but not visible. He pulled up his T-shirt and felt for them. Then he cut through the celestial material of his body with his obsidian blade. Even as he watched, the furrow began to close.

Just as he started to cut into the second runnel, he smelled frankincense and a silvery swirl appeared at the foot of his futon. "RAGPICKER!" intoned a voice.

Death quickly pulled his duvet up to his chin. "Lo, Jophiel. Don't suppose this could wait until later?"

"Later?" Jophiel repeated, before spouting one of the aphorisms the Custodes used to try to make sense of any word having to do with time. "We are when nothing was?"

"Nevermind."

Like all Custodes, Jophiel was timeless, existing then and now and at all points in-between. It made Death queasy keeping track of all those simultaneous existences melding together into a shimmering worm of his iterations: Jophiel as he first arrived and every Jophiel since with the Jophiel of now at their head. And they all talked at the same time. The copy at the very end of the worm would continue to shout RAGPICKER! in an endless loop until Jophiel went back Up.

He'd been the same when he'd first become Death. At the time, humans were still very sparse on the ground, so there was something comforting about the constant companionship of his past selves.

Then humans started settling and grouping together and reproducing at an alarming rate. The settling and grouping was followed quickly by plagues and wars and other large slaughtering events and Death had begun to find it confusing, always bumping into his earlier selves still spelunking around in the empty omphaloi of the already dead.

So he'd gone native, as Abdiel said with disgust, existing in one moment before moving on to another. Just him. Like a human. Except for the part about never dying.

Death hadn't told Abdiel about the other thing. About how he'd learned to make any particular moment stretch out infinitely. There had been a time when humanity pirouetted on the edge of extinction. With only 2,000 souls, Abdiel worried that Death wasn't being kept busy and signed him up for Group which was really just more Righteousness with the addition of Choir.

He hated Group.

"Abdiel is sending memoranda," announced Jophiel with the Custodes inability to conceive of any tense beyond the present. "You are not having the matter attended to." Then he indicated the discombobulated orange laundry basket and four intricately folded missives of celadon papyrus splayed across the floor.

Jophiel reached to the chain attached to the girdle around his robes. He pulled a pomander of chased mother-of-pearl to his nose. "Can we not be opening a window? The smell is absolutely sulfurous."

Then with his free hand, Jophiel reached once more into his robe and, pulling out a scroll, shook it open before passing it to Death.

CUSTODES RECTORUM
INDIVISIBILIS AETERNALIS ET IMMUTABILIS

Ragpicker,
On June 15, 2016 at 21:27:31:116, Mortal Standards,
you delivered the Rag of one Mary Molloy, although
the name on your list was clearly Molly Molloy. We
expect to see you immediately after purification.
Hallelujah,
Abdiel
P.S. read your mail, no one likes making these trips.

"WE ARE TELLING Abdiel of your coming?" asked Jophiel. "When you are purifying?"

"Yessss," Death said dully, his finger running once more over the scroll.

The sibilant had not yet left Death's tongue, when the Jophiel of now disappeared with a quick pop followed by a series of diminishing pops, until after one final disapproving RAGPICKER! the original Jophiel vanished, too.

Pop.

Death stared at the spot where Jophiel had been. With a sigh, he pulled himself up, tidied his bed, then went to his little bathroom and dropped a Dead Sea Salts and Sandalwood bath bomb into his tub before turning on the hot water spigot all the way. He made a few thousand pickups, allowing time and the water to run. When he returned, the tub was full. Stripping, he stepped into the scalding bath and scrubbed with a hard brush and myrrh soap. He dried himself with a fresh towel and pulled out the robes that he kept sealed in a dark green plastic suit bag.

They were clean and loose and disguised most of what he'd done to his body. He pulled on a pair of white Vans he'd taken after a mall shooting in Georgia and kept boxed up in the back of the closet for just this eventuality.

Then he jumped a few times until he grasped the bottom rung. It had been millennia since he'd last been Up, so he wasn't surprised that the ladder was more than a little balky. One more yank and it came down with a long squeal and a puff of dust. He started to climb.

"SISTE!" commanded a concerned voice when he was still a full league away.

"It's just the Ragpicker," called Death. "And yes, we have been purified."

He stopped to untangle his robe from the rubber bottoms of his Vans, then started again. From above, he could hear some muttering as well as the still echoing "SISTE!"

Where is our pomander? Puriel yelled at some underling because no matter how hard he scrubbed, the stench of the world clung to Death like gum to Doc Martens.

A few rungs short of his destination, Death shook out his robes, holding them down so they would be sure to cover his legs when he drifted Up.

"So, Puriel. Been awhile. How's tricks?"

"At Stewarding, we are hearing of error?" Puriel leaned forward with a kind of morbid curiosity before jerking back, his lapis pomander against his nose.

"You are not using the front peristyle."

"We know," said Death.

"You are using the back way."

"Yes."

"Yes."

The Peristyle looked exactly the same as it had last time he'd seen it. Four colonnades of celadon columns that stood in the middle of nothing. It was a pale, pointless reflection of architecture that sheltered no one and led nowhere. Not that there was anything to be sheltered from: There wasn't a sky, just an Above of celadon. There wasn't a ground, just a Below of celadon.

It all blended together at the horizon, a dizzying prospect with no discernible top or bottom or beginning or end. The Custodes like it that way. No top or bottom or then or now. No differences meant no decisions. No decisions meant no mistakes.

Death took a deep breath and started walking.

"The Back Way" was a vast emptiness leading to whispering Mangles where the real work was done. Death had read a phrase some time recently—within the last century, surely—about how no one wanted to see laws or sausages being made.

Death didn't really want to see how Rags were purified, either.

The hazy forms of Cherubim stood on either side of the Mangles feeding handfuls of struggling dark souls into enormous celadon rollers that sucked them in and by some process that even the Chief Administrator seemed unable to explain clearly, squeezed out the wanting and striving and trying that tormented them after their bodily captivity so that when they came out on the other side, they were still and bright, tumbling with other shining souls down troughs until they merged into the Mare Tranquilitatis, the Sea of Tranquility, ready to be released back Down, an unwitting soldier in the Custodes' struggle to bring back the stillness and grace of the Great Peace Before.

Death wasn't much for the Mare Tranquilitatis. But then he hadn't much cared for the Great Peace Before, either.

And he really didn't like the way the souls that he so carefully collected struggled against the Mangles.

"The Ragpicker are here," echoed a jittery Cherub, holding his elaborately chased and pierced pomander of rose quartz to his stubby nose.

"The Ragpicker is here," Death said sharply. "I am here."

"Ragpicker and I is here?" emended the blur, uncertainly.

All of the Cherubim held their pomanders to their noses as they watched Death walk past. One who had been feeding a Rag into a Mangle dropped his pomander and chased after it, leaving Nasreem Asif to wiggle silently between the giant rollers like a garter snake on a glue trap.

Death hurried past, his eyes fastened on the celadon under his Vans, until he reached the celadon door into the celadon room with confines hinted at by a slightly raised threshold but no walls. A celadon desk stood in the middle with the quite solid Abdiel. The Custodes' Chief Administrator rarely left his desk, which meant that Abdiel then was at his desk and Abdiel now was at his desk, so he coalesced into a comparatively firm shape, even if the outlines were shaky.

A celadon urn filled with scrolls stood on the left corner of Abdiel's desk. He kept a purified soul, opalescent and immobile, in the bottom of a long shallow dish on the right, so that he would always be reminded of what the Custodes were working toward.

Abdiel said nothing for a long time, just continued writing.

"So…" Death took a deep breath. "We made a mistake?"

Abdiel did not look up from his work.

"Do we remember Admonishments XIV?" Abdiel finally asked.

That was the other thing Death disliked about being Up. Someone always asking him about Admonishments and he'd rather let his studies lapse.

"**Oportet lavare manus?**"

"No, not 'employees must wash hands'? Think, Ragpicker."

"**Fregeris tu emeris?**"

"What in these circumstances would lead you to think of 'you break it, you buy it'?" Abdiel exhaled wearily. Then he took a deep breath and intoned "**Neglegentia inobedientia idem est,**" because Abdiel was known throughout the heavens for his intoning. "And why is carelessness the same as disobedience?"

Death thought back to his four failed attempts at Righteousness. He squinched up his eyes and thought, concentrating hard, but as hard as he concentrated he'd forgotten why a mistake was the same as disobedience.

"Because obedience is not simply doing a task, it is being devoted enough to that task, that you ignore anything that might mislead you," Abdiel snapped. "You made a mistake and were thus disobedient."

Abdiel's silver stylus flowed silently across the length of celadon papyrus. "We hear you breathing, Ragpicker. Hop to it. Or do you not have enough to do?"

BECAUSE SHE WASN'T DYING, Molly Molloy wasn't on his list. As far as the celestial accountants were concerned, she had died in Mt. Sinai and her file closed. Unable to track her down through any of the normal means, Death returned to Room 801, where Frank Spivak now lay. A nurse frozen in the moment of changing the dressing around Frank's port leaned her bottom against the chair where the girl had eaten Atomic wings only a few hours before. Frank had picked at his lunch tray, but hadn't touched the nutritionally balanced pudding "For Institutional Use Only," so Death rummaged in the big outer pocket where he kept his personal supplies and found his spork.

By the time he had reached the nurse's station, he had finished Frank's Nutritionally Balanced Pudding and threw the plastic cup in the trash, carefully licking off his spork before dropping it back in his pocket.

At the nurse's station, a wire-thin woman in purple scrubs

sat in front of a laptop. Death checked the frozen screen over her shoulder and got a whiff of her tropical melon body spray, which smelled nothing like the tropics or melons or bodies and made his nose itch.

Pulling on his rubber gloves, he moved the wire-thin woman's elbow and searched through the paper files until he found Mary Molloy.

Mary's ills were legion. High blood pressure, COPD, osteoarthritis, atherosclerosis. The list ran on and on. Craning his head, he found Mary's Manhattan Valley address, which was also the address of her granddaughter, Molly, who was listed as her contact.

He made a few stops. First to pick up the souls of a handful of miners in Queensland. Then running through the remains of a train wreck in the Belarus. In between, he dipped in and out of the rent-stabilized studio on 109th Street waiting for his schedule to coincide with that of the woman who was dead but just didn't know it yet.

Molly Molloy was in the tiny bathroom leaning over the sink and spitting out pink cinnamon-scented foam when he finally found her. He waited patiently for her to stand up so he could get a clear shot at her omphalos.

He had just started to slide his rubber-clad index finger and thumb under the waist of her pajama pants when her fist caught his jaw. Which wasn't the worst part. The worst part was that, as the bathroom was so small, he stumbled against the tub and lost his balance and grabbed at the shower curtain which pulled free from its rings with a pop-pop-pop-pop. He fell into the tub while the torn vinyl sheet of blue and green daisies floated over him.

"Ow," he said, feeling the squashed spot at the back of his head and when he looked up, the young woman was looming over him, menacing him with a toilet plunger.

"What are you doing here?" she asked, her voice as cold and

hard as the porcelain that had dented his head.

Death was flustered. This woman had agency, a thing he'd never had to deal with before and wasn't sure how to deal with now.

"I was trying to retrieve your Rag?"

"My what?"

"Your Rag. It's like your soul but, you know, scrottier."

She stared at him and he stared at her. "Are you a temp or something?"

"Attempt?" he asked, trying to puzzle out her question.

"No, a *temp*. Like a substitute. You could barely manage with my grandmother, who, by the way, absolutely everyone said should've died a decade ago. Then you sneak into my bathroom and try to kill me by manhandling my belly button. I don't think you have the slightest idea what you're doing."

"I most certainly do have the slightest idea what I'm doing," he said, with as much dignity as a man with his legs in the air being menaced by a toilet plunger could summon. "I've been Ragpicker for nearly 200,000 years and in all that time, I have never, ever *killed* anyone. Age kills, disease kills. Bullets kill. So do lawnmowers. They kill a weirdly large number," he said, momentarily distracted. "But not me. I don't kill anyone. All I do is facilitate transitions."

"'Facilitate transitions.' Is that what you call it?" The young woman straddled the side of the bathtub, the toilet plunger still hovering. "So seeing as I'm not old, not sick and there are no bullets or lawnmowers in my bathroom, you want to tell me what am I dying of?"

He raised himself slightly, trying to get at the pocket that was folded underneath him but Molly put one bare foot against his chest forcing him back down. Her foot was warm and had a beat inside that skipped like a stone on a still pond. When he inhaled, he caught a whiff of moss and salt and talcum powder.

"Just getting my list," he said, his other hand raised to the side. The girl's eyes narrowed. "It's in my coat."

Very slowly, he pulled the small silver scroll wrapped in fine celadon silk from one of his big outer pockets. "See?" He rolled it open until he reached a minuscule line of Aramaic. "That's you? Molly Molloy?" He held it up to her. "And it says you were supposed to die yesterday 21:27:31:116. Mount Sinai. Room 801. Cause of Death is listed as Chicken Wing."

"Chicken wing?"

"Well, so you see, there was powdered sugar on my coat? And your grandmother seriously did look like she was overripe and so when you were gagging, I was distracted and didn't put two and two together and come up with you choking to death on chicken wing. I made a mistake, I admit that, but the fact that you can talk to me proves that you're supposed to be dead." He moved his hips a little to make room in the tub. "People are only aware of me at the moment of death. You see me now and hear me now because you are on my time."

The girl's foot bore down harder and Death ran his mouth faster as he tried to explain to her about Mr. Steinhauer and the peculiar smell of old women dying in hospital beds and the mischief caused by Atomic wings.

"So you can see, I've got to get this sorted out."

"Or what?" Molly asked after a brief pause.

"Or *what* what?"

"What happens if you don't? Unless I'm very much mistaken, when you finish 'sorting this out,' I will be dead. Which is my least preferred option, so I'm asking what happens if you don't 'sort it out.' Does the world fall apart? Does someone else have to die in my place? You already have my grandmother."

Death stared up at her blankly. He didn't know how to answer "or what." You did what you were supposed to do *because* you were supposed to do it. End of story.

He didn't like the look in this woman's face. There must be

an Admonishment that would make her understand but he just couldn't think of it at the moment.

* * *

MOLLY TAPPED her bare foot against his chest.

How she'd known who he was, she couldn't say. Maybe it was the dreary regularity with which she bumped up against his disastrous consequences. He certainly did not look the way she would have expected. Smooth-faced with a long nose that was bent like it had been in one schoolyard brawl too many, he had pretty, very dark eyes, one of which was slightly larger than the other. Instead of the hooded gown or shroud of a more self-respecting reaper, he wore jeans and a faded T-shirt with eyes that stared out from the space between "Siouxsie" and "the Banshees." His thick-soled black boots had mismatched laces of black cord and brown leather.

And splayed over her bathtub was a long, much-repaired coat with a high collar that had fallen open to reveal the many tiny pockets of flowered calico and checkered gingham and paisley and damask all sewn in with sturdy black thread.

It made him look like a boy playing dress-up in his father's bathrobe.

Molly wondered if he remembered any of those other times he'd shown up and broken her life in half; those moments when she would grit her teeth hard and tell herself that she needed to start over again, only this time without quite so many mistakes.

"Get up," she said and held out her hand. Death struggled a little, then extended his gloved hand. Molly braced her knee against the enamel rim of the bathtub and helped him up.

He was disconcertingly heavy.

She led him into the single other room, a tiny living room with a microscopic kitchen near the door. There was a bricked-up fireplace and a paint-clotted mantelpiece supporting a collection of ornamental vases.

"What are they?" he asked when she pointed to them.

"What do you think?" she said.

* * *

DEATH PEERED CLOSELY. Each vase was sealed, making it useless for holding flowers. Each also had a narrow plate with a name and dates. The names were familiar to him, as all names would eventually be. He pulled open his coat and ran his hands along the many parti-colored pockets, searching for the faint resonance that each Rag left behind.

It didn't take him long to find the first two. He had picked up Sylvie Jean Kahn (1961 to 1996) and Keith Samuel Molloy (1958 to 1996) in the crushed remains of a gray Acura on the Tom Moreland Interchange. He remembered looking into the back at the sole survivor, a tiny girl no more than three, strapped into her car seat and buttressed behind a huge stuffed purple elephant.

Daniel Simon Kahn (1932 to 2003) had had a stroke beside the Whippoorwill Court swimming pool in a retirement home in Pensacola. While he twirled Daniel's soul between his fingers, a girl with tar-blackened feet raced across the hot asphalt. Death had retrieved Lucille Bloch Kahn (1935 to 2007) from a La-Z-Boy when she could no longer keep her heart working. There had been a girl lying on the sofa IM'ing SkadiKat98 to explain about how it was that Dylan Henrickson came to have his hand up her shirt.

Zachary Willem Adreux (1994 to 2011) was still a boy when he died, but he'd been alone. There was nothing in the *tableau mortant* that accompanied each retrieval that connected him to this woman. Thinking that there was perhaps something inside that might help him figure it out, he gave the lid a quick twist and looked inside.

Then he sneezed.

"Give me that!" Molly shouted, pulling the vase away.

A horrible idea struck him. Death had never given much thought to what mortals did in the time before death, but he'd given no thought at all to what happened to them after death. As far as he was concerned, it was like worrying about the packaging after he'd eaten the Ring Dings.

But he couldn't shake the feeling that the girl had kept the packaging.

"Is this the packaging?"

"What?"

"Are those the leftovers?"

"Do you mean remains?"

And Death began to panic.

"I god some ub my dose. I godda have a tissoo." He began searching around his pockets. "You godda tissoo? Ne'ermine," he said, shaking out a handkerchief.

He blew loudly and repeatedly. He wiped once and twice, sniffled a little, then sneezed again.

Molly stared at the thin, sniffling creature in her living room and wrapped her arms more tightly around Zachary, holding him in front of her like a shield.

"Knock, knock," she said.

"What?" Death asked, shaking his handkerchief with a snap.

"It's a joke. I say knock, knock, then you are supposed to say 'who's there?'"

"Who's there? You're right here. Why would I say who's there?"

"The interrupting cow."

Death froze for a moment, his folded handkerchief above his pocket. Then one half of his face rearranged itself in what she feared might be a smile.

"Oh, for the love of... That's not the joke." Molly put the vase named Zachary back on the mantelpiece. "Now, you're supposed to say, 'the interrupting cow who?'"

"It would seem to me that the absurdity of finding an interrupting cow on one's threshold would preclude further inquiry."

"Just say it, will you?"

"The interrupting—"

"Moo."

"But you didn't let me say—"

"Moo."

"Stop it. That's very irrita—"

"Moo."

Death glowered, his mouth in a tight line.

"Now you know how I feel. *You* are the Interrupting Cow. Every time I start something—every time I think, 'Now, my life can begin for real only this time, I won't make so many mistakes'—you show up. And now, because everyone else I know is dead, you're going to kill me."

"*I. Don't. Kill.*"

"I'm not dead, but if you 'sort it out,' I will be. So, yes, you do kill. You just have to be man enough to admit it."

* * *

HIS LIST WOULD HAVE to wait. Death was anxious, he couldn't shake the feeling that he'd been contaminated by Zachary. Even worse, there was something discomfiting in that girl's argument.

He took his clothes to Mrs. Kelly's big top-loader in Queens and his greatcoat to the organic dry cleaning place on Lenox. When that was done, he took his clean towel and clean flip-flops and his brush and a new bar of myrrh soap and headed to the Russian Turkish baths on 10th Street, one of the few places he frequented outside of work.

A handful of men sat frozen on the wood seats around the steamy, blisteringly hot room. They were naked under their towels. Death had been coming to the baths regularly since the late nineteenth century and preferred the company of the regulars, with their white wool caps and short robes and bodies that had embraced time in such interesting ways. There was a space next to a man who was the most regular of all. He'd once had clear true-blue eyes, dark blond hair, a taut body and smooth face. Now his eyes were bloodshot; his skin, mottled and tagged; his hair sprouted everywhere except his head—he even had a cloud of long curls on his bicep that encircled the rough tattoo of a sword-impaled heart with the name "Masha."

His body sagged effusively.

Standing in front of the stove, Death dipped his brush into the bucket of water and began to scrub. Once he rinsed himself off, he sat next to his friend with the bloodshot eyes, leaning forward like two of the other men were, elbows on knees.

He started to complain to his silent bench mate about the woman who refused to admit that she had choked to death on a chicken wing, the trouble with chief administrators and the looming possibility of Group.

Then, in order to be polite, he asked after Masha, nodding sagely as though his unresponsive friend had said something.

He started, looking at the man's bicep. He knew Masha's name because it was written on his friend's skin but without that, he would never recall it. Death had a prodigious memory for the names and circumstances of all of humanity's dead, right back to that first woman in the cave, holding her babies.

But he never knew the names of the living. He didn't know the name of his mistake which could only mean that this woman was—despite the Chicken Wing—still alive.

He quickly poured another clean bucket of water over his body and a second one up his nose.

He thanked his friend for listening, saying they should do it again sometime.

At home, he scrutinized his worn copy of the Book of Admonishments. Then he pulled on his white robes and his white Vans and went Up.

"You are being here still?" asked the censorious Puriel.

"No, we left. Now we are back. We must see Abdiel again."

"You are not on the schedule. You are having an appointment?"

"We have no appointment. What we have is a Question of Righteousness."

Puriel had been tasked with keeping corruption where it belonged which was Down. But a Question of Righteousness…? Abdiel was the legend in charge of Righteousness and would take a dark view of anyone who interfered with the dispensing of it.

"You are using—"

"The back, yes, we are aware."

Death jogged past the Mangles to Abdiel's office.

Abdiel could tell by the change in air quality that the Ragpicker had returned. He didn't bother to lift his head, just tapped the empty celadon urn on his desk. "Put it here," he said.

Death shifted uncomfortably until Abdiel rested his silver pointer on one line of text and lifted his head.

"Yes?"

"There's a bit of a problem," Death said.

Abdiel wrinkled his preternaturally smooth brow.

"The girl sees us."

"Yes?"

"Well…she accused us of attempting to kill her."

"We do not kill. It was the chicken wing that killed her. It's just taking an unconscionably long time to do it."

"Yes, but there's something else, Chief Administrator. We don't remember her name. Which can only mean she is alive.

Wait…I looked it up." He started flicking his dog-eared copy of the Book of Admonishments until he got the page he'd marked with a card addressed to Querida Vecina. "Here? In Admonishments XXVII?" He held it up high for Abdiel to see. "It says umm…" He craned his neck a little. "**Ad nobis neque initium neque finem vitae.**"

Abdiel shooed the book away, irritably. He had, after all, written Admonishments and could recite it from memory in any one of 10,000 languages, most of them long dead.

"It says it is not for us to begin or end life," Death clarified, helpfully. "And since she is alive now, if we take her soul, we will have ended her life."

Abdiel tapped his finger against his lips for a moment. "What is the short allegorical fable about the time before death?"

"The one about the food being terrible and the portions so small?"

"That's the one. Make clear to it, the smallness and terribleness of the time before death." Abdiel picked up the soft shining blob from the shallow dish on his desk and handed it reverently to Death.

"Here, take this soul. To illustrate the peace that will come after."

Death fumbled with the blob before slipping it into his favorite pocket, the pretty one made of periwinkle-dotted flannel.

"Ragpicker, Admonishments are clear on this point. We are clear on this point. The Custodes will do what we must."

Death flinched, feeling the threat inherent in that *we*. You or me, bub. It's you or me.

Metatron, the celestial scrivener and seraphic toady, entered the wall-less office laden with scrolls. He'd been a guest lecturer one of the four times Death had been forced to repeat Righteousness and his single contribution was, "When in doubt, ask yourself: 'What Would Abdiel Do?'"

But Death knew What Abdiel Would Do. He would march up to the girl and nab her soul. Fierce and sure, he would be unmoved as her limbs loosened and her screams lagged and her seeing eyes clouded with sadness and betrayal.

He wouldn't care that there was no one left to put her packaging in a vase on a mantelpiece.

Watching Metatron slither toward Abdiel's desk, Death suddenly lit up in inspiration.

"May we have until tomorrow?" he asked.

"When is—?" Abdiel hesitated, glancing at the face of his worshipful secretary, before saying, "Of course. Tomorrow is acceptable, but no longer."

"Tomorrow then."

"Tomorrow."

Death leaned back, letting himself go, his robes flapping around him as he fell.

He smiled to himself because while Abdiel had studied Tenses for Dummies and Rosetta Stone's Temporal Idiom, he had no more practical understanding of "soon" or "later" or "now" or "tomorrow" than a toddler had of googolplex.

CHAPTER 3

When Death picked up Mrs. Hurley at the DMV in Tempe, he grabbed a Sharpie as well. Then he popped by the woman's apartment but she was still there.

Back at the DMV in Tempe, Death picked up Mr. Rodriguez. After a few more retrievals, he returned to her apartment.

This time, she wasn't there.

So Death pulled on his rubber gloves and began his search, humming. *Vanitati et miserabili*—DeedahDeedah—*est tempus ante moooortem*, OhDeeDahDay. *The time before death is meaningless* DeedahDeedah *and miiiiiiiiiiserable*. OhDeeDahDay.

It always was: it was simply a question of determining exactly *how* it was meaningless and miserable. The tiny studio was rich in both. It was funny, he thought as he poked around, how the accessories required for the end of life tied so neatly to the ones required for its beginning of life: The walker folded into one corner next to the elevated toilet seat. The Geri-chair that supported a body unable to keep itself upright. In a sleeping nook was a hospital bed with bars meant to keep its occupant from falling out.

The little counter space that separated the Pullman kitchen

held bottles with nutrient-rich milks and two takeout containers filled with medicines and unguents. There were pills for osteoporosis, blood pressure, pain and incontinence. There were salves for eczema, yeast, muscle pain and fungus.

Above the drying rack that held a single cup and spoon was a clock. It was shaped like an old schoolhouse clock with a pendulum but was made from particles and plastic, took two AA batteries and said Montgomery Ward in flowing antique script. It ticked and tocked the seconds, though he would only learn that later.

He picked up the cup and smelled the whiff of char that meant instant coffee.

In the refrigerator were two browning bananas, a half loaf of spongy whole wheat bread, a bottle of applesauce, a carton of Parmalat and a yellow container that had once held margarine but now contained something pink and gray. Curious, he tasted it then spat it out into the white garbage can decorated with mustard-colored daisies.

The pantry had nothing but a few bowls and a score of cans of generic salmon which explained the pink and gray stuff that tasted so vile.

Across from the kitchen counter was a sofa covered with rumpled sheets and two pillows, where the woman herself must sleep. He sat down, his old coat spreading around him and felt the cushions that were still warm from her body and would stay warm, until he freed this millisecond to continue on and they went back to cooling as much as a hot day in June would let them.

In front of the sofa was a low table with a couple of baskets underneath and piles of paper on top. Carefully, he looked through the content of the baskets: several books, three pairs of jeans. A cardigan. Four long-sleeved T-shirts. Five sleeveless T-shirts. Three knit skirts. Several packages of tropical-flavored candies. Two bras and six cotton thongs. These last he touched with the shuddering queasiness of a tweenage girl with a flatworm.

Vanitati est, he thought, tearing open one of the candies, which looked like a lollipop without a stick. He popped it into his mouth. It was very chewy and not particularly good, so he spit it out into one of the napkins he carried in his pocket.

He thumbed through the piles of paper: A second notice from Health Tech Collects. Notification of Immediate Termination of Cable Service. Request for return of Social Security payment. Application for Part-Time Tuition Assistance Program for—he crooked his head to the side—the Paramedic Program at BMCC.

A pile of job applications.

Looking at the job applications, he pulled up the sleeve of his coat and using the Sharpie transcribed the woman's name to his wrist in big block letters.

MOLLY MOLLOY.

Then taking out his list, he retrieved a pencil and a sharpener shaped like Pikachu and a page of cheap brown paper all of which he'd retrieved from a school fire in Nepal.

> Molly, *he began.* This is me agin. I wan to shoe yu
>   something rilly rilly cool that will ~~klarefy clari-~~
>   ~~phie~~ make evereethng cleer. Meet me at—*Death*
>   *double-checked the underlined writing on his scroll*
>   —Bleker and Hutson at 19:48:16:456,
> Deth
> Ps
> Pls don be lat

HE REREAD THE NOTE, stretching out his cramped hand. Aramaic was so much easier.

* * *

WHEN SHE GOT HOME, Molly opened the pantry and stared. She no longer bothered to move things around in the vain hope that there was something hidden in the back. The avocado green can opener had something on the blade. She scraped it off with her thumbnail and rinsed it quickly before puncturing the can. Holding it tight, she twisted the handle until after the requisite number of turns (*scrch, scroch, scrch*), it was open and she could drain off the dusky liquid and pop some of the pinkish gray into a bowl. She sprinkled it with reconstituted lemon and sun-bleached dill then leaned over the sink and shoveled in each mouthful, tasting as little as possible.

Mary Molloy had bought canned salmon by the case because it was cheap, nonperishable and she was convinced that the calcium and Omega-3s had helped her live past her expiration date.

Taking two of the ancient restaurant mints that her grand-mother had hoarded in a red plastic container that still smelled like coffee, she had just started to pick off the wrappers that said Come Again! when she saw something on the chest that served as her dresser and coffee table and desk.

On top of her to-be-ignored pile was a grayish brown page with clumsy writing and atrocious spelling. The paper was rough-edged and smelled of smoke.

Next to it in a balled up napkin was a partially chewed condom.

Molly leaned back on the sofa and stared at the piece of paper.

"HELLO, MOLLY," said Mr. Medick, just emerging from next door. "Haven't heard the television recently. How's your grand-mother doing?"

"Dead," Molly said, locking the top lock. It was pointless to lie: the Medics had been waiting for her grandmother's apartment for fifteen years and too many people had seen the ambulance pull up in front of the building.

"So sorry," he said, fumbling for his phone, "for your loss." After a few quick swipes, he put his hand over the mic. "I have to take this."

The bronze strip at the base of the heavy outer door had come loose a few days ago and screeched along the concrete when she opened it. Molly stopped at the corner and listened to Alonso. Alonso had come into possession of a violin last year and had been gradually teaching himself to play pop tunes. Molly gave him two quarters because she hoped she could make a karmic deposit toward getting the job she'd just interviewed for and because she liked the way he played "Norwegian Wood."

A deflated yellow balloon with a smiley face got caught in the slipstream of a cab and bumped along behind it. Two fat drops fell from an air conditioner. The cement under Molly's feet rumbled as a train ran underneath. A dog tied outside a vape shop strained at the leash, barking for its owner.

Molly twisted her hair up so her neck could catch the tiny breezes that moved the heavy air. At 7:45, she was sitting on a bench near the intersection of Bleecker and Hudson watching people waiting for tables at a tiny restaurant called Fiorentina. The smell of wood smoke wafted from the chimney above.

A group of teenagers laughed under the jungle gym as though nobody could see them or hear them or smell the acrid smoke. A father and his little boy threw a ball back and forth over an awning. A middle-aged woman sat at the other end of Molly's bench with a huge bag of Cheetos and a bottle of water.

Gotta keep hydrated, she told Molly. Most important thing. Cancer comes when you're not hydrated. The cells, they dry up and get hard and make tumors. She sucked and her water bottle crunched.

A young skateboarder knocked into a woman in high heels. A policeman looking at the license of the fruit seller yelled at him to stop.

Then as if time was obeying the cop's command, it did. All of it: The annoying rap-a-rap-a-rap-a of a helicopter, the rumble-thunk of the skateboard, the rustle of leaves, the skunky smell from the jungle gym. Even the arc under a dog's lifted leg froze forming a pretty string of tiny amber beads.

"Hello?" Molly said quietly to the woman next to her, but her benchmate stayed as she was, her head back, her eyes closed, her face hardened around the lips pursed to her bottle. When the woman didn't answer, she pushed at her shoulder making her teeter. She didn't respond, just wobbled back into place. Even the bubble in her scrunched water bottle was frozen.

As her grandmother's apartment faced onto the back courtyard, Molly hadn't noticed the sound the last time he came. Now she realized what silence truly sounded like and that she'd never heard it before and didn't particularly want to hear it again. In this new, true silence, the slightest noise sounded outsized, like the flicked hem of a coat or a single footfall. Molly watched him, the thin man with hair the color of night and skin an indeterminate color between olive meaning golden brown and olive meaning green as he wove between the woman who had been knocked off her feet, but hadn't hit the ground yet and the young skateboarder who was twisting around to look at the policeman, his foot raised for a new burst of speed.

A little girl was watching the skateboarder with barely disguised envy, a bright red line melting down her wrist. Death stuck his finger into the cup and then deciding it was good, bent down and wrapped his lips around the swirl of cherry ice. He stopped to look at the phones of two teenage girls sipping iced teas by the blue lights at Fiorentina and then stole a handful of quenepas from the fruit vendor.

"So is this what you wanted to show me?" she called in the

city voice she'd developed since moving to New York. It wasn't loud, exactly, but capable of being heard over the blended back-drop of jackhammers, yapping spaniels, trucks going in reverse and the woman practicing scales in the apartment across the way. But in the absence of jackhammers and spaniels and trucks and scales, Molly's voice sliced through the silence like a street saw sending Death several feet straight up before coming back to earth with a thump and a fluttering of coattails, his quenepas rolling around the street.

"Don't sneak up like that!" he yelped.

"That's kinda rich coming from you, don't you think? That's all you do is sneak around and steal stuff. I'm sitting on a bench in the exact place and at the exact time of your invitation."

"Well, you almost gave me a heart attack," Death said, peev-ishly. He grabbed a new bunch of quenepas.

"Can you have a heart attack?" Molly asked, reaching into her benchmate's Cheetos bag. The woman wasn't objecting, and Molly did like Cheetos.

"I don't [blurp] I don't think so?" he said, pulling in a sharp breath. "But I do seem [blurp] to be having some kind of [blurp] attack."

Death raised a hand to his sternum, feeling the odd little convulsions rumbling through a chest that had no heart or lungs or anything but solid firmament.

"Hiccups. You should drink something," she said, shoving a handful of Cheetos into her mouth. Then she pointed a single neon orange finger at an iced tea on the table beside him.

"Mm [blurp] mm," Death said as he took a long, deep draw on the straw. He didn't stop to breathe or swallow and by the time he got to the bottom, the convulsing had settled and then stopped.

What would the girl would think when she saw her empty glass? Molly thought, then she remembered all the times she'd reached the bottom of a glass without being aware of how she'd gotten there. It made her wonder how many Diet Cokes and sweet teas Death had taken without paying.

"As entertaining as it is to watch you hiccup and drink iced tea, I actually..." She clenched her mouth before the words "have a life" could escape, hoping he wouldn't notice and maybe remember.

He gestured her to follow. As he passed the father and son, throwing the pink ball over the awning, he plucked the ball from the air and bounced it on the sidewalk.

Thock.

A teenage boy sitting on a bollard leaned forward, his arms folded across his stomach like he was going to vomit.

Death bounced the Pinky again. *Thock.*

A gray-faced older man stood behind him, one hand on the boy's shoulder, the other holding his phone to his ear.

Thock.

Just as Molly was about to tell him to cut it out, Death put the ball in his pocket, retrieving a pair of long rubber gloves instead.

"Right there." Death stepped around a big empty Suburban angled awkwardly across the lanes and headed for the crowd gathered at the side of the street.

It had seemed like a normal day filled with normal things, but then with Death pushing his way through the throng, Molly knew for someone this was not a normal day filled with normal things. She also knew that this wasn't going to be "RILY RILY COOLL" but before she could turn on her heels for home, she saw the man lying on the road, his well-groomed, dyed hair matted with blood. His skin—smooth and polished with a few incipient lines—losing color. He was wearing running shorts and a loose T-shirt scrunched up above a fledgling paunch. Someone, Molly saw with dismay, had lifted his head and slipped a stack of paper towels underneath. A few feet away were the ruined remains of a takeout coffee.

Death carefully fished in his pocket for a pair of ear plugs. "You may want to cover your ears," he said, inserting them with a twist. As his fingers jabbed into the man's abdomen, all the sound that had been absent—helicopter, voices, cars, sirens, the wind, birds, wheels, screams,—combined into a thunderstrike of noise that disappeared as soon as the black length of shadow left the man's bellybutton, leaving only Molly's New York voice yelling at Death to "PUT THAT BACK!"

"I can't put it back; he's dead."

Death had just begun to open up his coat when Molly lunged for the Rag in his hand, clutching it tight in her fist and pulling.

"You're going to stretch it," he said, loosening his grip. "They hate being stretched!"

Molly crouched beside the man and dropped the thing onto his abdomen, trying to push it into his belly button with her finger. The ebony puddle started to feel around tentatively like the cross between a Rorschach test and an amoeba.

"Wait, put your hands under his jaw like this," she said.

Death had just managed to take out one earplug when she positioned his hands at the man's jaw, fitting his fingers underneath so the man's jaw would jut out.

"Put your thumbs above his chin and don't move."

"I dropped my earplug."

"Don't. Move," she repeated.

She pinioned the man's soul to his belly button with one hand and pinched his nose with the other, covering his mouth with hers and counting out the breaths. Her hair fell over Death's hands. It felt heavy and warm, even through the protection of his gloves.

"Stay like that," she said. "You're doing a good job."

Death's cheeks started to feel hot. As she slid her hands to the dead man's sternum and started to push hard, her rhythm fast and steady, Death checked that the corpse's jaw was jutting just the way she liked it. When the Rag started to slither away, he pushed it back, though he knew it was pointless.

Maybe she would tell him he was doing a good job again.

The disgruntled Rag slipped out the other side and slunk away from its mouldering packaging. Death knew he needed to catch it before it got to a grate.

"I...I really need to get that," he said, indicating the slithering inky splotch. "I hate chasing Rags through sewers."

Molly searched for a pulse, for a breath, for anything that wasn't a body cooling under her hand. She slumped back onto her heels, her hands resting gently on his chest while Death darted after the slitherer.

"They're very slippery," he explained as he came back, the Rag held tight between thumb and finger. It had sprouted tentacles that flailed frantically searching the air, as they inevitably did.

Finding nothing, as they inevitably didn't.

"It's like he's looking for something," Molly said.

Death shrugged. "It's just what they do. They spend all of their lives trying and needing and wanting and then when death comes, they can't help themselves." He twirled it around and around until its tentacles knotted together and the dizzy splotch slid neatly into a pocket.

"Funnily, that's kind of what I wanted to talk to you about because after all that trying and needing and wanting, there is peace at the end."

He waited for her to answer but she was looking at the man's body that no longer had anything to do with life and was now just an empty shell.

"Do you want to see it?" he asked, already digging one finger into his loveliest pocket, the one made of soft cotton flannel dotted with periwinkles. "A soul at peace?"

"Naah, m'alright." Molly stood up and brushed her skirt. "I've got things to do."

Death looked up at her, his finger still in his periwinkle pocket.

He had prepared for a number of responses, pretty much any affirmation running the spectrum of Joy to Wonder. Honor, maybe.

What he had not prepared for was a mumbled, barely literate, "Naah, m'alright."

As he did not have a Plan B, he went ahead with Plan A and stood, the radiant soul fresh from his flannel pocket. It was a very soft, nearly weightless, opalescent blob. During the Six Dynasties when he'd been stealing quite a lot of poetry, Death had decided it looked like a Drop of a Rainbow.

"See?" he said and shook his hand, making the opalescent blob in his palm shimmer like a Jell-O mold.

"Looks like an oyster," Molly said, pushing her hair back.

Death sputtered. "No, it does not. It looks like a Drop of a Rainbow."

"Hmmph," Molly sniffed. "Don't know much about rainbow droppings, but I did work at Sam's Surfside in Pensacola so I know a thing or two about oysters."

"It is *not* an oyster," he snapped. "And you know what? I'm not sure you even *deserve* peace."

"Fine. Glad we agree about something," Molly said. "You don't want me to be an oyster and I sure as fuck don't want to be one, either."

"GAAAAAH," Death wailed. He plugged his fingers into his ears, intoning over and over, "**Non profanate nec linguam nec auriculum.**"

"What's that supposed to mean?" Molly said, but Death just intoned louder until she pulled at one of his hands and asked again.

"Neither tongue nor ears shall by filth contaminated be? It's Book of Admonishments Number Flurbityflur." He elided the citation number just a tiny bit, but in so doing he was certain he'd broken another Admonishment. Wasn't there something about "Thou shalt not pretend thou knowest Citation Numbers when thou plainly dost not"?

Molly stood up on her tippy toes and then rolled back on her heels. She sucked on one canine and narrowed her eyes. She looked different than she had when she'd told him he was doing a good job.

"Here's the thing. I've had a lot of those kinds of rules: No running, no yelling, no diving, no splashing." She moved closer and when she dropped her voice, Death had to lean in to hear. "No exposure above the knee or below the collarbone. No physical contact. No foul language. No lingering after school. No gum. No personal music players. No lights on after 9:30."

For reasons he didn't understand, a shiver coursed through the place where his spine should have been.

"I know what those rules are. Those rules are for people to hide behind because figuring out someone's story, why they do the things they do, takes time, takes thought. Takes work. I'm not putting up with that anymore, so here's the deal." Death looked at the tilt of her chin and had the feeling something bad was coming. "Do not come at me with the 'thou-shalt-not' bullshit of some dried-up old fart. Either ask me by your little cork-assed self or shut *the fuck* up."

"It's not the bullshit of some dried-up old fart." His hand flew to his mouth. "Now see what you made me do? You don't understand, when I make mistakes, things *change.* And you know what happens then?"

"No earthly idea," said Molly, looking like she couldn't care less.

"I get sent to *Group*," Death said, adding quickly, *"And I really don't like Group."*

Molly stopped, then stared, then pressed her lips together and creased her brow. A second later, she bent over in an explosion of laughter and Death felt himself losing control of the situation.

What, he asked himself, *would Abdiel do?*

"Do you know that short allegorical fable?" he asked brightly, remembering that Abdiel had actually told him exactly what to do. "The one about the food being terrible and the portions so small?"

"It's a joke."

"It's not a *joke*. It's a short allegorical fable about the Time before Death."

"And it is not 'the Time before Death.' It is life and you obviously know nothing about it."

"Young lady, I'll have you know that I have been doing this for nearly 200,000 years." He drew himself up as tall as he could, his voice deepening as he did. "I have experienced more of life than you can possibly imagine."

"Don't you 'young lady' me. Playing with our toys, wearing our clothes, eating our food and then stealing our belly button lint is *not* experiencing life."

Death slapped his outer pockets in frustration. That's when he felt the hollow bulge of the pink ball and launched it furiously into the sky. Molly watched it come back down and before it reached his hands, she plucked it from the air.

"That's mine!" Death said.

"*No, it's not,*" she snapped, and darted off through the unmoving forest of bodies with Death hard on her heels, his big coat streaming behind him.

She skidded to a stop right in front of the boy still looking expectantly at the blank spot where the ball had been. "It's *his*."

Death grabbed at it. Molly dropped it. They both lunged but Molly reached under a car and got it first. Death grabbed for it again. Molly shouldered him hard. Death stumbled back. She settled it into the boy's hands.

"Mine," he shouted.

"His," she hissed and her jaw set hard, her eyes narrowed and her nostrils flaring.

He raced around the boy, but Molly always managed to slide between them, her knees bent, her arms outstretched. He doubled back and stumbled over his feet, his legs tangling in his coat. He grabbed her arm and tried to pull her behind him, but she pirouetted and blocked him again. Everywhere he scuttled, Molly seemed to be there.

Billions of humans had failed at their attempts to stop Death, until Molly Molloy, a solid, but unexceptional player in the driveway basketball games at Odd Fellows Home for Teens, boxed him out.

Death was untiring and could have eventually worn her down. But as pickups had long been routine, straightforward matters, he had lost the habit of persistence and was easily distracted. So when Molly finally collapsed, her hands on her knees, panting heavily, the pink ball was still safely cradled in the boy's hands.

She wiped her forehead with her T-shirt.

Death couldn't help but stare at her belly button. Molly eyed him warily, pulling down the thin layer of jersey, her fists knotted in front of her.

He buried his hands deep in the big pockets and in the end, left without either the Pinky or Molly's Rag.

* * *

ALEX, the boy on the skateboard, twisted to see the woman he'd knocked down. Shit. A cop was yelling at him. He put his foot down for a new burst of speed and his heel slipped on the slick flesh and hard seed of a quenepa.

CHAPTER 4

"Of course, everyone heard about it," Bea said. "Those three go up on the stage. Make it like a splayed-out horseshoe."

Death picked up one of the huge risers from the floor of the room that served as both school cafeteria and auditorium.

"What seems to be the hold up, Neshama'le?"

Bea was the only one who called him 'little soul,' but then he was the only one who called her Bea. Everyone else addressed her as Beata Regina Caeli, Domina Nostra which had a way of interrupting the flow of any conversation.

"I made a mistake," Death said. He held the riser above his head and walked carefully up the low stairs. "But she keeps talking at me and she said I was trying to kill her, which I'm not, you know, it's not me, it's the chicken wing. Did I tell you she was supposed to choke on a chicken wing? Anyway just as I was about to pick her up, she hit me, bang, smack, right in the jaw and I fell down and she put her foot on my chest."

He rubbed his hand over the spot where Molly's foot had been.

"She wouldn't let me get up."

Bea raised an eyebrow while Death easily shifted the last of the long, massively heavy three-level bleachers to his hip, but she didn't say anything.

"I've tried reasoning with her, even showed her a soul…I mean she's holding it—grace, peace, an end to want and striving —and you know what she called it?"

"No idea."

"She called it an oyster." He lifted up the folding chairs. "Where do you want these to go?"

"In rows facing the stage," Bea said, pointing down to the chipped linoleum floor. "An oyster? Hmm. I went once. To the Sea of Tranquility. See what all the fuss was about."

"And?"

"Meh. Abdiel showed up, of course."

"Of course."

"He asked me what I thought. I said I wasn't sure that they were doing much good. He got all pious and said, 'Beata Regina Caeli, Domina Nostra' but then he added 'Sanctissima,' which is what he always says whenever I'm wearing jeans. Anyway, he said that was the point of Peace. It was not about 'Doing' anything; it was about 'Being.' I nodded as though I understood why he said 'Being' like it ought to be capitalized, but mostly I felt like maybe I should change my pants."

She tightened the buckle on the strap of her overalls. "He said he feared you were losing track of what your purpose was. Said he hoped that work would let up and you would find time to come back Up. Spend a little time in Venerating."

"You didn't tell him, did you?"

"About your 'me' time? Nooo. Not my business."

"Thank you for that."

"So tell me about this woman?"

"Nothing special. Not smart. Never got past high school."

"Hmph. I had no formal education and, if I remember correctly, you repeated Righteousness four and a half times."

"I was doing better the last time," he said, defensively, "but then I got sent Down again. And did I tell you she hit me? Oh, right. She put her foot right here." He rubbed his chest again. "Do you remember Alkippe the Virgin, who lived two streets over from you?"

"You may have mentioned her a couple of times."

"Well, she looks kind of like Alkippe. But she's not like Alkippe was. No virgin, that's for sure."

"Alkippe the Virgin was meant ironically." Bea put the pages into thirty piles. "Besides, virginity and morality don't have anything to do with each other."

"That's interesting, coming from you. What do you want me to do with the extra chairs?"

"It was a different time, Neshama'le," Bea said, "and I was fourteen. Put them in the back. Folded against the wall. If she's so unexceptional, why are you stymied?"

He set the extra chairs away neatly and then came back to sit next to Bea who was the Queen of Heaven and his only real friend.

"I don't know. That's the thing. Her life's a disaster and I don't understand why she's holding on so hard." Death started to bang against the stage with the heels of his boots. "She's just a mistake and you know I can't afford another one."

She liked Azrael. He was a good boy, though he was still given to intoning those dreary certitudes about life created by beings who had, after all, never lived it.

Just then, Bea got a strange prickling feeling in the sole of one foot. It was the feeling she got when something interesting was going to happen. She rubbed her toe against her arch.

She'd have to keep an eye on it.

"What are the kids singing?" he asked.

"Ni Wa Wa. Liang Zhi Lao Hu. The usual."

"No Kyrie?"

"They're only five."

"Just doesn't seem like a real program without a Kyrie."

Bea stretched from side to side and then took out the hair-band straining to control her ponytail. "Don't be so quick to dismiss her," she said, smoothing back her tight steely curls. "This may well be a mistake. Doesn't mean that it can't be a miracle as well. Depends on what you do with it."

CHAPTER 5

⁓

*T*he girl who was no miracle read over the checklist taped next to her mirror and removed one earring from her left ear. She dabbed at her eye shadow, hoping that she'd managed the balance between too minimal and too excessive. She checked that the stick and poke tattoo of two hearts joined by a strand of tears would be fully covered by her uniform. She made sure that the color of her control-top pantyhose was indeed Suntan and not some proscribed color like Nude or Buff or Taupe or Bisque.

Then she froze at sounds coming from the kitchen. There was a shake, a rustle and finally a ding like metal against porcelain. As quietly as she could, she picked through the trash and armed with her grandmother's ancient can of Lustre-Net ("Hair to Stay!"), she crept out of the bathroom.

A moment later, Death was dragged out the door and into the hall by Molly, who wore a bright red Niceville High T-shirt ("We Educate All Students!") and brandished a can of hair spray.

A spoonful of milky Peanut Butter Crunch dribbled down his chin.

"You. Do. *Not*. Break. Into. My. Apartment!" Molly shouted.

49

He fumbled for the box of cereal and still-open carton of milk that splashed as she shoved it into his arms. Then she slammed the door closed with her back and turned the deadbolt.

"I didn't break in," he called through the door. "I just showed up."

Molly pushed herself away from the door and went back to the bathroom. Still shaking, she drew an unsteady line under her right eye. She cursed under her breath and held a cotton swab under the faucet. Nothing happened. She opened the little window and leaned out. A wind-filled Key Foods bag had stopped mid-pirouette, its handles reaching into the air. Deaf old Mr. Shelton's television, his constant and only companion since his wife died, was silent.

She went back to the door.

"Are you still there?"

"Yes?" he said tentatively. "Can I come in? I left my spork and..."

Molly opened the door a crack, just the distance the chain allowed.

"I need a towel. I got milk all over my coat." He waggled his fingers through the gap. "Please?"

Molly knew she would not be having this conversation if Death had been Ancient, Imposing, All-Knowing and All-Powerful like he was *supposed* to be. But he wasn't Ancient—or maybe he was Ancient—but he certainly didn't seem Imposing, All-Knowing and All-Powerful. If he seemed like anything it was like an abandoned runty puppy in need of some serious house-training.

Molly's shoulders slumped. With a single finger, she pushed his forehead back, closed the door, undid the lock and opened it.

"Okay, but from now on, if you are going to come into my

apartment you will knock"—still holding the heavy metal door, she knocked on it—"thusly and wait for a reply."

"Why has one of your eyes got black around it?"

"Because I was in the middle of getting ready for my new job, when I realized I had an intruder. There's a towel on the refrigerator. Go ahead, clean off your coat, eat your cereal, whatever, and let me get ready for work."

She picked up a teeny tiny pile of clothes, topped by a large pair of socks, and stalked back to the bathroom.

When he was done, he called into the bathroom. "I cleaned the dishes," he said. Then he jiggled the knob but the door didn't open. "The door is stuck."

"How did you wash the dishes? The water isn't working."

"The water at my place never works either. Unless I leave. So usually I just turn the knobs and go and when I come back there'll be water in the sink. But I didn't want to leave because I wasn't sure you'd let me back in even if I knocked thusly. So I just used spit and polish."

"You what?"

"I'm perfectly sterile."

Molly made a mental note to wash every dish in her house.

"You have a place?" Molly asked, loading her stiffly dry toothbrush with toothpaste.

"Yeah," he said, checking the state of his coat in the corroded mirror above the mantelpiece. "135th and Adam Clayton Powell? Above Popeye's?"

"Really?" Molly said. "You have a place above Popeye's?"

"You sound surprised." He moved some of the ornamental vases to the side and pulled back his lips, checking his teeth in the mirror behind them.

"I guess," Molly said. "If I'd had to imagine your place I think I would have imagined something more…more epic?"

"It actually is pretty epic. I can see the line at IHOP from my window."

He carefully rearranged the containers holding her parents back to their space in the center of the mantelpiece. Then he picked up the single pewter urn to the side, the one belonging to Zachary Willem Adreux.

"So what's your job?" he asked, shaking the urn against his ear.

"Entertainer," Molly said. She spit the last of her toothpaste into her dry sink.

"Broadway?" He put Zachary back.

Stepping out of the bathroom in her Suntan legs, her hot pink shorty shorts, her white socks scrunched down around her ankles, she pulled at the bottom of her black tank so he could read *TaaTaas!* in hot pink letters splayed across her full breasts and beneath it the smaller *An Eatery* that when she let go of the hem would disappear into a rosy shadow on the cantilevered underside of the push-up bra that Dave the Manager had suggested would pay for itself in just one night.

"You look, umm—"

"I know exactly how I look," Molly snapped. She pulled a loose dress over her uniform and put her hair into a ponytail so that it would stay neat on the trip to work.

"Molly?"

"Hmm?"

"Why did Zachary kill himself?"

Molly's eyes flickered toward the mantelpiece. Her chin trembled and she went back to the bathroom, locking the door once more.

He called her name until he remembered about the knocking thusly, but Molly didn't answer. Then he put his ear to the door and listened to the quiet snuffling sound.

When the door finally closed behind Death, Mr. Shelton's television blared, the Key Foods bag twirled out of sight and Molly continued to cry.

CHAPTER 6

Taking off his gloves, Death entered the room full of forgotten people and watched Bea gently stroke the clawed hand of a Mr. Patel who had spent the past decade losing his memory. She sang to him. She was always singing something. Recently it'd been Motown.

> Remember me as a breath of spring
> Remember me as a good thing.

"Did you finish the cistern?" she said without turning.

"All cleaned out and ready."

"Help pull him back up, will you? Oh for crying out loud. You don't need gloves. What do you think you're going to catch?"

"I don't know...It's just always"—he pinched his nose—"'Ooooh Wagpickuh. Wheah is my pomanduh?'"

"Dear me, Neshama'le, you aren't developing a sense of humor, are you?"

"Was that funny?" he asked, settling Mr. Patel.

"Mildly amusing. Why do you even go Up? I don't unless I absolutely have to."

"I never used to, but now because of, you know, everything…"

"Unhun. So you heard about the report?"

"What report?"

"Apparently you told Abdiel you'd bring this soul to him tomorrow?"

Death mumbled something and scuffed his boot along the painted concrete floor.

"Well, in the several days since you told him that, he has come to have doubts and asked Rogziel to get him a definitive answer on what is meant by 'tomorrow.'"

"Yuh-oh."

"Exactly."

"He says that if he finds out that tomorrow is already past, he will descend from on high and retrieve the Rag himself."

Death stilled and stiffened, looking distractedly at Mr. Patel's right foot.

"But…but that's not for him to do. She's my mistake. Not his. Mine. Besides, she's not talking to me now. I want that settled before she's transitioned."

"Not sure what one has to do with the other, but why's she angry with you? Aside from the obvious bit about trying to kill her. There's an extra pillow in the wardrobe over there."

"I am not trying to kill her," Death said, stomping irritably over to the warped wardrobe and searching under thin waffle-weave blankets until he came to a pillow. "You're going to think this is crazy: she keeps the scraps in jars in her house." He handed Bea the pillow.

"Scraps?"

"You know. I forget what she called them. Leftovers? No, remains, that's it. Anyway, I looked inside one and it's got this powder that's..." He grimaced. "All I can say is don't get it up your nose, it's worse than ragweed. At least Zachary is, maybe the other ones aren't as bad."

"What were you doing sticking your nose in there?"

"Well, she had all of these vases for like"—he held up his hand, carefully touching one finger at a time—"for five people. Mostly family except for one, Zachary, who killed himself but when I asked her why he killed himself, she locked herself in the bathroom and stopped talking to me."

Bea looked at the thin slip of a tin wedding ring Mr. Patel had made when he first married his wife in the bad old times and the gold wedding ring that he'd bought to celebrate better times. But then she'd died only nine months into those better times.

"Death is always hard for the people left behind but suicides are the hardest of all. Since you don't know anything about death, just try to be a little sensitive."

"She said the same thing! What do you people think I've been doing all this time?"

"Bookkeeping, little soul. Bookkeeping."

When Death started to object, Bea put a finger to her lips. "Neshama'le, you know how fond I am of you, but you are out of your depth here. And a quick tip? Don't call them scraps."

Death stretched out one empty latex glove. It exploded back with a loud POP.

"Why do you do that? Rub his hand?"

"Because in the beginning when we understand nothing else, there's touch. And at the end, when we understand nothing else, there's touch."

* * *

HELLER SUSSMANN WAS MORE than a little blind. He was in the middle of opening his door, one hand framing the lock, the other scraping with the key near the keyhole. His stooped shoulders were covered with a worn greatcoat of dark gray cotton drill that had originally belonged to Gustave Maria Zellberg until Zellberg was deprived of both it and his divine spark at Passchendaele.

Death, who had taken both coat and spark, was splayed out across the industrial carpeting in a color that was called Blue Spruce, his face hard against the crack under the door of the apartment down the hall and across the way from where Mr. Sussmann stood.

Molly hadn't answered the many times he had stopped by her door and knocked thusly. Thinking that perhaps she was still angry about Zachary, he carefully draped his coat over Mr. Sussman so nothing would fall out of his pockets, then he pressed his long nose to the tiny crack under the door. With one huge breath, he sucked in all of the air in the room, rolling it around in the various cavities in his head, until he was quite sure that she wasn't there.

He sat up and draped his arms around his thin legs. In his limited experience of Molly, she'd never been gone this long and it was making him restless, like when he forgot a word and couldn't stop worrying until he remembered it again.

Maybe Abdiel had already gotten her? Well, it solved the problem, that was true. And he should feel happy for her: It wouldn't have been painful and it allowed her to transcend her coarse earthiness. She'd go through the Mangles and then her soul would go to the Sea of Tranquility, waiting, ready to return, a teaspoon of peace in a messy world.

Really, he told himself, he just needed to know. Know that he had no more obligations and that this episode was really and truly behind him.

What was that word that he'd read recently in pamphlets while eating at the hospital cafeteria in Camden?

Closure. Yes, he needed closure.

Maybe he'd be allowed to hold her soul, all radiant and unstained? Though that could be tricky because once they went through the Mangles they were all exactly alike: young, old; woman, man; bearded, clean shaven.

He could ask to feed her Rag into the Mangles. The Rag would still feel like her, it would still resonate as who she'd been. Then he'd be able to remember her name. Then there would be closure.

But she wouldn't be able to see him and smile at him or talk to him and tell him he'd done a good job. So maybe he did need to transition her. Then they could talk one last time. And then there would be closure.

But she didn't want to be transitioned and probably wouldn't smile at him. She definitely wouldn't tell him he'd done a good job.

If they'd only known how to look, millions of New Yorkers would have caught a millisecond glimpse of Death that day. Though they might not have recognized him in the slim, beard-less young man with the long dark gray overcoat flapping open around his jeans with the hole at the pocket, sturdy black boots and a T-shirt announcing that he'd **HAD A WHALE OF A TIME AT BUFFY'S BAT MITZVAH**.

Death never paid much attention to what people looked like; he only knew the sonorities of their souls. But his chest tight-ened every time he saw a tall woman with a full figure and long brown hair who reminded him a little of Alkippe the Virgin. There were too many in New York City and next time, if there was a next time, he would pay closer attention to her details.

As the day passed, the pricking irritation ripened into some-thing warm and then hot and then fiery so that when he finally found Molly collapsed on a bench in a garden behind a church on Barrow Street, he yelled "I wasn't ready!" and stomped his foot and Alpha Lupi, though it had long been on the list of supernova candidates, shattered with a violence and suddenness that shocked even seasoned observers.

Molly jolted at the sound, then slumped back again with a sigh.

Oh, he thought, and crouched in front of her. He smelled the mix of cassis and moss and salt. Under her bowed waist, the straps of her bag were wrapped around her wrist and both hands grasped her phone stopped in its countdown at 2:37.

Tentatively pulling off one glove, he licked a finger and held it near her open mouth until he was sure he felt her breath. Still squatting down, he looked at her more closely. He'd seen many different kinds of brown hair during his search. As he looked at Molly's hair he knew it wasn't chestnut or amber or dark chocolate. It was very medium brown. It was, he decided, the exact right way to do brown hair.

She looked less like Alkippe than he'd originally thought. Her eyes drooped a little at the corners and her face was more rounded and her cheekbones less pronounced. Her nose which was neither aquiline nor pert, came down farther leaving not a lot of space before the intrusion of her upper lip which was thinner than Alkippe's. Her lower lip was fuller and had the remains of a scar just to the left of center.

They were, he decided, the exact right way to do lips.

With his still-gloved hand, he moved her arm. Hunched as she was, the heavy curve of her breasts nearly met the bulge at her midriff. Her thighs, he noted, were thicker than they like them these days—

Molly started to topple. He caught her, forgetting about his one ungloved hand, and his bare hand touched her bare arm.

He shivered. He'd done it at the beginning, touched the bodies. But that was before Admonishments were modified to include something about **Terrena divinis {aliquid aliquam}**

non contaminantur, which commanded that celestial and terrestrial should {yada yada} not contaminate.

They didn't get more terrestrial than this. Death's sensitive fingers felt the steady salt tides of her blood, the air currents of her breath, the mineral seams of her bones, and above it all the skirling thrum of the spark that held the little world of her together.

He squeezed onto the bench, so that she could lean against him. His naked fingers barely touched her arm, but it was enough to feel every shudder, every rustle, every wounded breath while she slept beside him under the dappled light of a tree on a bench in a garden behind a church on Barrow Street.

IN THE BEGINNING, when we understand nothing else, there is touch.

* * *

MOLLY HAD to run faster if she was going to make it in time. There were no doors or windows, only those damn walls textured with sharp nubbins of grit that tore at her skin as she scraped against them. The stairs had no landings, but they changed directions. She kept running forward until she smelled the wood stain and pine cleanser that made her thoughts scream. The swampy smell of the cushions on the patio furniture made her body ache.

There it was, the sleeping porch with the same struts that supported the same balcony and the legs dangling there. She pressed her face into the damp cold jeans that smelled like piss and braced them as best she could.

"Those who live only to satisfy their own sinful nature will harvest decay and death."

. . .

SHE COULDN'T BREATHE.

Because Death knew nothing about bodies except for those that were about to find their final release, Molly's tight scrabbling at his chest, her short uneven gasps of breath made him worry that maybe he'd broken her.

He poked her forehead with his finger. She sucked in a deep breath and held on tighter as her lungs and brain fought off the heavy prickly fug. The denim-clad legs that smelled of piss gave way to a thin chest clad in cotton drill that smelled of sandalwood and soot.

She looked up. There was no swollen tongue or purpling cheeks or single staring eye. Just the hairless face of a man who looked hardly older than a boy.

There was a familiar prickling around her cheekbones and Molly knew that her face was flushing with the peculiar mottling that made her burn even hotter. Pulling away, she smoothed her shirt and tugged at the strand of hair stuck in the dried saliva at the corner of her mouth.

"I...I had a dream," she mumbled, her mind still reeling unsteadily.

"Are they nice?"

"Can't recommend them, no."

She bent low over her backpack, her hair falling on either side of her face. "What are you doing here?" she asked, trying to hide her discomfort in the pointless reorganization of her bag.

"You kept not being home and I wanted to know where you were."

"Well, here I am," she said and pulled out a large plastic bag with her tiny black and pink uniform, a smaller clear plastic case, a water bottle, her textbook.

He fingered the smaller clear plastic case. "I've seen these before, but I've never known what they do."

Having only bought the stethoscope two days earlier, she'd barely had time to use it herself.

"Here." She unraveled the rubbery tubing. "You put these in your ears. No the other ears."

"I've only got two ears."

"I mean you've got it backward. That's it."

Sweeping her hair back, she put her fingers on either side of the bell and held it to her chest. The currents that he'd only felt before were loud and much more complex. When she moved her hand, the sound changed from a lush and liquid knocking to an insistent rustle of velvet rubbed first one way and then another.

She could tell by his intent expression that he heard. She breathed deeply so he could hear how the sounds changed yet again. "Now give me your hand."

Death held out his hand, the one with the glove. She pushed up his sleeve and saw her name written in Sharpie on the inside of his wrist. "I remember the names of the dead. But I can't remember yours. That's how I know you're not dead." He peeked at the block letters inked onto his wrist. "And that you're Molly."

She put the bell to the spot right above her name and looked at him expectantly.

He knew what she wanted, so he nodded because he didn't have the heart to tell her that he didn't have a heart to hear.

Then she carefully packed away the stethoscope while he thumbed through Prehospital Trauma Care, quickly skimming over the compound fracture or the unevenly dilated pupils or the head wound. He tapped an image of a chest with a thick pinkish-gray blob extruding from a bloodied torso. "Ahhhh, Rosario Morales."

"So I take it he didn't survive?"

"No."

"Pity," Molly said and slung her backpack over one shoulder. "Where are you going now?"

"Subway. I've got to get to work. I'm trying to negotiate a

61

better schedule, but right now I've got two full days of work sandwiched between three full days of classes. That's why I've been coming here. Take a quick nap."

He fell into step beside her.

"Can I ask you something?" she said.

"I guess?"

"Do you remember every death?"

"Yes?" He hoped this wasn't about Zach.

"Do you remember the crash that killed my parents?"

"Ahhhh," he said, trying to hide his relief. "Yes."

"I think...I think it was pretty bad? My grandmother—I lived with my grandparents after that—would ask me from time to time if I remembered anything—*anything*—about it. She always looked anxious when she did."

Death scratched absently at his chin. His memory was stacked with bodies in every state of disease and dismemberment, but he understood why her grandmother hoped Molly'd been spared that particular remembering.

"Never mind. I don't really want to know."

Molly never talked about the accident and her grandmother worried that she'd seen something that she was burying deep inside and would haunt her. Molly was haunted, but not by what she'd *seen,* rather by what she'd heard.

She'd been dozing behind the giant purple bulk of a stuffed animal—she could remember only yellow tusk or horn so she tended to think of it as an elephant or a rhinoceros—but she could hear her parents' heightened whispers.

Her father was exhausted and angry. It hadn't been his idea to help his in-laws move into a retirement community all the fucking way in Pensacola.

"Shhhhhhh," her mother had said, before calling back softly, "Molly?"

Frozen by the anxious interest of children who fear there is more to life than they have been told, Molly didn't answer.

"She's tired."

"Well, she can sleep. I'm the one who still has to drive all the fucking way to Pensacola."

"She didn't need to sleep with us. We could've shelled out an extra $20 for a trundle. But you—"

"And we could've stuck to our plan. The plan was no kids until we both had jobs we wanted in the same city. "

"For the last time, it wasn't some great conspiracy. I didn't mean to get pregnant. It was simply a mistake."

"But we had a plan, Syl. You promised. No children until—"

The only thing she remembered about the crash itself was the big crunch and feeling like she was being thrown forward and pulled back at the same time. Then she fell into a big hole of purple acrylic that made it hard to breathe and impossible to see. She buried herself deeper into the cloud of white stuffing as voices yelled around her. Then she went absolutely still when a loud grinding noise attacked the door next to her.

The door came off and a man angled his body around her and held her cheek with his hand and whispered to her not to look.

He let her play with his tongue depressors.

"You lived at a retirement home."

"Hmm? What?"

"I think you lived at a retirement home? I think I saw you when I transitioned your grandparents."

"Not a retirement home." Molly lifted her chin and in a loud pseudo-baritone announced, "Vivarbo: *The* Place for Active Adults in Pensacola."

"You Intone very nicely. Did you take classes?"

Molly looked at him and laughed. "You're funny sometimes. It's just that's how the advertisements sounded. They were all over the radio. Luckily my grandparents got in before the sponsors realized that the contracts said 'Owners' must be fifty-five or older. They changed it to 'residents' so that there wouldn't be any more kids, but I was grandfathered in."

She looked at Death expectantly and he looked back with a bent and baffled grin.

"It's another joke," Molly said. "It always made my grandmother laugh. You don't get out much, do you?"

"I get out loads," he said. "Any place you think of, I'll have transitioned someone there."

"Have you ever 'transitioned' an extraterrestrial?"

"*No*, and why do you say it that way, 'transitioned,' like you don't believe it?"

"Because it always irritated me when people would say that my parents 'went to a better place' or my grandfather 'came to the end of his journey.' They died. I kind of expected that you, of all people, could manage to avoid the euphemisms."

She stood there at the top of the subway stairs looking down at the young man stilled at the bottom with his arms bent and his right foot high above the step and knew that he'd sprinted on ahead of the other passengers spilling from the train and as soon as Death left, he would pump his arms some more and his foot would find the step and he would finish his race with the stairs.

"You let me sleep, didn't you?" she asked, twirling her MetroCard between her fingers.

Death shrugged and nodded at the same time, making him look, Molly thought, like the Josh Becket MVP World Series bobblehead doll her grandfather had promised would be worth a fortune someday. Unfortunately when that someday came, Molly went to share a room with four other girls in a group home and Josh Becket went to the dumpster.

"Well, thanks," she said, "for letting me sleep." She started down the steps to the subway until she got halfway down. She stopped and without turning added, "And for not killing me."

"I don't—" he started to call after her, but she was already gone.

And he was already in Vasundhara Enclave when he finished the sentence.

"—want to."

YUH-OH, he thought. *This is going to be trouble.*

CHAPTER 7

Death had barely sent the laundry basket up when it came down again with a thump and spilled a bridal veil stinkhorn fungus made of folded celadon papyrus.

It was a valued art form but opening the thing took forever.

CUSTODES RECTORUM
INDIVISIBILIS AETERNALIS ET IMMUTABILIS

Ragpicker,
We require your presence in the Now. Not the Here-
    after. The Now.
Hallelujah and don't try to pull a fast one,
Abdiel

HE STARED at the intricate lines and complicated folds of the page cupped in his hand. Then he stared at the robes in the bag on the hook attached to the door leading to his bathroom.

Looking at the page again, he dropped it to the floor. He

opened his pantry and scanned the boxes of things that were dried or canned and required no cooking. At the top, on its side, was a big bucket of Bowser's Bacon Jerky Bites. The manic green cartoon dog on the front sometimes made him wonder if they were meant for bipeds but they could do him no harm and he liked them.

After stuffing a handful of Jerky Bites into each of the outside pockets of his greatcoat, he jumped and grasped the bottom rung of the ladder. It hung lower now that he'd been using it so often.

He was still several leagues short of Up, when he heard Puriel screeching.

After rooting around in his pocket with one hand, Death crammed several Bacon Jerky Bites into his mouth and kept going.

Puriel was nowhere to be seen when he cleared the top rung. Instead he was greeted by a covey of panicky low-level Dominions wildly swinging smoking thuribles. Death wasn't sure whether Puriel had forgotten to pass along the usual instructions to use the back or whether speaking required passing air through their bodies and that was something they were simply not willing to do.

The tumbling mass of flunkies with their smoking censers surrounded Death as he walked toward the main campus.

Even the celestial incense could not disguise such powerful earthly fetor of his century-old greatcoat plus Bacon Jerky Bites, so when the multiple presences of the toadying Metatron opened the door of the wall-less office, they did so with a stick. Metatron scurried toward the back muttering something about Abdiel's expected return. The door slammed behind him.

Death pulled out another Jerky Bite.

"What is that stench?!" came Abdiel's voice from a distance.

"Ragpicker," replied Metatron's quickly diminishing voice as he raced to anyplace far, far away.

"Metatron?" Abdiel called. Receiving no answer, he tried again more insistently. "Metatron! We need our pomander!"

Abdiel finally opened the door, his mouth and nose hidden behind an orb of pierced silver. With his free hand, he waved frantically at the air around him.

"We apologize, but your summons was of such urgency that we did not dare delay over the usual ablutions," Death said.

"Aulllhhhhhhh." Abdiel moved toward the back of the office, and tried not to breathe. "Wagpickah? What is Admonithmenth I?"

Death knew the first Admonishment. It was the only one he was really clear about but something had happened to him and to his horror, he heard himself offer up, "**Non conspuentibus**?" And while the Chief Administrator was very weird and prissy about spitting, he wasn't weird and prissy enough to make it the First Admonishment.

"NO!" shouted Abdiel. "**Obedentia thuper omnia.** Obedienth above all. Above *all*. It hathe been noded—"

"Noded?"

"NODED!"

"Oh, *noted*. Sorry, go ahead."

"It hathe been noded that you ha' oppodunity to wetwieve its rag—"

"But you said we had until tomorrow?" Death said, flourishing the skirts of his greatcoat and lowering himself into Abdiel's spare chair.

"Nah my chaiw! Do nah thid in my chaiw!"

The Custodes's Chief Administrator rolled back, right out of the floorplan that constituted his office and breathed deeply through his pomander. "We had Rogziel do some research on the subject of tomorrow," he hollered across the distance, "and we are increasingly of the opinion that tomorrow has already passed."

Death thought a moment. During the course of his interactions with humanity, he had learned many avoidance strategies: cowering, threatening, pleading, bribing, brownnosing and, of course, chess.

He decided on the brownnosing.

"In TIT," he started, using the acronym for Temporal Idiom for the Timeless used by all those who had taken it, "most wrote, 'We have returned Salafiel's lyre tomorrow.' But one—and only one—wrote, 'We *will* return Salafiel's lyre *tomorrow*.'" He didn't mention Abdiel by name, because the art of brown-nosing lay in not being too obvious.

Abdiel tapped his silver pointer on his celadon desk and then unwound a scroll sitting in celadon urn. After tracing many lines of script with his pointer, he sighed. "Rogziel does admit to some confusion among scholars as to exactly when tomorrow is.

"We are trusting, Ragpicker, that in this, as in all matters, you will choose the path of righteousness?"

Death pushed up the hem of his sleeve above the two looping curves at the very top of Molly's name. That thing that had been happening to him that he couldn't quite identify, happened some more.

"Or what?" he asked.

"WHAT?"

"Just asking…what happens if we choose another path?"

Abdiel's eyes narrowed. Azrael had gotten this way once before and they were still paying the price for it. Abdiel rose, standing surrounded by his Glory of stretched and shimmering ether. *"There is no 'or what'!"* he boomed. "Do we have to remind you of everything that has happened because of your choosing? We will not t—"

Death pounded at his chest, loosening a burp redolent of Bowser's Bacon Jerky.

"'Scuse me."

Abdiel turned a silvery gray and fled toward the East Buildings. Death stayed until he was sure the Chief Administrator was gone and then let himself fall.

CHAPTER 8

*I*t was a long fall from the celadon monotony of Up, through the dark constricting emptiness of Limbo, before reaching the parti-colored chaos of Down. Death munched on another Bacon Jerky Bite and thought about all of the times he'd been super, super busy and would inevitably get an elaborately folded celadon radiolaria or Horsehead Nebula. Surrounded by blood and dirt and destruction, he would sit down and unfold the celestial missive.

CUSTODES RECTORUM
INDIVISIBILIS AETERNALIS ET IMMUTABILIS

> *Ragpicker,*
> *Well, that was certainly a disaster.*
> *Hallelujah,*
> *Abdiel*

BEA WAS the only one who saw the things that weren't disasters. She called them miracles. She always said the problem with miracles was that they were subtle and needed both tending and interpreting, while disasters were big and loud and in your face and smelled bad.

Death was increasingly unsure what Molly was: she wasn't small, but she wasn't big either. She was loud, but he'd certainly heard louder. She was often in his face, but not in the way that really bothered him. She smelled like the combination of fried food and cassis shampoo and yeasty beer and cherry Chapstick and he liked it.

No matter what Abdiel said, he did have a choice, and he needed to know whether Molly was a disaster or a miracle before he made it.

He landed with a thump in Times Square and walked the rest of the way.

* * *

"YOU SHOULD CHECK ON TABLE FOURTEEN," said Dave the Manager. "See if you can help."

Molly shook her head. She'd noticed the table before. It was a birthday party for a man who was only a couple of years older than she was. She'd taken an instant dislike to him.

She didn't like the way he wore his hair. She didn't like the way he leaned against the booth, his arm draped over the back. She didn't like the way he ordered more alcohol and more food than a football team could possibly consume. She didn't like the way he raised his glass to other guys' dates. She didn't like the way everything he said seemed to end by a splayed hand and the words "without me." And she really didn't like the way he called for "Sienna, baby" who was worried about her sick toddler at home with her sick mother, without bothering to turn his head.

"There are already two girls there," she said, pointing to

Dawn who was swiveling her hips in the orbit of her hula hoop to the enthusiastic hoots of table fourteen.

"Besides I've got a party going for Carl here, too."

"Yeah," said Dave the Manager, "but I want to make these guys happy and you look prettier than...than...a plate of hot cheese fries."

"You have quite the way with words, Mister Dave," she said and batted his hand away with her own hula hoop. "No employee contact on premises. Your rule."

"Molly." His voice dropped to a whisper. "Can I drive you home?"

"Not tonight," she said, smiling brightly even as her heart sank. "Sorry, darlin'. Carl's calling for me."

Dave wanted more guys like table fourteen. More of the young, self-assured Masters of the Universe wannabes. But Molly could size up a room better than anyone and she didn't care about the demographics of the restaurant. She knew that a tableload of Big Swinging Dicks would take everything given them as their due.

Carl, on the other hand, was over forty. By that age, guys in his field had either made it big or they hadn't. Carl and his friends hadn't and he knew it, but having a pretty girl flutter around him would make him feel better even if just for a night. He wouldn't take it as his due and at the end of the evening, Carl would say "thank you" and he would tip.

It took only a second for Molly to establish a rhythm with her pink plastic hoop, then Gina, the bar trainee who was going to school for social work, handed her a pitcher and a glass. Molly expertly poured a glass, never losing her swivel.

Carl and his friends applauded loudly as Gina reached across with empty glasses and Molly reached back, the glass full.

"Gina?" Molly asked, holding out another full glass, but Gina had faltered, the applause with her. Deron Williams froze on the screen, the basketball midthrow.

There was a soft staccato tapping at the front door.

Molly held her hand in front of the now-static air of the AC and sighed. "Come in?" she called.

When nothing happened, she let her hula hoop drop to the floor, put the glass she'd been holding down in front of Carl's friend who was frozen feeling again for the e-cigarette in his shirt pocket, and walked toward the glass door.

Through the frosted glass, she could make out the outline of the thin man in the big coat, not that she needed to.

"This is a public place," she said, holding the door open. "You don't have to knock."

"Oh," Death said and walked into the breastaurant at 34th Street.

"Notice anything?" Molly was holding her chin up high and her shoulders back. Death's eyes widened and he quickly looked away, turning the silvery color that Molly suspected was embarrassment.

"Not those," she said. "My necklace."

He looked more closely at the thin strand of silver and the tiny pendant that said "Molly" in cursive letters and peridot.

"My grandfather gave it to me when I was little. I haven't worn it for years."

He read it out loud, but it didn't come out as Molly, like it was written. It came out as *Molly*, like he'd been taught in Venerating.

It sounded nice, she thought, part sigh, part secret.

Molly stopped in front of table fourteen, laden with plates of food in shades of gold and beige and brown and dotted with little tubs of sauce overlapping one another. She had just taken a bite of chicken wing, when she felt the back of her shorty shorts creep up the way they so often did. She twisted a little to the side, so she could reach around and pull them down and with the twisting, the chicken wing started to go down the wrong way and she coughed the tight, airless cough of the choking.

Death had studied the thousands of posters ignored by the millions of people until it was too late, so he knew to wrap both arms around her waist, one fist at her sternum and jerk up hard.

She really did need a lot of tending, Death thought as she sucked in a long desperate breath.

"Wow," she said softly, when she'd recovered. "Thank you, really. But I think that's it for me and chicken wings. Never knew they could be so vindictive."

As soon as he let her go, she rearranged her uniform, while Death popped in a cheesy tater tot that was way too hot and would remain too hot until it was time for him to leave. Molly poured him a still-icy beer from the pitcher belonging to the shiny men who thought they were the Masters of the Universe.

* * *

"I GUESS I just assumed you could hold your liquor. Some liquor. Any liquor," Molly said from the coffee station. She reached under Cassie's outstretched arm and poured two mugs of hot coffee.

"Hey, Dee. Do you like milk?"

"Whaa?"

"Milk. In your coffee? Sugar?"

"I lig everything, Molly."

"Yes, well, I think we've established that."

"Molly. Molly. Molly. Molly."

He liked her name. Even more, he liked what she'd called him. Tired at the end of a long shift, Molly had dubbed him Dee, which was so much better than being called Ragpicker! or Azzzrael the way Abdiel did, like he was holding something distasteful in his mouth that he couldn't spit out because there wasn't a trash can.

Or Death, the way humans said it, freighted with whispered terror.

"Goddit now," Death said, jerking around, his big coat swaying frantically. He slammed the hula hoop forward and then back and then forward until after a little more jerking, it slithered once more to the floor.

"Enough of that. Here." She gave him the coffee mug and took the hula hoop. "I'm tired, and I still have another hour on my shift. I really need you to pull yourself together."

"Do i' one more time?" he said.

"If I do, will you promise to get out?"

"Promise."

Molly twirled the hula hoop around her hips and swiveled expertly as the little ball bearings inside made a steady shwish-shwish that that always brought back the feeling of hot concrete under her feet on the sidewalks of Vivarbo. ("Covered toed shoes are to be worn outside at all times," quoth Mrs. Kulamaa. "Exercise equipment is only for use in the designated fitness areas," echoed Mr. Moskowitz.)

"Molly? Why's zat man staring at you so hard?" Death asked, pointing toward Dave who was staring at the place where Molly had been and would be again as soon as she figured out how to kick the drunk personification out of her workplace.

"Because like you, I made a mistake. I make a lot of them."

"What was your mistake?"

"We had—have—a thing. Dave and me."

"A thing?"

"Just…a thing. You know. Sex."

"You are with child?"

"Don't be ridiculous. It was supposed to be a one-night stand or something, but I stupidly told him I didn't have any family and it made him feel like I was a damsel in distress—that's what he said. He has this house in Teaneck with two bedrooms and a sunroom that could be made into a third and his younger brothers are married with kids and he starts to think…I don't know what, exactly, but…

"I was stupid and now because he's my manager and I need his help with the schedule, I'm stuck. It's what comes from pissing where you eat."

"You urinated on the table?"

"Oh, for the love of ... You have simply got to sober up. It's just an expression about the inadvisability of mixing bodily needs—like sex and work."

Yes, he nodded, suddenly sage. This he understood and could address. He reached back into his years in Righteousness for the proper Admonishment that would help her avoid such mistakes as urinating on tables.

"**Flamma**," he intoned, in a voice that smacked of sobriety but was not sober, "**radix doloris est.**"

Molly rolled the hula hoop back and forth, listening to the ball bearings that were the only sound in the silence. "And that means what exactly?" she asked, her voice suddenly cool.

He could almost hear the hair on her neck bristle. But now that she was asking, he realized that he didn't want to translate it.

He pulled up the high collar of his coat and buried his mouth in it.

"Dee? What does it mean?"

He couldn't bear it if she started to say this new name in that old way.

"Passion is the root of suffering?" he mumbled softly and shoved his fingers in his ears just in case.

But Molly didn't scream. She looked up at the ceiling for what seemed to Death like forever. "Suffering," she finally said, "is the root of passion."

With the insistence of someone who spent four and a half eternities failing at Righteousness and was finally sure of something, he said, "The Book of Admonishments says very clearly that passion is the root of suffering."

Molly propped her hula hoop against a chair, then she

stretched out her back and one after the other, circled her stiff ankles. "Well," she said wearily. "The Book of SAT Prep says that the root of the passion is *pati*. To suffer. So suffering is the root of passion. And until you know something about either, Do. Not. *Ever*. Admonish. Me. Again."

She took his wrist and pulled him after her to the door. He was strong, but Molly had been fighting with Death her entire life and wasn't about to stop now.

He stumbled over a chair and clutched onto a wood-paneled pillar for support.

"Wait, stop. Please ...Molly. I need to think. I want to think. It's just that I've been told 'no' for so long, that now I can't even remember whether there's supposed to be a 'yes' at the end."

* * *

SEE, now this is interesting, Bea thought, watching Death weaving on his unsteady legs, talking so earnestly to the tired girl in bright pink shorts outside the breastaurant on 34th St.

* * *

BY THE TIME DEATH LEFT, Molly was exhausted. She even dropped the remains of a plate of curly fries. Then when she leaned over to pick them up, she saw a ragged, shale-colored shadow creep farther under the table.

Molly got down on her hands and knees to the perfunctory smatter of applause from the guys waiting for final call. Reaching past a shriveled curly fry, she stretched her arm out long, her head against the bench, until she felt the coolness of it on her finger tip, felt it swirl swiftly up her arm over her shoulder and into her shirt.

She jerked back, sitting on her heels, and looked into her

bra. Only one guy bothered to whistle. The Rag pulled itself small between breast and bra and shivered there.

In the staff room at the end of shift, the entertainers—because that's what they were called—peeled off their perkiness in layers. The smile that was so automatic was always the last to come off.

It stayed when Sienna worried that her mom wasn't doing well and wasn't sure how much longer she'd be able to take care of the baby. It stayed when Gina complained about homework that she had waiting for her at home. And it stayed when Molly distractedly wiggled out of her shorty shorts and felt the dead woman's soul clinging to her underwire.

* * *

THE APARTMENTS above the Popeye's at 135th Street and Adam Clayton Powell Jr. Boulevard had no names on the buzzers, only numbers. Molly peered through the tiny cracked square window of safety glass crisscrossed with wires. The wall on the right was lined with mailboxes. Straight ahead she could see a staircase, lit by a flickering fluorescent light. She tried banging on the door, but that just got her a furious diatribe from someone clearly unfamiliar with Admonishments.

She wrote a note on a corner of her Soft Tissue Damage test and folded it up, writing DEE in big block letters on the outside. Then she settled herself into a booth at IHOP.

"I don't suppose you're going to eat anything," asked a woman with dyed mahogany hair, a blue striped shirt and an orange badge that said Colette. She held the limp menu in her rough and reddened hands.

"Just coffee, thanks."

The restaurant, like most twenty-four-hour places at a remove from tourist hubs, served an eclectic crowd. In a booth near the divider was a man with a trench coat and formal shoes but no pants who was holding his phone to his mouth and whispering sentences that all ended with the word "explain." A shell-shocked woman pushed a stroller up and down the aisle, stopping occasionally to grab a sip of coffee before the stroller's inhabitant noticed and started screaming.

Only the stoners in the corner were eating anything.

Molly checked on the soul a few times, but the man with no pants left off begging to watch her, so she stopped and bent over the EMT test prep she'd loaded on to her phone. Collette was under strict instructions not to let anyone sleep at the tables but just as she was about to shake the girl awake, Death slipped under her arm into the booth.

"You really have her?"

"Yes."

His hands shook as he reached them across the table, his eyes pleading in his gray and waxy face.

"How are you feeling?" Molly asked.

"I can't think. There's a balloon right here behind my eye. This"—he circled his palm around his torso—"feels like a cake with a hole in the middle. And I lost her. I've been searching everywhere. What if she'd crept into a hole or...?" He clutched at his mouth. "Can I see her?"

"She's safe," Molly said, lightly feeling the underside of her right breast. "I can feel her, but I think she's afraid to come out."

Death reached out to the skin above Molly's cleavage and below her necklace.

"What are you doing?" Molly said, slapping his hand.

"She'll know it's me and won't be afraid."

"Yeah, well, you're not copping a feel. I'll go into the bathroom—"

"No! Not here," he said, his hands clenching into tight pleading fists. "They have drains in the floor. You don't know how slippery they are. If you drop her, she could go right into the sewer and it would take me forever to find her."

In the end, Molly agreed to follow Death to his apartment, and dislodge the young woman there.

Collette finished shaking Molly. Molly put her money on the table and stumbled over a pothole on 135th street. The bright lights above the Popeye's sign hurt her eyes. Death opened the door and led her up the tightly coiled stairs. The long hall in the second floor was lighted with fluorescents that gave everything the bright joyless pallor of a morgue in a poorer corner of the former Soviet bloc. The only thing that broke up the expanses of boiled-cabbage green were dark red doors and a faded poster advertising the Seventh Annual Shower of Stars at the Apollo with Sad Sam emceeing.

Death lifted the poster and slid his fingers along the back of the frame. His brow started to furrow and he slid his fingers up and down until finally he emerged dusty and triumphant.

"I don't usually bother with the door, so it's been a while."

He stretched out his fingers and then fiddled with the key, putting it in the wrong way, putting it in the right way but not far enough and after a couple of minutes, Molly wrapped her hand around his and slid it in easily turning it the right way, while simultaneously twisting open the door knob. His eyebrows zipped up. He smiled in triumph; Molly smiled because she didn't have the energy to come up with something more original.

He really did need a lot of tending.

Beyond the open door wasn't a bachelor pad exactly. Just the home of a guy who lived alone: a futon with two pillows and a Buffalo Bills comforter that still bore the soft indentation of a body. A tiny unfinished pine table with a single chair stood next to the Pullman kitchen. There was a single bowl and spoon on the drainboard. And a huge ancient-looking cabinet of intricately carved, cracked wood with a pair of slightly warped doors at the top and another pair at the bottom. Two metal straps held the doors closed, each with a lock.

On top was an upside-down lime-green Cake Taker. Once he had emptied his big outer pockets into the Cake Taker, he shifted carefully out of his greatcoat.

"Hnh," said Molly, sitting on his unfinished pine chair, her head resting on his unfinished pine table. "That's interesting."

The table felt powdery and smooth against her cheek.

"What's interesting?"

"You don't have a belly button."

When he looked at his utterly smooth featureless torso, that peculiar silvery sheen spread across his face. He pulled down his shirt.

She watched him lay his coat out across his futon. He started coaxing the souls from each pocket, dropping them into a big orange laundry basket lined in pink and blue flannel.

When all the pockets were empty, he turned to Molly.

"Are you ready?" he asked.

She didn't say anything.

Death got on his knees in front of her. "Hey," he said again. "Molly?" He held his hand above her chest, hoping that the Rag would jump to him the way she had when he'd first come to her. She didn't because now she wasn't in a tortured body; now she was with Molly, who'd found her and kept her safe and dragged her exhausted self across the city in the middle of the night, all for a young woman to whom she owed nothing and who could do nothing for her in return.

Death picked Molly up easily. He cradled her head on both pillows and folded his Buffalo Bills blanket over her.

He retrieved his sewing box from under the futon and moved aside the black iron-on patches, black thread and spare black laces and picked out a thimble and a box in yellow and red that said, "Luminous Safety Matches, Made In Sweden" but contained needles.

Sitting on the wood chair, he sucked on the end of the thread and squinted. When he'd threaded the needle, he checked every pocket and repaired the one that had a hole through which the little soul had slipped and the three that were starting to weaken. The pockets had been replaced often over time; the coat itself was becoming threadbare and he would need a new one soon. But he had time. He always had time. Not like Molly who was always wrung out from days crammed full.

Not like Molly, who was always living, always dying.

Hanging his coat on the back of his chair, he sat down next to her. Hesitating at first, he finally reached around her front and pressed his fingers to her navel, pinching and pulling until the ebony shadow emerged. He hadn't reached deep or pulled hard, but the breath still streamed from her body with a sigh. He let go quickly and lay back, his bent arm cradling his head, and stared at the ceiling. He pulled out a length of his own soul. It was particularly stretchy and near the surface and numinous.

Maybe Molly didn't do what she was supposed to; maybe she was coarse and crude and earthy, but how was she worse than the indifferent Cherubim with their sparkling souls? The ones who would feed her Rag into the Mangles, only stopping to make sure she was securely between the rollers, before turning to the next and the next. Not even caring that Molly had been turned into a fucking oyster.

He started to panic and turned on his side and arranged his body so that it paralleled the awkward curve of hers. He lowered his nose until he could suck in the heady smell of sweat and yeast and nachos and coffee and loam.

He wrapped his arm around her. Sometime in the long stillness of this moment when no one was dying, he settled his hand on Molly's breast until the frightened soul found him and curled around his fingers.

CHAPTER 9

*M*olly was long gone when Death noted with alarm that his soul had developed a tendril. He could feel it right in the middle of his chest. It didn't hurt, but it was irritating and when he pulled it into the open, it squirmed like a salamander on hot asphalt.

He couldn't help picking at it.

* * *

"You're a doctor, right?" he asked the psychiatrist who had been called in to assist in the chemical restraint of a man who had shanked another inmate. "What do you think this is?"

He pushed his fingernails against his chest, and pulled out the silvery strand.

"Should I cut it off? Or do you think it will just go away on its own?"

The doctor looked steadily at the hypodermic in his hand.

Then Death rubbed the tendril between his fingers and his teeth gritted. He let it go and with a slight thrrrip it sucked back under his skin.

"You're absolutely right," Death said. "I should check with Molly. She'll know what to do.

"Thank you, Dr. Pataki, you've been very helpful."

Death left as soon as he'd slipped the Rag of the dead man into his pocket, leaving Dr. Pataki to pump his killer full of ketamine.

* * *

HER SHIFT WAS NEARLY over when Molly heard the nerve-shredding scream. She ran to the back to find Kitchen Lyle turning the cold water to high while Manager Dave held the hand he'd burned while trying to clean out a clogged burner orifice on the Fryolator. Molly turned the water down to a gentle stream.

"It's not bad," she said. "I'll get the first aid kit."

"Look at this," he said, showing her the second-degree burn the size of a silver dollar. "It's huge. I mean no offense but I need to see a real doctor." Her molars tightened together in the back of her mouth and her jaw stayed clenched as he hailed a cab accompanied by Kitchen Lyle and a bucket of ice.

She wasn't particularly surprised when Dave called back to say that neither he nor Kitchen Lyle would be back for break-down. She could only imagine the ER triage nurse's eyes sliding over a second-degree burn the size of a silver dollar before returning to the overdoses, heart attacks and penetrating trauma.

Molly promised Dave that she would help out. She would do the kitchen for double time and Sunday off so she could study for her Obstetrics test.

Slipping out of her tight black tank and tiny pink shorts and those damn Suntan pantyhose, Molly pulled on her black leggings and an old, loose T-shirt.

She leaned on the metal counter and turned on the speaker

that Kitchen Lyle had left stuck to the white tile backsplash. She synced up her phone and pulled on the thick rubber gloves. After filling a big bucket with hot water and detergent and bleach, she scraped the heavy grill with a wire brush and pushed it into the sink. She filled another bucket and washed the surfaces with hot sudsy water mixed with bleach and opened the refrigerator.

"Hey, Molly," called Gina, who'd helped close out the front. "I'm out of here."

Molly blew her an air kiss with her big black glove covered in soap and the combination of milk and watery blood that had spilled and coagulated at the bottom of the refrigerator.

She scrubbed the mats and duckboards and set them against the wall.

She danced around the mop, her hips swaying, singing into the handle, her eyes closed. When the music stopped, she pulled off one of the big gloves and leaned over the counter, her hips still shifting to the song she kept humming. Her phone was old and sometimes glitched and needed to be restarted. She pushed the power button. She pushed it again.

Death didn't say anything at first. He just wanted to watch her hips sway and listen to her torment the minor melody.

"Molly?" he said finally. She whipped around, her face falling as soon as she saw him.

"Hey, what happened?" she asked, pulling off one glove. "You look freaked out."

"It's your name. Molly. I know your name. I didn't have to look at your necklace or here," he held up the block letters on his wrist. "I just know it. Molly."

"Okay," she said, squeezing her mop in the wringer. "Isn't that good?"

"I'm not sure. Usually, I can only remember the names of the dead or the undying. The living are not my business. I..." He rubbed his chest where the tendril had started to pop out all on its own, twisting and churning through his skin. He put his hand over it, rubbing it distractedly through his thin T-shirt.

"What is that?"

"I don't know. That's what I came for, because I figured if anyone could tell me what it was, it was you."

Molly slid the mop into the graying, soapy water and, holding her gloved hand behind her, kissed Death gently on the cheek because that was just what she'd needed to hear. A declaration of faith, a recognition of worth that made up for Dave choosing Kitchen Lyle and his bucket of ice.

He pulled down the loose, ragged collar and Molly leaned in for a closer look. "I really wish I could help but I've never seen one. Does it hurt?"

"Doesn't hurt, but I'm always aware of it. This is the first time it popped out by itself, though."

The thing strained from his fingers, stretching itself thinner and thinner until it was a shimmering thread reaching toward her. Cautiously, she touched it with the tip of her finger and it shot up, twirling around her, making her skin tingle but not unpleasantly. When she pulled back, the tendril collapsed and retreated, thrrrrrippp, back into Death's chest. "You go to pretty rough places," she said, rubbing her finger. "Are you sure it's not a worm or something?"

"It can't be. Remember how I told you I was perfectly sterile? I mean that. My body can't support life. Can you imagine what would happen if I were a vector? I transition someone dying of Ebola and within a week I've visited over a million places. What a disaster that'd be. You guys wouldn't stand a chance."

"Well, ummm, I guess all I can say is keep an eye on it and let me know if there are any changes. Not that I can do anything but at least I won't worry. Right now, I've got to finish up, so...?" She pointed to the speaker on the wall. "I like to have music when I work."

Death didn't want to leave. He wanted to stay with this

woman who might worry about him. He watched as she spread a coating of ointment over her hands, paying special attention to the cracked skin between her fingers, before pulling on her heavy gloves.

He searched around his mind through the playlist he'd accumulated during his millennia in Choir trying to find something with a beat that matched the swaying of her hips.

Molly brushed the grills and swung her hips while Death washed the vent top filter and sang *"Labia insurgentium et cogitationes"* at the top of his lungs.

"Look at my enemies whispering and muttering against me all day long. Sitting or standing, they mock me in their soooooongs."

* * *

"No, I've never seen one," Bea said poking at the tendril. "I presume it doesn't hurt?"

"No."

"How long has it been like this?"

"A little over a week. And now I have a little one right here." Death let go of the big tendril at his chest and squeezed the spot under his cheekbone with the nails of his two index fingers until a tiny tendril popped out.

Bea tilted her chin up and leaned in for a closer look. She shook her head. "If you were a man, I'd say it was a guinea worm, but... Have you asked Zerachiel?"

Death said nothing.

"Neshama'le, you are going to have to go Up. You can't avoid Abdiel forever."

"Maybe you could do something? They listen to—"

"I cannot contravene Admonishments, you know that."

"It was my mistake. They should punish me, not Molly. And see that? I know her name now. I know her name. Molly Molly

Molly Molly Molly Molly Molly Molly Molly Molly Molly Molly."

"Ahhh, hmmm. Did you show your Guinea worm to Molly?"

"Yeah, and it just popped out all by itself. I thought it was pretty creepy," he said, picking absently at the tendril at his chest, "but luckily she was okay about it. She even gave me a little kiss right here." He rubbed the spot at his cheek where the Guinea worm had just been and smiled dreamily.

Yuh-oh, thought Bea. *That's going to be trouble.*

CHAPTER 10

*M*olly had been two when her father had insisted that his dying mother see her only grandchild.

Grandma Molloy was still dying the next time Molly saw her after sixteen years and thirty hours on a Greyhound bus that started in Pensacola with changes in Mobile and Atlanta and Fayetteville and Richmond. She carried nothing but a backpack, the ripe smells of many different lands, and a big duffle bag filled with the remains of her mother, her father, Grandma and Grandpa Kahn, and Zach, the first boy she'd ever loved and the last.

"What took you so long?" Grandma Molloy snapped. At first Molly thought that her grandmother had mistaken her for yet another hired caregiver sent by the Agency. Then she realized that the waspish woman knew exactly who she was.

Unfortunately for Grandma Molloy, Molly was not from the Agency and was absolutely done with accommodating. So when her grandmother said she DID NOT want to see those urns on her mantelpiece, Molly rearranged her Geri-chair so the urns stared at her back while she watched *Wheel of Fortune*.

"Fucking morbid," Mary Molloy had muttered.

Now Grandma Molloy was on the mantelpiece in a small cardboard box with printed block letters that claimed it was a TEMPORARY CONTAINER but wouldn't be.

Her granddaughter sealed the box up with duct tape and then shoved it into the duffle bag that had carried her bottled family and her canned lover north so she could move them to the Lower East Side, an apartment on Grand Street to be exact.

Molly pulled at the ancient Run-D.M.C. T-shirt that had fit Zach so nicely. It strained over her breasts and gapped at the waist, but she would never throw it out. She couldn't afford to be profligate with her memories.

The Medicks next door had bought her grandmother's rent-stabilized apartment with her in it. They got it cheap because Mary Kathleen Molloy couldn't be moved, but everyone knew the old woman was standing on Death's threshold, her hand firmly on the door knocker.

After the birth of their son, the Medicks made the strategic mistake of asking after Grandma Molloy's health.

If they'd known her grandmother a little better, they'd have been more discreet. Her last years were fueled by canned salmon and spite and if it hadn't been for the powdered sugar on Death's lapel, that combination would have allowed her to survive her husband, her son and her granddaughter and quite possibly all three Medicks.

Molly was much more practical and took the $5,000 the Medicks offered her to leave expeditiously and without getting the courts involved and used it to pay the security deposit on an apartment above a Middle Eastern bakery.

She started to pack what she could do without. Mostly a few books from the days before she read everything on her phone. Books filled with the endless notes she'd written assuring her young self that there was a world outside of the tightly circumscribed world of Vivarbo and the strip mall populated by Straynes Deli, a Piggly Wiggly and the drugstore that said Rite Aid, but most of the residents at Vivarbo still called Eckerds.

Looking through them, seeing the vocabulary words, the notes on historical figures and places, she felt almost embarrassed by the pretensions of the dreams she nursed at Vivarbo, encouraged by the inmates, well, two of the inmates, her grandmother and her friend, Mrs. Thibaut.

She looked at the box that she hadn't opened for years. It had been interred in her underwear drawer because it was marked fragile and it seemed right somehow to store it with the things that her housemother at Odd Fellows called "Delicates."

Picking away the packing tape, she pulled up the top flap and carefully slid out a polished column of wood on a pedestal. There was a glass window that looked onto a painted blue sky and a tiny tree with tiny leaves and a little mirrored pond topped by miniature ducks. Next to it was a woman in a long dress and a man in a frock coat followed by two tiny children.

At the bottom was a tiny envelope that said

To Molly Molloy
Jacqueline Thibaut's Best Friend.

The bit of Scotch tape she'd used to attach the envelope to the base had started to get crispy and peel off. She held the envelope, feeling the bump inside. Finally she shook out the key and cupped it in her hand.

Kids at elementary school teased Molly relentlessly about living in a nursing home, no matter how often she asserted that Vivarbo was *"The* Place for Active Adults in Pensacola."

The one time she'd invited a friend over, Ava hadn't known that you had to use inside voices, and inside movements, even when you were outside. She hadn't known that the pool was not for swimming, but for bending side to side with a noodle in the morning and for sitting next to with large visored hats in the afternoon.

Ava had gone home in tears.

Mrs. Thibaut was one of the few who'd never clucked disapprovingly. Never complained about how loud she was. Never yelled at her to slow down. Even the caviling claque at the swimming pool would keep their grumbling to themselves when Mrs. Thibaut was around.

Mrs. Thibaut introduced Molly to Ella and Satchmo and Django and poker and cribbage. Her young friend reminded her of her own mischievous daughter, Natalie, who needed to run and fly when she was Molly's age. She jumped on the bed and squirmed and struggled even while she slept, the blankets always ending up in a puddle on the floor. She could never walk down the stairs, but with one dirty hand pressed to the wall, the other holding tight to the banister, she would fly down an entire flight without touching a single step.

"*Ça suffit!*" Mrs. Thibaut did a wicked imitation of the old sow of a concierge. "*Tu me gonfles.*"

Then Mrs. Thibaut died. She was very, very old, but Molly was heartbroken anyway. A bald, paunchy man came and while Molly stood at the door, the horrible stranger pawed through Mrs. Thibaut's belongings.

"Who are you and what are you doing here?" Molly had said, yanking a picture from his hands.

"I'm Robert Thibaut, Jacqueline Thibaut's son. And who would you be?"

"I am Molly Molloy. Mrs. Thibaut's friend," Molly had yelled. "Her *best* friend. Where is Natalie?"

Robert stopped for a moment, put another neatly wrapped rectangle into a box, then he turned to the girl in front of him with a considering look. "Natalie has been dead for decades. She and my mother's first husband died in Sobibor." He pulled a new piece of paper from the pile and continued to wrap the old framed photographs.

Molly stumbled across the threshold and as soon as she got home, she confronted her grandmother who had assumed that Molly, like everyone else, knew Mrs. Thibaut was a Holocaust survivor.

"And there's a man there. Robert. He says he's her son, but she never talked about him. She only ever talked about Natalie."

"Robert can talk for himself," her grandmother had said. "Natalie is the one whose life needed remembering."

Molly had been at school when Robert dropped off a cardboard box marked fragile. The envelope taped to the outside was addressed

To Molly Molloy
Jacqueline Thibaut's Best Friend.

She put the key into the back and wound it up and watched as the woman in the long dress and the man in the frock coat and the two children slid in a circle around the tiny tree with the tiny leaves and the little mirrored pond topped by miniature ducks and the music box pinged "What a Wonderful World."

* * *

AT EXACTLY 6:00, she got the first knock. She picked up the chipped enamelware filled with pumpkin-shaped peanut butter cups and looked through the peephole. Medicks, husband and wife, stood accompanied by a costumed creature who must be their son, the zitty, hulking, odiferous manchild, Vince.

She opened the door.

"Trih o Tree" came a voice muted by preteen angst and gray-green latex. Behind him, Vince's parents weaved back and forth, straining for a better view of the apartment.

"Would you like to come in?"

"No," they said in unison. "We really couldn't."

"It's fine. But I'm in the middle of packing."

While the Medicks, who really wouldn't dream of snooping around the apartment, took out their graph paper and pencils and measuring tapes, Vince pawed through her candies with his all-too-human hands. His voice, still muffled behind the gray-green latex with bulbous yellow eyes and a gristly smile on a skeletal face, asked something. She had him repeat it.

"D'yo ave anythin' else?" he mumbled more slowly this time.

"It's what I like," she said. "What are you supposed to be anyway?"

"Depp."

"What?"

"Deathhhh," he repeated, holding the mouth of the mask closer to his face.

"Hunh. He doesn't look like that at all, you know. He's actually kind of handsome."

From the bathroom Mrs. Medick fell silent in the middle of asking whether the pipes were original.

The only sound was someone knocking thusly at her door.

"Hey," Molly said, concealing Vince behind the opened door.

"Hey," said Death, closing the door and revealing Vince.

When he jumped, Death achieved a velocity and loft well beyond the carrying capacity of mixed-income, post-war housing in New York City. When he landed, there was a concavity in the ceiling and a slight indentation in his head.

"Wow. Do you need an ice pack?"

"I'm okay," he said, massaging his head back into shape. "What is that?"

"It's Halloween. You know, Trick or Treat?" She held out the big bowl and Death helped himself to a pumpkin-shaped peanut-butter chocolate.

"I like these," he said. He always forgot there was more to this holiday than people drinking too much, putting on masks that drastically limited their field of vision and getting into cars.

"Take more. There aren't really that many little kids in the building anymore and the big ones are too cool to go Trick or Treating."

Death nodded toward Vince, his hand frozen above the candies that were no longer there.

"He's a beard. His parents just wanted to get a look at the apartment. It's an old mask."

Death popped the melty chocolate candy into his mouth.

"He's supposed to be you."

Why, he wondered for the umpteenth time, were all the images of him so creepy and cadaverous? He had nothing to do with what happened to the body afterward. Its decay was prophesied at the moment of birth when the mother's body pressed into her baby the microbes that would support the body's defenses and allow it to feed. At the moment of death, those symbionts—the maternal gift—became opportunistic, migrating through the body's corridors and turning it into muck. If anyone should be blamed for what happened to the body, it was good old mum.

"I told him you didn't look anything like that. Told him you were kind of handsome, even." She chuckled to herself and Death wondered if she chuckled because she thought it was true or because she knew it wasn't.

He wiped his hands on one of the stack of napkins he had in his pocket, then sat on the sofa and started moving around cards she had splayed out on the low coffee table.

"I take it you don't know how to play Solitaire?"

"The only game I know is Obedience." He continued to move the cards around, quickly swirling them into curve after curve until it looked like a nautilus. "I was never much good at Obedience."

Molly's smile faded. "How do you play it? With Legos?"

"Legos? Well, no. Someone tells you to do something but it has to be...Here, it's easier to just show it." Death scanned her little apartment until he saw a box of oatmeal.

"Open the box of oatmeal."

"Why?"

"Just open the box."

"Tell me what I'm doing it for."

"Because that's how you play the game."

She took the lid off and looked at him skeptically.

"Now shake it."

"What? R'you nuts? It would spill all over the place." She popped the lid back on. "Why would I do that?"

"*That's the point.* Obedience is about doing something without having to know why. Are you sure you played before? Because you're even worse at it than I am."

She sealed the oatmeal carton shut with packing tape.

"That's not how we played Obedience. Mrs. Newton—she was the housemother at Odd Fellows—she would spread out Legos on the floor. We had bare feet and a blindfold. Then Mr. Newton would give us directions. The better you were at following instructions, the less your feet hurt at the end."

She put the oatmeal in the box that was heavy with books.

"Zach"—she gently touched the pewter vase—"he just walked straight across."

Molly carefully put the music box back in its cardboard then wrapped it in one of the sheets of spare bubble wrap she'd been gathering from the recycling room.

"Molly?"

"Hmmm."

"What are you doing with all the boxes?"

"What does it look like I'm doing?" She pulled at a piece of tape and tore it with her teeth before wrapping it around the bubble wrap. "I'm moving."

Death stilled.

"Moving? What do you mean you're moving? You mean you're leaving?"

"This isn't really my apartment. I found a place downtown."

The smell of the air never changed when Death was around. If it smelled like canned generic salmon when he arrived, it smelled like canned generic salmon when he left. But now the combined fragrance of stinky preteen and peanut butter cups gave way to something bright and burny. "When were you going to tell me?" he said in a hollow voice that reached well beyond the narrow confines of her apartment. "Supposing I came later and knocked thusly on the door and nobody heard me?"

He looked at Vince's malignant mask.

"It makes me feel very...very shaky and spicy."

"Angry, maybe?" Molly said.

"Yes, angry, but also shaky and not spicy. More cold and heavy?"

"Sad?"

"Yes, sad. Sad. You made me sad." He stormed over to Vince, slapping his hand and the peanut butter cup he'd been holding while pawing around for something better in Molly's candy bowl. "I want him out of here. I don't want to see him anymore."

This is what happened, he thought, when you disobey Admonishments. You felt spicy and shaky and cold and heavy and angry and sad. He didn't like it. He wanted to go back to before, before he even felt Curiosity, the disastrous first feeling, and Shame, the second feeling, that put a leash on it.

A hand rested against the middle of his back, utterly steady and still. "I'm sorry," she said. "I didn't know it would bother you so much, otherwise I would have told you earlier. But I'll tell you now."

She told him everything about why she was leaving and where her new address was and when she was moving and her hand and her voice sucked away all the shaking and the tendril at his sternum was met by another at his back and still more that knit him all together in one warm and wistful and wanting whole.

He didn't bother to ask Molly what the feeling was that he was feeling because he already knew.

Yuh-oh, he thought. *This is going to be trouble.*

CHAPTER 11

❧

*N*ow the Geri-chair was gone and Grandma Molloy was in a plastic bag in a cardboard box sealed with packing tape. She'd been cheap and crabbed in life, she could be cheap and crabbed in death as far as Molly was concerned.

She'd gotten a van without a man, because a man was time and a half.

Mr. Costo, the super, had said he would help her move her mattress and sofa and coffee table down to the van for $100.

On the day, Mr. Costo clarified that he'd meant $100 *each* and stood in his door watching the furious Molly struggle down the stairs with a box of books too tightly packed and too heavy. She banged the door open with her hip.

The air felt thick and still and then she saw the old gray coat draped over the rearview mirror.

"I'll get something else," he said and ran up the stairs.

"Dammit." She put the bulky box down and ran after him. "Be careful. They're really heav—"

A thin pair of legs poked out from underneath her sofa which was being steered down the stairs like a bulky bag of helium balloons. His head poked from the side. "Open the door?"

Molly ran back down the stairs. Turning the sofa, Death bumped it into the door frame and then turned it slightly to ease it through the narrow passage. Balancing it on one knee, he freed a hand to push his hair back from his face.

And, like always, it took no time at all.

As she drove toward her new apartment, Molly imagined the super's smirk fading when he finally gave in to his curiosity and pushed open her unlocked door only to find it empty except for three cans of generic salmon.

Molly drove south and double-parked the van directly in front of the Palmyra Bakery, blocking in a man whose car was in turn blocking a fire hydrant.

But now that Dee no longer looked quizzically at her belly button, his fingers twitching; now that there were no more lectures about peace or transitioning or anything else hinting at a future as an oyster, Molly enjoyed having a friend who had time for her. Real time. Not the truncated meetings with friends from work or school that were rushed because they—and she— were all busier than Death.

Not only had he moved her heavy furniture, he sat on her sofa and discussed earnestly whether it was better to look into the setting sun, or have it at your back.

"If you don't like it, we'll change it," he said. And they sat there eating warm lavash and pita and things with za'atar sprinkled on top that they'd picked up from Palmyra downstairs, leaving a twenty under the counter man's fingers.

The only thing left was the duffle bag filled with her potted family and canned lover and the boxed grandmother. She didn't want them in the back room, the bedroom, because they would block the fire escape and more importantly the roof over the ovens, which she'd already begun to imagine as her own private terrace.

She decided to figure it out later, after she had cleared her head. But for right now, she needed to recycle the boxes and take a shower.

Death volunteered to deal with the boxes and promised to come back after she'd taken her shower, in case there was anything else.

Molly headed into the bathroom. It was small and outdated and perfect.

She leaned over and soaped up her hair again, making sure to get her scalp, replacing the sweat with the cassis-scented shampoo. She squirted more onto a clean kitchen sponge because she hadn't been able to find her soap when the water froze midair and someone was knocking thusly on her front door.

"Be out in a second," she said.

Molly scooped just enough of the drops dangling in the air to rinse her face. She ran her toothbrush through the heavier drops hanging like unpicked fruit under the faucet and brushed her teeth.

Then she pulled on her favorite bright red T-shirt that said

NICEVILLE HIGH
WE EDUCATE
ALL STUDENTS!

and served as both pajamas and loungewear which were really the same thing, only one was worn during the hours when one could acceptably be sleeping and the other when one shouldn't.

"What happened to your hair?" Death asked when she opened the door.

"I got the 'rinse and repeat' stage all right but the water stopped before I got to the 'for best results, follow with...' stage."

"Do you need me to go away?"

She shook her head and sat on the sofa with her back to the ever-setting but never set sun, running her fingers through the knots.

Death watched her struggle her way through the tangled mass, then he stretched out his slight hands. "Can I try?" he asked. When Molly didn't say no, Death put his fine fingers into the damp softness. He wiggled and stretched and pulled gently until the stubborn tangle was gone. Teasing out the knots turned out to require much the same technique as teasing out a reluctant soul.

She leaned against his shins and as he worked; he felt the cool surface of skin, the warmth of the flesh underneath, the softness and slightly sticky dampness.

Molly found herself relaxing as his fingers untangled her hair. She curled her arms around her bent legs. She leaned her cheek against her knees and let his hands whisper against her neck and the spot above her ear.

"I miss him," she said, staring at the jar on her floor.

It was the first time Molly had talked about Zach, even though she hadn't said his name and Death continued drawing out the knots in her hair, hoping that perhaps it would unknot other parts of her.

MOLLY KNEW ENOUGH to know that there were much worse places than the Odd Fellows Home for Teens.

It had been founded by Mr. Newton, a builder, who at the bottom of another housing bust, was looking for a calling that was less cyclical than residential construction in Florida. One that wouldn't suffer when the Feds decided they could no longer afford to insure people who insisted on building in flood zones.

Then he and his wife hit on the most recession-proof undertaking of all: unwanted children.

He built a three-story house with rooms on the top for the boys and rooms on the bottom for the girls and an apartment in the middle for the Newtons complete with a lovely patio from which they could see the Choctawhatchee River.

Underneath the patio was a sleeping porch where no one ever slept. Instead, Mr. Newton, who'd paid a small fee to be ordained online, hectored the children in his care while his untended wife nodded and drank diet peach iced tea.

Every dinner started with the lobbing of questions on the day's sermonizing. Molly, who was twelve when she arrived and ached with hunger, quickly figured out that the questions could be interchangeably answered with almost any disapproving quote from Paul ("For to set the mind on the flesh is death").

Because underlying everything at Odd Fellows was the assumption that anyone in their charge had to be guilty. Not of any particular sin, but just in an intrinsic way that allowed the Newtons to keep believing in the Plan of a Just God.

They condemned everything from the way Nevaeh styled her hair to the comic books little Kai read to the songs Molly sang when she thought she was alone. ("While we live in these earthly bodies, we groan and sigh...")

Molly didn't groan or sigh. She either quoted Paul or she kept her mouth shut. After four years, she had stress fractures on six molars.

When Zachary Willem Adreux showed up, Molly had only eighteen months to go. A little younger than Molly, Zach had been abandoned as a boy and then punted from one foster family to another. He'd had run-ins with the law and Odd Fellows was his last stop before heading to a high-risk facility.

Molly knew when she looked into those black eyes that this skinny, horny boy was going to be nothing but trouble. He was a born provocateur. He couldn't keep his mouth shut, not with the Newtons and especially not with Molly whose rigidly maintained appeasement pissed him off. He didn't accept her philosophy of accommodation until life could begin for real.

Life was already for real, he'd told her in one of the hushed and angry conversations over the dinner dishes. After months of hectoring, he called her a prude and she said shows what he knew, she'd been having sex with her child psychologist since she was fifteen.

She nearly cracked another molar waiting for Zach to crow or make fun of her. He didn't, though. Instead, two nights later, he picked the security gate outside the girls' room and took her to the sleeping porch.

Trying to seem tougher and cockier and more sure of herself than she was, Molly told him about Dr. Thorsten. About how he'd taken her virginity while she held onto the doorknob of his office so there wouldn't be any stains on the recently reupholstered therapeutic couch. How sessions always ended with her holding on to the doorknob. Then he would hold out the tissues and tell her to make an appointment for next week. She didn't tell Zach that she made ecstatic sounds just to get him to finish, but he seemed to know.

She hadn't had sex, he said after a while. She'd been fucked. Fucking, he said, is just masturbating with an audience. He knew because when he didn't care about a girl, he fucked her.

Don't let yourself be fucked, he said. Not by anybody.

Then he got up and helped her back through the window and sealed up the security gates.

He moved with the quiet of a kid who knew all about breaking out.

Their hushed conversations over the dinner dishes were less angry after that. Two months later, they met again on the sleeping porch and for the first time, Molly was not fucked. And the next morning, they listened attentively to Mr. Newton ("Put to death, therefore, whatever belongs to your earthly nature: sexual immorality, impurity, lust, evil desires...") knowing that his cushions were still damp with the sex and sweat of the airless Panhandle night.

Molly knew that love based on Rawness and Need and Worthlessness and Sex was a mistake, but being a mistake didn't make it any less real. Any less miraculous.

Until they were found out, confirming all of Mr. Newton's worst suspicions. He called them many things that a more mature, less small-minded man would have avoided.

Molly cracked another molar. But Zach hit him. Mr. Newton called child services. Both of them were locked into their rooms. Zach, Mr. Newton said with relish, would be sent to a secure facility.

She stood by her window, with her bag packed, waiting. She was waiting there still when little Kai started screaming from the sleeping porch. Molly banged on the door until her fists bled and finally someone opened the door and Molly ran to Zach's legs dangling from the rafters.

"Those who live only to satisfy their own sinful nature," Mr. Newton intoned, his head bowed and hands clasped, "will harvest decay and death."

It was only after the paramedic loosened her fingers that she realized the pee-soaked jeans against her cheek were cold.

Molly felt nothing at all. She felt nothing as she started the long walk toward the Choctawhatchee River. She felt nothing as she waded into the river. Why? The whole time she lay there in that thick warm water she tried to imagine why he'd done it. Because he was afraid of going to the secure facility? Because he wanted to make Mr. Newton sorry? Because she had stood by grinding her teeth and hadn't said anything, anything at all? He had broken out; why hadn't he run away?

Or maybe he had.

Just like she was.

She imagined what they would make of her death. Another disapproving quotation from Paul and then... nothing.

The soupy yellow Florida sky met the soupy yellow river in a foretaste of oblivion. Not just for herself but for her parents and her grandparents and Mrs. Thibaut and Natalie and Zach because their stories—the stories that lived inside her—would be gone.

So.

She waded back to shore and back to Odd Fellows, her clothes covered in beigey-yellow silt. Ignoring Mrs. Newton's questions, she showered, changed and then reached under the bed in the room she shared with girls who were at school and pulled out the duffle bag that held her mother and her father and her grandfather and her grandmother and strapping on the backpack that was still waiting where she'd left it when Kai screamed, she hitchhiked into Pensacola and picked up the cardboard box containing Zachary Willem Adreux.

She used the money she'd saved from Sam's Surfside and hopped a bus for New York City and the sick and spiteful grandmother who had never wanted her, but who knew Molly was the last chance to stay out of a state-run nursing home.

* * *

"It's not your fault," Death said.

She started because she hadn't remembered talking.

With one last long stroke, Death smoothed her now unknotted hair. He sat for a long time looking at the buckets of scraps on her coffee table.

"Where do you want these?"

The five urns fit neatly on the windowsill in the living room. The box stamped TEMPORARY CONTAINER went in the closet, next to another box marked SEASONAL CLOTHES.

CHAPTER 12

*N*ow, Molly thought. Now, her life would begin for real. And this time she would keep the mistakes to a minimum.

This time she had her own apartment. With her name on the lease, with her money paying the rent. There was no one to die and leave her suddenly homeless. Really, there was no one left to leave her. They'd all up and done it already and she had no intention of adding anyone else to the lease of her existence.

She shook out the shower curtain and sucked in the dangerous PVC off-gassing of new beginnings. Opening the bedroom window, she climbed out onto the rooftop that extended over the ovens of the Palmyra Bakery on the first floor. She listened to a singer lament in a language she didn't understand to the strains of a stringed instrument she didn't know and watched the morning glories in the box next to her window twist tight around themselves in the late afternoon sun.

Lavash and sumac were the smell of life beginning for real.

. . .

THE NICEST THING about her apartment was that roof near her bedroom window. She'd imagined using it in the summer, but as it was above the ovens and was poorly insulated, it was going to be hell in July.

On an early November day when the sun was bright if low and the temperatures in the seventies, it was just about perfect. Molly took out a big ratty old quilt and the sunscreen and the book she'd picked up from the box marked TAKE ONE LEAVE ONE on the window ledge of the Suds 'n' Stuff.

She tied up her hair and loosed the back of her bikini, so that when she wore her halter at work, there'd be no line. She remembered the time at the Whippoorwill Court pool when she'd swum the entire length of the pool with one breath, and she'd popped out of the pool desperate to see if anyone had noticed. Mrs. Falkenfleck had noticed and thrown a towel over her. "Make yourself decent," she'd hissed, pointing to the blue and white gingham check swim suit top with the white eyelet ruffles that had shifted to the side.

As far as Molly could tell, her exposed seven-year-old nipple looked exactly the same as the ones gracing Timothy Falkenfleck, Mrs. Falkenfleck's nine-year-old grandson who'd come to visit the week before and whose naked top half had elicited no demands for decency whatsoever.

Molly poured lotion on her back and thought of Zach shaking the cheap drugstore brand sunscreen and how it came out spitting into his dark hands and he rubbed it slowly until it coated every part of her from her bare breasts to the tips of her ears, protecting every part of the body that he would love and cherish forever. Til death do us part.

Then she lay down and let the sun penetrate the cool air at her back and the cumin-scented heat from the bakery ovens penetrate her front and fell straight through the deep sleep into trudging up those endless stairs ending in the urine-soaked jeans that she tried so hard to push up, up, up, until maybe she'd be able to push him back into life. This time the hands didn't pull her arms away, they pushed her arms down against the graveled roof coating.

Fighting through the heat and grogginess, Molly twisted her hip. A man in work shorts and a dingy tank stumbled. Molly twisted the rest of the way and kicked him hard in the torso. He tried to stay upright but his unbuttoned and unzipped shorts had fallen to his calves.

There was a sound behind her like canvas sails or leather wings that flew over her. As the man continued to stumble backward, Death's hand shot out toward his navel. A lengthening black shadow stretched between them then snapped just as the man's body disappeared from view.

Molly scrabbled toward the low masonry wall at the edge of the building, dragging her quilt around her as she went. Cautiously, she leaned over to look at the body caught midfall. His eyes were still open, though even motionless as he was, she thought there was something missing from them.

A woman holding a bag of groceries with oranges on the top looked up, shock not having yet registered.

A man sitting on the hood of a car had started to flick the ashes from his cigarette.

"You...you killed him," she whispered. "You said you couldn't but you did. I saw it."

Death twirled the Rag in the way he did so it would slide easily into one of his pockets. "I was supposed to pick him up down there," he said, nodding toward the sidewalk. "Only I got him here, instead."

Molly looked back at the man, his startled face surrounded by thinning, wind-puffed hair, his penis equally surprised above the shorts looped about his ankles.

I was supposed to pick him up down there.

Down there, where he would eventually hit, and his skull

would crack and his blood would flow and the lady with the groceries would scream.

I don't kill. Bullets kill. Old age kills. Disease kills.

Molly Molloy kills.

Or at least she was supposed to have killed. She was the one who had kicked the man and sent him stumbling back, his shorts falling awkwardly, when Death extracted his soul.

"Why?"

Death shoved his hands in his big outer pockets and shrugged. "I didn't...I didn't want it to be your fault?" he said cautiously.

They looked at the sun that would remain framed by towers along the East River until it was time for someone to die. Across the street, a woman leaned out of the window looking at the woman who would eventually scream at the man who would eventually hit the sidewalk.

Molly leaned her head on his shoulder and Death suddenly worried that his shape wouldn't hold and that he would burst into a million tiny pieces and surround her, coalesce around her, but he managed to hold it together while she pulled on her red T-shirt. Then he walked with her to find the lady who sold churros along Essex Street.

Death got four churros while Molly got a horchata and stuck five dollars into the woman's paper cup because she wasn't a sneak thief. Molly was three blocks away when the man's body hit the sidewalk and the woman screamed and the oranges rolled into the street and the ashes from the end of the cigarette floated down.

CHAPTER 13

*B*y closing on Wednesday, after three full days of classes and four nights of poorly remunerated beer slinging, Molly was exhausted. She fell asleep immediately on the subway, clutching the phone that started buzzing a half hour later, so she wouldn't miss her stop. Another half hour later, she washed out her body, her hair and her two uniforms. The sturdy, dark-blue, long-sleeved shirt and sturdy dark-blue multi-pocketed pants of her EMT trainee uniform and the flimsy tiny pink and black and Suntan entertainer's uniform.

Then she collapsed onto her bed, her hair still wet and spread over a double thickness of towel that was all that protected her pillow.

"Molly?" said a worried voice. "Molly?"

"Blathafak?" said Molly, starting upright.

"I kept knocking, but you didn't answer."

Molly curled up with her pillow over her head and whimpered.

Back when he first came Down, humans had frequently used guttural modulations to comfort each other. He wouldn't call them songs, exactly. He'd spent an eternity in Choir and knew exactly what songs were. They were about Holiest of Holies and Praise and Eternity and usually ended with an Admonition on repeat.

Looking at his exhausted Molly, Death remembered his favorite. It started out slow and a little awkward but very soft.

Sum in aliena provincia...

I am in a foreign land, distraught in my misery. All means gone. All pleasure vanished.

Not that Molly understood the words. She reached out with a hand that was rough and warm and had whorls at the knuckles and freckles on the webbing between thumb and forefinger and veins under the skin, and tendons running connecting fingers to wrist and a burn at the pulse point. Her hand relaxed in his own that was so very, very featureless, unless a celadon undertone could be considered a feature.

He watched Molly's body sink deeper into the pillow and into the bed next to him. This was easier, he thought, this still life, this little death, without all that perplexing waking agency. His hand fluttered across her body, feeling her soul soften inside the border of skin that isolated her. He touched her hair and leaned over so that he could feel the damp cool heaviness of some strands and the dry warm lightness of others against his lips.

HE WASN'T sure how long he'd been sitting there frozen in that fraction of a second, but eventually Molly woke up refreshed and recalibrated. She smiled and thanked him and offered to make him coffee, but the water wouldn't run and the gas wouldn't turn on.

Night after night, Death would look for that instant in time when no one was dying and hold Molly in her apartment on Grand Street, humming her the gentlest songs from Choir while the tendrils around his body grew longer and thicker and more numerous and one, the first one, that had grown longer and thicker and broke out from his chest and touched her skin. As soon as it did, Death felt the ever-searching movement of life and the ever-unravelling movement of mortality.

* * *

NECIE, who was just finishing her shift at BICU, looked around for the source of the unmistakable sound of a hand hitting skin. It was the brown-haired girl, the slightly blowsy one with the old-fashioned name, who was still hanging around hours after that devastating first ride-along.

"It was a joke, Molly," shouted the man next to her also in the EMT trainee uniform. "If you can't take a joke, there's no way you have the balls to handle this job."

Molly. That was it. She worked as a waitress? A bartender, maybe.

"Say it again." Molly's voice was haggard, but her hand had disappeared to his undercarriage. "And you won't have any fucking balls either."

The man jumped away and yelled for Necie over the girl's shoulder. "You!" the man said to her. Necie could see his name now. D. Storval. "You're a witness. I want this reported in her write-up."

"What was I witnessing, exactly?" Necie was tired and wanted to get home but she didn't know D. Storval and Molly had stayed after her shift, changing into scrubs on top of scrubs so she could sit as near as she could to the little boy who, if Necie knew anything after fifteen years in the Burn Intensive Care Unit, was not going to live through the night.

Molly said nothing, but Necie thought she could hear teeth grinding.

"That she hit me, assaulted me."

"Hunhunh. Just out of the blue, she hit you?"

"I made a joke. It was nothing."

"I'm tired, Storval, so you better talk."

"The kid in BICU, you know the crispy—"

Molly's hand cracked against his other cheek.

The sound was still vibrating through the hall when Necie dropped to her knees. "My contact," she said dully, "I cannot see a thing without my contacts." She enunciated every word, making it perfectly clear that even if she could see without her contacts, she wouldn't.

D. Storval marched away to find their Preceptor. Molly said nothing, just stood in the doorway, watching another group assess little George, like they were going to find anything different. Like they weren't going to find full thickness burns or 90% total body surface burned or inhalation injury or head trauma.

Necie knew the story, she'd heard variations on it before: something cooking too long on a hot plate in a tiny apartment. Mom asleep in front of the television. Little boy who was too big for a crib, but still confined to it. Per procedure they took both, though they knew the woman was already dead.

Now the little boy was in BICU, alone, with a Foley catheter, a tube pumping humidified oxygen delivered through a slit in his badly burned neck. Swan-Ganz catheter. Two drips at his groin, trying to rehydrate him. Molly was shocked at the way his body had swollen in the hours since he was picked up. His legs were elevated to try to counter edema.

She sat at the foot of his bed, her hand on his ankle, the only part of his body not burned. More than one nurse had told her that the paralytic drip meant George wouldn't be able to hear anything she said, which was fine, because most of her stories were about dead people: mischievous Natalie, stalwart Mrs. Thibaut and the crotchety inmates at Vivarbo. Zach and the younger but equally crotchety inmates of Odd Fellows. It seemed important anyway that there be some sound other than monitors and the woosh of the ventilator and the opening of sterile dressing and the distant sounds of phones and of announcements and of gurneys in the hall.

She was almost relieved when the quiet came, expanding to the very edge of nothing, broken only by the tread of the heavy boots and the soft humming and the papery rasping of her own scrubs on top of scrubs and of her ragged breath in her ears.

"Molly," Death said, looking shocked. "What are you doing here?"

She said nothing, just looked at him with swimmy eyes and swollen throat and took off her masks and held little George's hand, even though she wasn't supposed to, because now it didn't matter.

Death understood and in one step was at George's side. He bent down whispering in the boy's ear and before his hand touched the bandages around his belly, a pale gray shadow stretched up for his fingers.

A momentary blast of sound, of monitors and phones and squeaking rubber soles and the wobble of rubber wheels and clicks and whistles. Then it all went away and when Death gently coaxed the shivering Rag into his pocket, Molly's tears plashed warm and silent on the little bandaged hand.

Uncertain what to do, Death stood beside her, his hands cupped in front of him. Molly took off her gloves and pulled his hands open before gently stroking the gray splodge. "It was his time," Death whispered and Molly stretched her hand smelling of latex and touched Death gently on his lips, silencing him. It wasn't a "shut up" kind of silencing, more like an "I know" kind of silencing.

First he looked at her hand on his lips and then at her face. Her eyes were red and rimmed, her forehead lined, her nose pink and splotchy. Her hair was tied up into a puffy blue hair cover. Sweat beaded around the rim of her scalp.

And Death who had seen everything—everything—in this

world, knew that he would never see anything as beautiful ever again. In her face, he started to see both the wonder of life and the cost of his bookkeeping.

She patted George's hand one last time and stood, her exhausted, all-too-mortal body listing dangerously. Death's arm shot out for her and gathered her to him. She leaned her forehead against his thin chest and cried long and loud. She sobbed messily and incomprehensibly in her helplessness.

He curled his arms tighter around her and her body relaxed into his and she started rocking slightly. Death rested his cheek on the top of her propylene-covered hair and smelled the exhaust and rotting leaves and the peculiar combination of moss and yeast and salt that he recognized as corruption but sucked in with one hungry breath after another.

He felt the soft heavy press of her breasts through her scrubs. He felt the smell of lemon and tea on her breath. He felt the light glinting on the almost invisible hairs of her cheek. He felt the sweat and the sound of her caged hair.

He let her body mold more closely to his and buried her face into his neck under the veil of his dark hair, her lips still wet with tears.

He felt her hip against his and then it happened.

When he had whittled away at his calves and thighs, he couldn't just throw out the leftover bits of the condensed empyrean that made his body. So he stored the excess at the apex of his legs.

It was never meant to be anything but storage or maybe decoration so the spot didn't look quite so empty. But then another tendril tore through the center of his ornament, joining the thousands of others that now littered his body like the poppies in Flanders that April when he stopped by to see why he was no longer needed.

Feeling the rise against her hip, Molly knew that whatever else he said, he was a man.

The monitor screeched its monotone cry for help and Molly stumbled forward into the empty space.

CHAPTER 14

*D*eath needed to keep busy. He stopped taking the long breaks for food and poking at humans' stuff; he'd even stopped with his own chores and now he was down to his last clean T-shirt ("Three reasons I love being a Grandma: Justin, Leanne, Alex").

He needed to keep his mind occupied so, as soon as the woman's Rag (puerperal fever) was safely stowed in the Black Watch tartan pocket, Death took out his list and ran his finger carefully under the next name. One pickup after another, after another, after another. Like he was supposed to. No distractions or complications.

"Neshama'le?"

"Bea?"

Metal rings slid across a metal wire and Bea stuck her head out of one of the makeshift rooms.

"Who were you here for?"

"Bacia Odu."

Her lips tightened. "Can you move her out to the courtyard?

"

"The courtyard?"

"*Yes, the courtyard.*" She pointed toward the square in the middle of two buildings and what looked like a makeshift machine shop. "Come back when you're done and we'll put Tibyangye into her spot."

"Just leave Bacia there?"

"Since when are you worried about the scraps?"

"Not *worried* exactly," he mumbled, "it just seems..." But he picked up the already festering body of the woman who had died so soon after her son. He hadn't bothered with his gloves for days.

The gloves had never been about spreading anything, they'd always been about avoiding corruption, but he knew now in the deepest part of himself that it was too late.

Bea went about her work comforting the living and bossing him around. He did what she told him without comment because he could tell she was in a bad mood and because the busier she kept him the less time he had for thinking.

"You want to tell me what's wrong?"

"Nothing's wrong. Do I seem wrong?"

"Not w*rong*, just quiet. I've known you for a long time now and I've never seen you quiet."

"Nothing's wrong."

"Hmmhmm."

Death stared down at the packed dirt floor.

The *thick-thack* of the sandals she often wore bounced around the silent cement block clinic with its tin roof. "Are you coming?"

He followed after her as she wove through the makeshift walls made of sheets.

"So tell me, Neshama'le. What ever happened with that young woman?

"Nothing."

"Nothing? Really?"

"There's nothing wrong, okay? I have a lot of work to do."

But before he could shift his weight to the leaving foot, Bea's hand shot out. It was pudgy and covered with the liver spots that were rewards for many years spent working hard in the searing sun. "I am your friend, little soul. As far as I know, the only one you've got."

"I don't want to talk about it."

"Too bad, Ragpicker, because I do." Her eyes flashed and when Bea's eyes flashed it wasn't just bright and lively, it was bright and filled with potentially devastating discharge of electrons. "What happened to this woman and don't make me pull rank."

Death's shoulders slumped further forward and he muttered something.

"Speak up."

"I wanted to lay with her."

"Lay with her?"

"Yes."

"Did she?"

"Did she what?"

"Did she want to lay with you?"

He blushed so furiously that his face blazed like mercury. "I don't know. I... See, this is why I didn't want to talk about it."

Bea frowned, her eyes going to his zipper. "Can you?"

He pulled his coat closed around him and said nothing.

"It's no secret that you've done things to your body: your nose, your eyes, your—"

"*Oy.* How many times do I have to say it? It's the smell. I had to change my nose, to survive the stench. I had to change my eyes, to see. It's *dark* down here."

"You tell yourself what you need to, but when you carved up your legs, you added something? Don't roll your eyes at me. Since when do you roll your eyes? Everyone else sees you in robes, but I've seen you in jeans and I'm not a fool. I did have *seven* more children."

"I…There were leftovers. I couldn't just leave little pieces of empyrean scattered around. Someone could have fallen into it or whatever."

"You know, you could have given yourself love handles or saddle bags," Bea said, with a loving pat to her own full thighs. "You can pack a lot of overage into these things, let me tell you."

He probably should have, but like the Intimate Male catalogs he used now, the antique statuary he used as his models didn't focus so much on beer bellies or muffin tops.

"Well, I didn't, okay? It was only supposed to be an ornament and—"

"Be very gentle. Her insides are…not in one piece."

He looked down at Tibyangye, a skinny little girl in the blood-stained diaper. His chin trembled slightly. He had seen so many girls and women and men, too. Invaded, torn.

"You see?" He looked at Bea with his despairing eyes. "How could I ever…ever do this to Molly?"

Bea was holding Tibyangye's tiny fingers. They were rough with the calluses of a weathered old woman and the gnawed nails of a little girl. When she looked back at him, her eyes were bleached white. It's what happened when she was furious and the power inside her began to roil and foment. Her voice changed, too, becoming low and hollow and huge and filling up the world.

"How can someone so old be such a child?" it cracked. "Listen to me, Azrael."

Death didn't like it when she called him that and cringed.

"This is not love and it is not sex. This is violence. It is cruelty. Lord's Army, my ass."

Bea took a deep breath and when it exhaled, her voice was soft again. "Little soul, if you think you're doing something *to* Molly, then you should be very afraid. But if it is something you are doing *with* her, that she wants, then stop being such a prude."

He felt the girl's soul begin to unravel under his touch. "Bea?" he whispered cautiously. "I will have to take her soon."

With a crack, Bea's body exploded upward, her hair flying wide, black as night around her before it burst into flames. The blue of the sky folded itself around her and as her hands swept through the air, her fingers tore open the atoms in the air until her aura hurt Death's eyes.

Death curled into himself, his eyes closed, as the blast of thick ionized air blew past him, sending his coat and his hair flying straight back from his shoulders.

Just as suddenly, the roaring stopped and a soft hand patted his cheek.

Squinting just in case, he saw that Bea's eyes were warm and brown again and she looked not angry but sad. "She's in a lot of pain and there's nothing to give her for it. Just..." She stroked the little girl's arm. "Just don't be late."

Death didn't hesitate long before leaning toward Tibyangye, his fine fingers hovering above her navel.

"I am here, little one," he whispered. "If you need me, I am here."

Which was all it took for the gray Rag to leap from the girl's body.

Bea watched him slide her gently into a pocket. Watched as Tibyangye's tortured face and body relaxed.

"Neshama'le?" she said, her voice gentle against his mind. "I think it's possible that after all these uncounted eons, you may actually be growing up."

CHAPTER 15

$\mathcal{M}$olly really had no choice but to tell Manager Dave about her change of address.

He had, predictably, been furious that she hadn't consulted with him. He would have helped her look. Made sure landlords didn't take advantage of a woman alone. Helped her carry heavy things.

"It's not just that; my sister-in-law, Maureen, won't even buy a throw pillow without me," Dave said.

"I didn't want to bother you."

"It's no bother. If you don't rely on me, who can you rely on?" They continued to talk at cross purposes while he worked on next week's schedule.

Dee had stopped coming by ever since he'd held her at BICU. So there were no more Latin songs while she crammed eight hours of sleep into a fraction of a second. Without it, she couldn't deal with more nightshifts Sunday through Wednesday, so she took a deep breath, pressed her breast against his shoulder and told him the address.

And she knew it was a mistake the second she did it.

Dave had immediately made it very clear that he was unimpressed by her little apartment. He didn't like anything about it. Didn't like the location. He didn't think much about the Palmyra Bakery downstairs. ("What's that smell?") Didn't care for the size. ("Cozy is not the word I would use.") Or her furnishings. ("We'll go to IKEA.") Or her wall hangings ("Anatomy of the Female Abdomen and Pelvis," "Anatomy of the Male Abdomen and Pelvis," "Understanding Asthma"). And he hated her five urns lined up on her living room window.

"Damned morbid," he'd said.

Then without asking, he'd written his name in Sharpie as her emergency contact on the File Of Life magnet stuck to her freezer, which irked her most of all.

She'd left Dave watching TV while she went into the bathroom ("No window? Y'should fix the door."). Under the steaming water, she whispered the invocation that had accompanied all of her mistakes and bad decisions, which were usually the same thing.

Stupid, stupid, stupid.

AFTER HER SHOWER, Molly pulled on her sleeping T-shirt and clean underwear and stretched her neck to the side, slowly drying out her thick hair. While she procrastinated, she stared at a face in the mirror that looked tired and cynical and calculating. It was, she knew, the face of a woman who was about to get fucked and didn't want to.

She gently patted the muscles between her eyebrows until the little lines there relaxed and put some acne cream on the zit forming under her chin.

Then she unwrapped the shiny smile she usually reserved for work. The woman in the mirror now looked perky and enthusiastic and not at all cynical or tired or calculating. Until she made it to her eyes, but there was nothing Molly could do about that.

She kept smiling as she left the bathroom, still squeezing her hair in the towel. She kept smiling as she took the Montgomery Ward plastic clock down from the picture hook on the wall to check the batteries. Double As. She kept smiling as she put it back on the wall.

No man looks quite right hunched over his crossed legs, his thumbs stuck in the hem of one sock, the softness of his stomach compressed and oozing. Dave had achieved a state of demi-turgidity that made him look like a half-filled windsock, when Molly heard a sound like the flapping of a sail, followed by the noise of the delivery truck backing up outside and the tick-tock of her plastic clock.

As soon as Dave saw Molly standing at the bathroom door, he pulled himself up and pulled off his sock. Then he sucked in his stomach, straightened his back and came toward her with an arch smile. He pulled at the tie of her bathrobe.

Stupid, stupid, stupid.

MOLLY LEANED back on her bed wondering if she shouldn't paint the ceiling a darker color. She'd seen it once in a magazine that had been tossed in the recycling of her old apartment.

Having rejected her explorations of his body, Dave had told her to relax: He was older, experienced, and knew what he was doing.

Molly was younger and experienced and knew that was bullshit, because men who told you they knew how to satisfy women, never did. He gave six kisses to her left breast, and bit her nipple too hard, which made her cry out. He smiled at the unrehearsed evidence of his technique.

Then he started some frantic rubbing between her legs and Molly started to moan just to get it the hell over with.

Never let yourself be fucked, Zach had told her. But she had and she was doing it again.

When it was the hell over with, Dave leaned back with an expectant, complacent smile and Molly lay on her back thinking not of death with a small 'd' which was her nemesis, but of "Death" with a big "D" who was supposed to be her friend.

She curled as far away from Dave as she could, her second pillow clasped to her chest and tried to make sense of the muddled needs of her body.

Dave was still there in the morning, stretched out wide and possessive across her bed and Molly just wanted to scream at him to GET OUT, but instead she turned her back to him, silently mouthing stupid, stupid, stupid, stupid.

Get your hot prickly knee out of my back.

Stupid, stupid, stupid.

"Time for breakfast, sleepyhead," he said with a light smack to her ass.

Molly didn't want to make him comfortable. She didn't want to introduce him to her local spots. They certainly weren't going to be cooking in her apartment.

Dave complained about the line at the IHOP at 135th Street, but Molly refused to leave. Even though it was freezing, she put her hands on her hips, holding her wool coat back, hoping the bright white letters against bright red background would be visible from the apartment above the Popeye's.

Even at the glacial pace, they were slowly approaching the door. Molly invited a family with small crying children to cut in front. Then a man whose wife was in a wheelchair. Then—

"DavePartyOfTwo. DavePartyOfTwo," called the frazzled hostess.

Dave ordered an egg white tomato spinach omelet ("hold the cheese") and a fruit salad side. PartyOfTwo ordered Bananas Foster Brioche French Toast with whipped cream. And sausage. "She doesn't want whipped cream," he said to the waitress. "Extra whipped cream," Molly said, cupping her breast where a soul had cowered last time she'd been here.

Misinterpreting once more, Dave slid back into the booth and slipped his knee between her legs. He didn't move it even when the waitress handed Molly's Bananas Foster Brioche French Toast with sausage to Dave and Dave's tomato spinach egg-white omelet ("hold the cheese") to Molly. Molly switched plates without saying anything.

Stupid, stupid, stupid, thought Molly, her throat tight. The French toast was too hot and she gagged.

Death pounded her on the back and once he was sure he didn't need to hold her by the heels and shake her, he slid into the booth across from Molly, shoving Dave roughly into the corner.

He started chewing at the back of his thumb.

"Where have you been?" Molly asked, looking at the anxious face across from her. "I've missed you."

"I've been busy," he said, his legs bouncing and jouncing.

"Unless there's a plague I haven't heard of, you shouldn't be any busier than usual. Are you avoiding me because of what happened with your cock?"

"*Gaaah.* Don't say that! It's not a cock, it's just an ornament. I had leftovers that I had to put somewhere. It's not supposed to *do* anything."

"Well it did. *You* did."

Molly looked thoughtfully at the forkful of French toast. It was still too hot, because she hadn't learned as she would eventually that French toast that was too hot when Death first appeared would remain too hot until he left.

"I liked it," she said, spearing a banana and dipping it in whipped cream.

Her lips were still stained in sweet cream when Death darted across the table toward her, his mouth hitting her own so hard that their teeth clashed. He pulled back, rubbing his incisors with his tongue.

Molly paused for a second to make sure that her front tooth

was still firmly rooted in her jaw before she swallowed.

Then she pushed the plates away and leaned slowly toward him until they were close but not touching. She exhaled and Death felt a warm current of cream and the tropics tease his lips. His mouth opened. She licked her upper lip and brushed it against the full sensitive part inside his lower lip, the part that was usually hidden, and his eyes closed and he lost sensation in every part of his body except that tiny bit of his lower lip.

Molly drew back.

Death whimpered and looked at his featureless hands with no little whorls at the knuckles, no tendons, no blood vessels, no roughness around the fingernails he'd carved and buffed during the Age of Enlightenment.

He put his hands back on his jouncing legs, and looked at the inanimate Dave. At the arm hair and the bits of fat and the mole on his neck and the freckles on the webbing of his hand and the nipples making tiny tents in his shirt.

He was a man, who knew Molly's body and had used some of Molly's time and Death became unaccountably angry, shoving the man's inert bulk hard against the side of the booth.

Molly grabbed his arm. "Stop," she said in a voice of soft command. "Leave now and I'll come find you."

And Death vanished.

"—no kind of job for a young woman?" said Dave, looking suddenly confused at finding himself scrunched into the corner of the booth.

Molly opened her mouth and tried desperately to remember what they'd been talking about. He'd been telling her about all of the things she didn't want: the tiny apartment above the smelly bakery. The shoddy neighborhood. Now, he was telling her that she didn't want the grim job, by which he meant paramedic, not TaaTaas!

"Wow, you really vacuumed down that whipped cream," he said.

Then he froze again, his eyes partly closed, his eyes partly opened.

"When?" Death asked, still twirling a soul into a pocket in his coat.

"Today," she said. "At 3—"

He nodded and disappeared.

"—o'clock?"

"'O'clock' what?" asked Dave. "What are you talking about?"

Molly wanted out of this conversation, out of this relationship, out of this lie she'd woven to get a better work schedule. There were far worse people than Dave, but she wasn't the person for him. Dave wanted someone who needed him and because Molly knew death with a small "d," he assumed she'd cling to security. But it was precisely because Molly knew death with a small "d" that she knew how rare and precious life was and was trying hard not to compromise.

"You know Sienna?" she said, with a sudden flash of inspiration. "She's always had a—"

"3:00 isn't going to work," Death said pushing Dave's omelet to the side and drawing his finger down his long list. "Can we say 3:00:23?" Death asked.

"Fine," Molly said. "That's fine."

Death held his finger at a line of tiny writing and wrote an arrow with his stubby pencil.

"Are we good now? 'Cause I'm really having a hard time keeping track."

He rolled up his scroll and put it in his big pocket.

"Sienna always had a what?" asked Dave. "What is going on with you? It's like you're high or something."

"A crush. Sienna's always had a crush on you," Molly blurted out before the next interruption. It might be true. She wasn't sure it wasn't, but she also knew that the best flint to desire was the desire in another's eyes.

"Where?" Death asked.

"Your apartment. I'll be at the front door."

* * *

Dave stared at Molly, who was looking vague again and blurting out more words that had nothing to do with the ones she'd started with. His mind wandered to Sienna. A crush? He hadn't really thought about Sienna that way before. She had a baby, a daughter, he thought. He remembered that she'd stopped nursing to get the job. He was surprised by this observation, because it meant he had been thinking about Sienna that way. Noticing her breasts.

And why not? She was pretty. He vaguely recalled she'd asked for time off because her mother was—sick? Dead?—and she needed to take care of her daughter. That she was in danger of losing her—her mother's—apartment? Something.

Molly looked at him again with a helpless, addled stare and silently rubbed her temples.

Dave signaled for the waitress.

Sienna. Pretty name.

CHAPTER 16

a t 3:00:23 Death arrived at the narrow metal door with the diamond shaped window next to Popeye's.

"Have you been waiting long?"

"Got here at three."

"Sorry about that," he said, patting his outer pockets nervously. "Can you hold these?" He dropped a couple of dollars and more foreign bills into her hand. A crumpled butterfly made of wire and pale green gauze and glitter. A set of keys. An unopened but blood-spattered bag of M&Ms.

"What are you looking for?"

"Keys."

Molly held up the keys.

"Not those."

Finally he found other keys that were not old and heavy and tied together on a piece of string, but smaller and more modern and threaded on to a key ring with half a broken heart bedazzled with red rhinestones.

Then he took back the old keys and the M&Ms and the gauze butterfly and used the keys on the ring with the half a broken heart bedazzled with red rhinestones to open the door.

Okay, so he was weird but when Molly questioned the shattered remnants of her own heart, those remnants didn't say what they usually did.

They didn't say, "Stupid, stupid, stupid."

Upstairs Death dumped his key and his currency into the upside-down Cake Taker on the old chest. Molly plucked out the butterfly, feeling it was too delicate for such rough company.

He looked nervously around his tiny apartment with no shades and straightened the chairs and a pile of magazines next to his bed before mumbling something that she couldn't quite hear.

Retrieving the bright orange laundry basket lined with pink and blue and white striped flannel, he sat on the side of the bed and coaxed each little black or gray or white shadow out of the tiny pockets.

There was something about him, hunched over the little puddle in his palm, that was so gentle and made her want to touch him. But as she straightened out the pale green gauze wings of the butterfly, she remembered when she caught a cabbage white on the grounds of Vivarbo and held it in her cupped hands, feeling the soft whisking of its wings against her palms. One of the pool ladies said she'd as good as squashed it, touching its wings like that.

Bent all the way over until his chest touched his thighs, Death was more like a beetle than a butterfly with that big heavy coat held tight to his body like a carapace. But Molly wasn't the kind for ripping wings from beetles either.

Once she'd smoothed out the butterfly's wire wings and straightened out its wire legs, she stood on the chair and twisted the butterfly's legs around the darkened bronze chain supporting the old hanging lamp.

It fluttered when she blew on it. Death stopped what he was doing and watched her, yearning.

Custodes were often called angels by humans who didn't know any better. But Death did know better. And he knew that the only real angel he'd ever seen was this one, in black leggings and a bright red T-shirt that promised wisdom to all the students of Niceville High.

Steeling a body made of the forces that held the universe together, he shifted out of his coat, feeling the familiar, comforting weight leave his shoulder, the shield of the high collar stripped from his neck. It slid from his back and down his arms. His hands clutched involuntarily at the cuffs, but then he let go, his fingers spread wide against the frayed lining.

He hung it carefully on the hanger by the door, then he walked over to Molly and when he took one unnecessary breath, all of the air in the little apartment moved. The chain swung and the butterfly fluttered and Molly smiled and Death held out his arms to her. She put her hand to his slight shoulder and he told her to watch her head as he lifted her down.

She slid her body against his, then reached her fingers to the flat plane of his chest. But he covered her hand with his, stopping her.

With the wisdom of waitresses, Molly knew when to intrude and when to be silent and she waited for two long minutes until Death twitched a little.

"There was a fire at a bridal shop last week. Do you know Yarmouk?" he asked. But Molly didn't know Yarmouk and shook her head. "I needed to get the owner's son-in-law. He was buried under all this lace and that stuff burns so fast. Then I found a body in a badly charred suit, I wasn't paying attention I guess, and didn't notice until I turned him over to find his omphalos."

"His what?"

Death touched the area midway between what would be a sternum and what might be a pubis if he had either.

"Belly button. Navel."

"Yes, anyway he didn't have one because it was only a plastic model."

"I...I'm sorry?" Molly said, because he seemed to need sympathy, even though she knew he'd seen worse.

"It looked like me, Molly. That's what I look like. I don't look like Dave or Zach or anyone you're used to. I don't look real but..." Now he pressed her palm to his chest and stared out the window at the deepening shadows of 3:00:23 on a November afternoon. "I feel real. At least I feel a lot. Too much sometimes."

She moved her free hand to the strangely firm and fluid skin of his exposed arm.

"I never thought you would be like other men. Look, fucking...take your fingers out of your ears and listen...Fucking is what happens when you're just going through the moves. Someone once said to me that when you do it right, you're starting over as though it was the first time for both of you."

He looked at Molly's fingers that were cracked on top and red in between because the air was dry and she was constantly washing things.

"Was it Zach who said that?"

"Does it matter?"

"No, I suppose not."

Molly smoothed the black hair back from his face. He looked up, startled.

"What I'm trying to tell you is that none of what happened before matters." Then she looped his hair behind his ear, and when she had, she left her hand alongside his face, feeling the slight nervous hitch against her palm. With her thumb she smoothed his cheek. Then drew her fingers slowly across his chin and down the smooth column of his throat and around the back of his neck.

Gently and chastely, she leaned into his mouth, until Death sucked the heady mix of mint and Molly.

Her hands crept under his T-shirt (The Cult) and he waited

for her to feel his complete otherness and cringe. Nothing happened. Molly let her hands take him in. There were no dips and nobs where the spine should be. No bumpy finial of the collarbone. No crisscrossed bulges of muscles. No nipples. No veins, hairs, wrinkles, scars.

No navel.

She let her own entirely mortal form touch him, sliding her leg between his thighs. Well, she thought, that is certainly solid enough.

His legs clamped around hers and he put his hand to the back of her head and pressed his body against hers. His fingers sunk deep into the Lycra-covered flesh of her leg.

The air sparked electric around her when Death's mouth took her. She'd kept her eyes closed when she was fucking Dave, but now, she kept her eyes open, watching a wildness take hold of her unearthly lover.

His tongue entered her and tasted.

Molly kissed him back, opening him up, feeling his oddly smooth and dry tongue, feeling the unified backs of his teeth. Tasting the air of eternity, while her hands explored.

Every touch of the cool silkiness of his skin made the need to feel it against the warmth and stickiness of her own living flesh a burning ache.

"I want to see you," she whispered.

"You see me now," he whispered back.

"All of you. The way you are."

Molly followed his eyes as they flickered warily to the stack of magazines on the bedside table made of pilfered milk crates.

The corners were ripped like kiosk owners do to mark magazines that are past their date, but Molly could still see what they were: *GQ*, *Esquire*, *Maxxim*, with their pictures of implausible men and impossible women and Molly turned his chin toward her. "You," she said. "I want to see *you*." And she slid his shirt up, high on his chest. "Help me," she said and he grabbed the hem and threw the shirt to the floor before hunching, his arms crossed protectively across his chest.

She ran her hand over the place where his clavicle would have been. His cool, dry skin almost felt like it was there and not there at the same time, like touching water. Real, but not quite solid and when she kissed his skin, it undulated beneath her lips. Then she nipped near the spot where his nipples might have been and his back arched.

Molly smiled against his chest, then slid her hand to his jeans and the pulsing ridge under the roughness of his zipper and with a practiced flick of finger and thumb undid his button. With a careful pull, she dragged the zipper down, her hand curved around his crown.

"Please," she whispered though no one would ever hear her.

In late November at 3:00:23 across the 41st Parallel North, the shadows are deep and long, but not like the ones that consumed Death as he stepped away from Molly.

After his jeans shot across the floor, he hung back, a whisper of brightness in the shadows.

Molly knew that if he was not like the implausible men of the magazines, she wasn't like the impossible women either. Heavier, softer. She worked hard, but worked *out* not at all. And she ate sausage and Bananas Foster Brioche French Toast with Extra Whipped Cream and curly fries with cheese.

Ever since Zach, who had loved her, Molly had been careful to slip out of her clothes under the cover of dark or of blankets.

Keeping her eyes on where he had been, Molly slowly and deliberately removed her red T-shirt, her black leggings, her matching peach-colored underpants and bra with their smatterings of slightly tattered lace.

Naked beyond the absence of clothes, she raised her arms out to either side and waited as the glow began to re-emerge from the hall of shadow.

Molly steeled herself. She knew what he was seeing: her

somewhat lopsided breasts, the stretch marks at her hips, the hair she tidied up with a razor in the shower when she thought of it and not often, the swelling at her ankles that had become semipermanent now that she spent most of her day on her feet.

He saw all of it and loved it all. And when the shadows disappeared, he wore nothing but the look of a man who knows firsthand what a miracle is.

He held out his arms, too, and when they came together, the immortal and eternal with the mortal and dying, they were alike: nervous and needy but convinced that their improbable joining was absolutely right.

Death's ornament jutted against Molly's pelvis, his arms folded around her and with no effort lifted her, his hands cupping her ass, his fingers growing toward her hidden spaces.

She leaned into him, feeling the stillness and constant motion against her skin.

Death, it turned out, was a quick learner. She'd given him a few suggestions, pulled him back from something he'd tried with her armpits that she didn't much care for.

Then Death learned how to cheat.

Molly, he discovered, had tendrils of her own. Since she had a corporeal body and he was just solidified empyrean, her tendrils were trapped inside her skin. But if there was anything he knew, it was how to read a soul. The tendrils recoiled when he licked her armpit, so he didn't try that again. Other moves, though—like when he swirled his tongue along her inner arm or the base of her throat. When he sucked long and gently at her nipple. When he slid the crown of his ornament against her fluid opening—then the tendrils moved against her limits, stroking at his skin and making Molly shudder.

She could not feel his tendrils in the same way, but Death encouraged her explorations in any way he could. He loved all of it. This body that had been nothing but a stupid, unsanctified hobby, felt holy under her hands and her tongue and the weight of her full flesh.

She started working the line leading from the nascent ribs she could only just feel with her soft and sensitive upper lip to his abdomen, to where his belly button should have been, and then to his ornament. He began to twist and clutch at the blankets and whisper necessary words in a language she didn't know.

Her breasts softly caressed his skin and caught on his generous ornament which, though missing blood vessels or seams or ridges, still became heavy and larger when she suckled him.

It was taking far too much will to keep himself in this form.

She kissed him on his forehead, and swung her legs over the bed.

"Don't go," pleaded a voice coming from everywhere at once. Death grimaced, seemingly as shocked as she was. He took a deep breath and when he spoke again, it was as he always had.

"Please, Molly. Please."

"I'm not going. I just need to get a condom."

"A what?"

"A condom. A prophylactic?" Molly offered hopefully, stumbling a little as her toe caught in the Bills' comforter.

She rustled around in the inner pocket of the outer compartment of her backpack until she found the tropical-flavored condom that she always kept there just in case.

"Dee?"

Death was staring at the ceiling, his mind filled with the millennia he could not unsee of pulling Rags from bodies skewered on the cocks of men.

He flopped over on his stomach, his ornament pinioned beneath the strong forces of the universe.

"Talk to me."

He stared at the ancient chest he'd had for millennia that now seemed no more than the blink of an eye.

"I can't."

"You can't talk to me?"

He shook his head. "No, the other thing. What you want me to do."

Above the chest was a tea-colored water stain in the shape of a ginkgo leaf left when the upstairs neighbor's dishwasher overflowed.

"Why?" she asked, trying to disguise the disappointed chuff of air.

"You are a miracle, Molly. My miracle. I don't mean you belong to me, I mean that not everyone gets a miracle, but I did and you are it."

"Okay?" she said, more confused than before when she'd presumed he'd had a change of heart.

"I've seen so much…" He sucked his lips in between his teeth and hunched tighter into himself.

Molly waited and then thought and then knew. Everything ended with death but he'd seen nothing of the multifaceted narratives that brought people there.

Clearly whatever he knew of sex ended badly.

She propped her chin on his shoulder. "I know you would never hurt me," she said, his hair caught on the rough skin of her hands.

Then she kissed him chastely on the cheek just under the outer corner of his eye.

His eyes closed and he stopped breathing, feeling each successive touch of her soft lips against his skin, waiting now for her to get closer. Willing her to touch his lips with hers, but waiting as though she had all the time in the world.

He pursed his lips and exhaled and the little gauze butterfly she'd tied to his lamp fluttered and he looked over his shoulder to see if she'd noticed, but she hadn't. She was watching him.

Finally, he turned onto his back and Molly kissed him gently. She took her time touching all the places where the markers of manhood should have been: A collar of bone would have stretched from shoulder to shoulder. The knot of gristle would have interrupted a man's throat. The vestigial nipples hidden by hair.

She didn't shy away from his smoothness and under her tongue and teeth and touch, he felt differentiated, almost as though he had shape and form and the bit where the vestigial nipples should have been didn't feel the same as the place along his lower belly where his cock strained.

Though when she left it all felt empty again, desolate.

Molly reached for the shiny orange foil packet, shaking it between two fingers.

"Do you know what to do with this?" she asked holding it out to him.

"Yes," he said. He hadn't liked it before, but he would do whatever Molly needed, so he opened up the packet and ate it.

In PSR B1620-26, a circumbinary planet circling a pulsar and a white dwarf, a partly chewed mango condom launched into orbit.

Molly didn't know about PSR B1620-26, she only knew that —circumbinary planets or no—her single condom had just become irretrievable.

She looked crestfallen.

"Was I supposed to share?" he asked.

"No. Well, yes but it's too late now," Molly said, swinging her legs over the side of the bed. After sitting for a moment with her shoulders hunched, her palms buttressed on the mattress, she pushed herself off.

"I suppose I should get going," she said, and Death panicked.

"Wait, Molly!" He turned away from her and hit his hand to his chest. "Give me a moment to see if I can find it. It wasn't candy?"

"No, it was a condom. You're supposed to put it on your…" She pointed toward the join of his legs.

"On my ornament?"

"Yes, to prevent diseases and pregnancy."

"Oh. *Oh*. But…remember I told you I am absolutely sterile. Nothing lives on me. I could lick necrotizing fasciitis, I could drink—"

"That right there…?" She tapped his lips with her finger. "Not date-night material. Look," she said as she started poking around in the sheets, "I'm willing to trust that you don't carry diseases, but I can barely hold myself together. The last thing I need is to get pregnant. Have you seen my underwear?"

"Molly…I am immortal."

Molly chuffed out a deep breath. "Well, bully for you," she said. "That's not going to help me find my underwear." Then she knelt on the floor looking under the bed.

"You don't understand. Like I told you before, it is not permitted for us to end life, but we are not permitted to begin life either. Only those who die are allowed to create something that survives them. It is meant to be a consolation. We have no art. No literature, unless you count Admonishments and I'm starting to have my doubts about that.

"And we have no children."

Death kissed the place on her jaw where a strand of her hair had stuck to a dot of whipped cream and banana and sugar and felt the recalcitrant tendril immediately reach out beneath skin and hair and whipped cream and banana and sugar.

Bit by bit he teased each tendril alive and while he did, his own tendrils erupted from his body until they filled the space between them with pale strands rather like children's hands when they play with glue, clap their palms together and create intricate cathedrals of milky threads.

Molly saw this and took it in stride as she straddled his hips, lowering herself onto him while she fell into the black that stretched beyond his pupils and into his sclera and through the night sky and beyond the bright of newborn stars and the even brighter newly dead ones, kept staring past the thinning lights and though she couldn't know it, right to the blackness of the beginning.

With every one of his unnecessary breaths, Molly felt the air inside the little apartment, and with it the world's currents.

As the air filled with static, Molly's hair rose above her as charged and wild as the blood in her womb. Death plunged deep into her and made the tendrils inside her follow his thrusts until his back arched and her back strained and her body pulsed around him and inside of him. Then in the dingy little apartment above the Popeye's, Death's soul reached out and touched Molly's.

She groaned hard and dissolved into his dark infinity of time and space, knew it for the loneliness it was. Though he was inside her, she was more definitely inside him and held his loneliness to her until he pulled himself back together and lay facing her, his knees tucked up, touching hers. He stroked her hair and her skin, repeating her name endlessly with more veneration than he had ever been able to muster through centuries of Veneration.

The blackness of his eyes had contracted to a pinpoint again. Molly smiled and stretched slowly, grateful for her body's limits after feeling the infinite.

Death lowered his head on to his upper arm and watched over her, immensely grateful for his first experience of the finite. He felt her soul soften, becoming almost liquid, the halfway point between the solidity of wakefulness and the airiness of death.

Then that first strand, the one in the middle of his chest, erupted, thicker than all the rest. It was strong and insistent and snaked around past her hand, prodding and searching.

And when it found her omphalos, Death yanked at it, reeling

it back with his fist, but it simply attenuated until it was no more than gossamer and then...then another thread, this one as black as the black between stars reached from Molly's belly button and touched his iridescence.

As soon as it did, Molly sighed and Death fell long and hard in the two ways that he was able to. He fell in the way that led Abdiel to threaten an odious eternity spent in Group. And he fell in love.

Sleepless, Death watched over her deathless sleep and loved.

He touched the mole on her neck, and the fullness of her tangled hair and the breast that sagged softly as she slept and the lines on her forehead.

It's so easy, he thought, for the all-powerful to be generous, so easy that it is meaningless. Here, with Molly who had so little but shared her time and her self anyway, Death knew that he was closer to divinity than he had ever been.

CHAPTER 17

*I*t was still 3:00:23 when Molly woke up and Death kissed her tightly clenched lips. Her tongue found the fuzziness of her mouth and pushed him away. Hopping out of bed naked and glorious, she recovered her clothes ("have you seen my underpants?").

She retrieved the Ziploc bag that held her toothbrush and her work makeup and the disposable freshening-up cloths that she used to make the transition from Molly Molloy, learner about head trauma, to Molly Molloy, Hula-Hoopist and server of curly fries.

She got the spare pair of underpants from the bag with her shorty-shorts and tighty-tights and closed the door to the bathroom. She flicked at the switch, but without time, the electricity didn't flow, so the only light came from the dim perpetually excited electrons of the two nightlights Death kept plugged in the socket where men used to plug in their electric razors and now plugged in their hair dryers.

In the mirror, Molly smiled. For the first time in years, her body felt well and truly loved. Her skin was stroked and caressed and though her thighs were free of sticky residue, her core was full and she knew she hadn't been fucked.

She tried her mantra out but as soon as she said the first stupid, she knew it hadn't been.

Her hair was a cloud of static that crackled when she pulled her comb through it.

"The seltzer is for rinsing," Death called out. Molly used some disposable wipes and brushed her teeth. She checked the pimple that had been forming under her jaw, but was now mostly gone. She put a little concealer on the remnants.

Back under the low shadows of mid-autumn, she found Death dressed again in black jeans and a T-shirt (Johnny. Joey. Deedee. Tommy) utterly engrossed in one of his collection of ancient men's magazines.

She looked over his shoulder to one yellowing page that showed a man with a cigar and an eye patch being sniffed by a woman with extravagantly puffy hair. The other page said:

When she touched his shoulder, he startled.

"I think I was supposed to take you to a movie."

Molly giggled, then gently pulled away the magazine and set it on the stack on his milk-crate bed table.

"Oh god, don't read those," she said. "If you need to know something, just ask me."

"I don't usually. I mean read them," he said. "I get them for the pictures. See?" He opened the magazine to a worn and dog-eared page of a sloe-eyed man with a mullet and a chiseled torso pulling off his tank.

"Okay? Though not really?"

"Right there, see the ribs?" Then he reached over to the obsidian knife that had been obstructed by the stack of magazines. He splayed his fingers to either side of one of the runnels he'd been working on for the past decade and stabbed.

Molly screamed and yanked it away, covering the spot with

her hand. Even before the stone blade chipped against the brick fireplace, his flesh began to seal under her hand.

"Don't worry about me," he said, pulling her hand away so she could see that the flesh was already knitting together. "I'm just making improvements, Molly. I do it all the time."

A sob broke out. She couldn't help it. She knew that he was immortal, but she also knew that everyone she loved died and that the one man she had loved as a man, had died by his own hand.

"*Well, don't,*" she snapped and wiped her nose against the heel of her palm. "I like you fine just the way you are so don't you ever, *ever* do that again."

Death was used to anger. He'd heard enough rants that started with "Ragpicker!" before proceeding to some obscure and easily flubbable point of doctrine. But Molly wasn't angry with him, she was angry *for* him.

He grabbed her to him and rocked her, murmuring songs that used to be Bea's favorites but their practitioners had died centuries ago, taking with them whole rich cultures and religions that no one even knew should be missed.

Then he leaned his head against hers and smiled like a fool, because Molly Molloy liked him just the way he was.

HE WOULD HAVE STAYED that way for a hundred years, but Molly needed a shower and something to eat that wasn't Peanut Butter Crunch.

They checked their calendars for a time when she was between shifts and nobody was dying, then after one more long and lingering kiss, Molly closed the door.

Once he was absolutely sure she was gone, Death plucked out the stretch of peach lace he'd stuffed in his pocket. Holding it to his corrupted lips and to his profane nose, he craved.

CHAPTER 18

*T*uesday, after what seemed like an eternity of war and murder and disease that wore more heavily on him than before, Death met Molly at a multiplex because it had nine options and was conveniently located near to Molly's subway line and around the corner from a vehicular homicide.

Afraid that she was running late, Molly got off the train the stop before, so she wouldn't be trapped underground when the world and the wheels stopped turning.

She was still two blocks away when it did.

She absorbed the silence and the odd freedom from fear. No car or bicycle or person was going to touch her. On the other hand, she had to dodge the tiny sparrow frozen in his ascent from the hamburger bun in the gutter to his nest in the hollow crossbars of stoplights. And the plastic bag hovering at the intersection. And a sticky novelty gummy hand that a little boy had dug out of his goodie bag.

She plucked a particularly beautiful yellow leaf with a bit of green and peach from the air and put it between the pages of Goldfrank's *Toxicologic Emergencies*.

The door to the movie theater was propped open against a

man's burly back. She tried to close it so the heat wouldn't escape, but then she realized that the man was heavy and the heat stayed where it was, a warm and butter-scented wall.

She passed into the warm and butter-scented wall and wandered through the silent montage of children and adults and teenagers until she heard metal scrape across metal. Under the murals of children playing outside and against the red and white stripes of the popcorn machine, she saw a slim figure scooping vast shovels into a bucket. He shook bright yellow salt from a plastic shaker until the popcorn glowed neon.

"Maybe that's enough with the Flavacol," said Molly, who had worked at a bowling alley one summer and knew how thirsty it made you.

"There's also two sodas." He gestured toward two half-filled cups with stiff crystalline columns connecting them to the fountain. One was brown and one was transparent. "You take whichever you want. Oh, and I got Jujubes." He took a swig from the bright green box dotted with colorful dots and handed it to her.

"Not until I've got dental coverage."

Death took the spork from his pocket and pushed the column into the cup before angling the cup out from under the spout. Molly prodded at the tiny bubbles submerged just under the surface with a straw.

Even though Molly had suggested that he not to rely on advice from twenty-year-old men's magazines, he really had no one else to turn to, so he had memorized the article titled "From Smitten to Committed" in *Men's Monthly*: "When giving your girlfriend a massage pay special attention to her bottom!" "Tricks for making her believe you like going down on her!" and "No matter how independent she may appear, she wants you to pay for her!"

He trotted over to the cash register, making sure Molly was watching as he fished out some of the wilted currency he kept in the shoe box under his bed and lined it up on the counter of the AMC Magic on the corner of 125th Street.

They ended up in Theater Five in the front row where there were still seats. Molly nestled the bucket of popcorn between them and sodas in the cup holders. Death stretched out his legs.

Molly stared at the screen and the basement vault where the masked Peter Parker dangled suspended by the silvery strands of webbing slung between what looked like shipping containers.

"You know there are supposed to be more of them," Molly said.

"More of what?"

"Pictures. They're not single moments. They're like a gajillion pictures and they all tie together into stories that move. That's why they're called movies."

"How many is a gajillion. Is it more than 108.234 billion?"

"Any time someone tells you a made-up number ending in -illion, it just means a lot. Not like 108.234 billion which is pretty weirdly specific. And I'm not sure I want to know why."

"That's the number of people who have died."

"Like I said, I'm not sure I want to know why."

The man next to him had taken the hand of the girl next to him. He looked cautiously at her face, to see if she was objecting, but her head was tilted toward the man's shoulder, so Death stretched his hand palm out figuring that if this was the right thing to do, Molly would know.

She put her hand on his and wrapped her fingers around his and he did the same, feeling the little heartbeat and the reviving swirl of her subcutaneous tendrils.

"Can you tell me what this story is?"

"Well, I haven't seen this particular version, but it's pretty famous and I have seen others."

"So it's part of the canon?"

"Yes. Definitely. If there's a canon, Spiderman is part of it."

Then she began to tell him about the canon of Spiderman

and the radioactive spider and how he's trying to stick up for the little guy against the man.

"Which man?"

"*The* man. It's like someone super powerful."

"Like God?"

"Not *that* powerful."

Death hadn't really considered why they were called movies. He just knew that when he went there, he felt an ill-defined sense of inclusion. People weren't talking to each other using words he couldn't hear, or making plans they would rather he was not a part of. They were all doing what he was doing: staring at the screen. Together.

Now it turned out he had missed something after all. There was a story with one thing leading to another and in the end there was an Admonishment that Death had never heard, and doubted even Abdiel was aware of:

With Great Power Comes Great Responsibility.

"Does everyone have a story?" he asked as they started for the door.

Molly fed the last few kernels of popcorn into her mouth with the practiced motion of a girl who ate a disproportionate number of meals standing up.

"Yes, everyone has a story, though they're not neat like this. Our stories, the real stories, have a beginning you have no say in, a middle made up of a crapton of stupid decisions, an end no one is ever prepared for and no moral to make sense of it all." She pulled out her MetroCard and shrugged. "You just do the best you can and hope it's enough."

After they had parted ways and Death had continued around the corner to the vehicular homicide, he pondered the little girl on the scooter who was already under the car, but not yet under its wheels.

What was her story? What was the story of the woman reaching toward her? Molly said everybody had a story. They were messy and sometimes painful and sometimes joyous, but whatever it was, he had begun to feel that these stories were incomprehensible in the single moment of his meeting, when he put his fingers to their belly buttons and wrote FIN.

He draped his coat over the side mirror of a parked car and lay down on the cold asphalt, but just as he was reaching for the girl's omphalos, a foot kicked him away, not hard, but enough to startle him and make him bang his head on the chassis.

Before he could recover, he saw the girl's terrified face slip away to the other side.

Molly settled the little girl in her mother's arms and stood in front of them, arms crossed, making it clear that if he wanted to get to anybody's omphalos, he was going to have to go through her.

Once again, Molly Molloy, that solid but unexceptional player in the driveway basketball games at Odd Fellows Home for Teens, boxed him out.

"Mahleeeeee," Death pleaded, wringing his hands. "You don't understand. This is my job. I can't keep mucking everything up."

"You're right, I don't understand. So why don't you explain how one little girl's life will muck everything up?"

"Not everything. It's not about her, she's just a symptom. I—we—are trying to bring peace to the world. Like the Great Peace Before when things were easy and there was no pain, no want, no destruction. Before I made my first mistake and it all spiraled out of control."

Then he repeated the Admonishment he had just learned from the Canon.

"With great power comes great respons—"

"Oh just don't," Molly said. "Hold this," she added, tossing him her bag and while Death fumbled to catch it, Molly slipped under the car, wedging herself tight against the front wheels.

She didn't know much about temporal mechanics, but she knew that at the fraction of the second when Death removed a soul from its body, time started up again. The woman's tears would fall, the light saying "Wait Wait Wait" would flash and the speeding car's wheels would turn, crushing her.

"Dammit, Molly!" Death spat out, squatting next to the car that had been speeding through the stop light and would be again.

"You know what's easy, Dee?"

"What?"

"Dying. Deciding that the wanting, the pain and the spiraling is too hard and you're just going to step off. And you're going to leave people, maybe only one person, behind."

"Are you angry with Zach?"

"Yes, I'm angry with Zach."

"But you love him, too."

"Yup," she said. "Pretty miraculous, right? I can hold on to two messy feelings at the same time. Like, I can be pissed as hell with you but care for you all the same."

Then Death lay down on the asphalt, his hand to her face.

"Are you going to leave the girl alone?" she asked.

"Yes."

"Promise."

"Yes."

"Pinky promise?" And she snaked her arm out from under the wheels that were still hot from the friction, her pinky hooked. Death kissed it.

"Good enough," Molly said and began to inch her way out until Death could grab hold of her. Her armpits were damp.

Then with a sudden terrifying crush of noise, he disappeared.

The car ran over the scooter, the little girl screamed hysterically, and the mother held her tighter in her arms and sobbed.

* * *

APOLLO SORIANO, who was having a hard enough time with his second day at the snack counter of the AMC Magic at 125th street, stared at the blood-stained Yuan notes from the South Kwong Industrial Bank lined up on the glass case in front of him.

CHAPTER 19

*D*eath slung his laundry bag over his shoulder and popped over to the garage in Bayside, Queens where Mrs. Kelly kept her enormous top-loader. Mrs. Kelly had twins in high school who occupied the full spectrum between Emo and Goth, so she had never noticed one more pair of narrow black jeans or T-shirts with incomprehensible band names. Especially since they were always gone as soon as the dryer stopped.

"You can't keep doing this."

Death pushed his Bauhaus T-shirt deeper into the sudsy water.

"Mrs. Kelly's never noticed before."

"You know I'm not talking about the laundry, Neshama'le. I'm talking about the woman."

Death felt the ether where his heart should have been contract. "Why? What did Abdiel tell you?"

"I don't care about that old geezer. I have eyes. I can see what's going on."

"But you said..." he started defensively. She *had* said. She'd said don't be a prude. "I'm not hurting her. Don't let me forget my washcloth." He closed the lid with a bang.

"I know what I said, but I hadn't imagined that you would do this."

"What? What am I doing?"

"I didn't imagine that you would stretch every second you spend with her into days, which is fine for you. You're immortal. If you shoehorn a thousand years into a day, what difference does it make? But she isn't. She isn't immortal. If you keep this up, Molly Molloy is going to reach twenty-eight with bifocals and sciatica and a constellation's worth of liver spots. She is dying. That is what she does. I've changed my mind and I'm telling you now that if you're not going to kill her then you need to let her live."

* * *

MOLLY FRETTED a few days before heading up to Popeye's. She slid a note under the bent metal draft stopper.

Time marched on, unimpeded.

A week later, Sienna came to TaaTaas! with little Aria. Dave dropped everything and as they walked toward his office, Dave stroked Aria's cheek. The toddler smiled with her tiny-toothed smile and Dave looked anxiously toward Molly. She tried to keep the relief from her face, because she knew that guilt was even better leverage than misguided pity.

The next day, before work, she waited by the brick-colored metal door with the tiny cracked square window of safety glass crisscrossed with wires, staring at the wall lined with mailboxes until someone opened the dinged up door and then she pushed in after him. She slid another note under Death's door.

Time marched on, unimpeded.

By the end of a month, Molly was sad and furious and was finding it hard to concentrate during the Cardiac Emergencies session. She'd been paired with a trainee with the unfortunate name of Edwin Salad. Edwin had packed a lot of living and a lot of beer and peanuts into his thirty-two years, which Molly saw even before she'd opened up his shirt for her assessment. His chest was covered with hair below the dark tan line at his neck. Except on the lower left side, where it looked like flesh had been scooped out with a grapefruit spoon.

When she put the bell to his heart, there were no sloshings or thumpings. She moved the bell around and a shadow fluttered across the room accompanied by a sound like the flapping of canvas sails or leather wings and Molly looked toward the high window.

"You fucking coward," she screamed.

"I served two tours in Iraq." Edwin's voice echoed deep and cold over the cacophonous sloshings that had just started emanating from his heart.

Molly signed up for any extra Emergency Department and Ambulance rotations she could get. She did her studying in the waiting room of the Trauma Ward.

Then old Mr. Rodriguez downstairs went into cardiac arrest. Almost inevitably during one hospital run, they picked up someone like Mr. Rodriguez. He was unresponsive. No breath. No pulse. A neighbor had been pushing at the skin of his chest in slow even strokes to the beat of one Mississippi. Two Mississippi. Three Mississippi.

He turned away with relief as Molly took over.

"Isn't that kinda rough?" he asked as Molly got full compressions to the much faster rhythm of the BeeGees.

Ah Ah Ah Ah Ah until she'd gotten up to thirty and then pulled out her pocket mask for two breaths at Stayin' Alive. Stayin' Alive.

She helped get Mr. Rodriguez into the ambulance and sat in the jump seat, with a clipboard in her hand, watching more experienced EMTs stick pads to the side of the old man's chest while the other used a bag valve mask.

"Analyzing heart rhythms. Do not touch patient," the Automated External Defibrillator said. "Shock advised," it said. "Charging. Stand clear of the patient. Deliver shock now. Shock delivered."

They were about to give up to call it in and get permission to stop resuscitation, but Molly knew what Death looked like and knew he hadn't come yet for Mr. Rodriguez. She insisted that they try again and when they did, his heart started.

CHAPTER 20

*S*ometimes, when he was with Molly, the thrumming of the tendril had made Death feel like he was growing a heart. Now it felt like a catastrophic absence and very notable void. Not in that stupid if-you-look-long-enough-into-the-void-the-void-begins-to-look-back-through-you way of that middle-class Saxon schnorrer.

No, this void was like that first one, the great absence that had gotten him into so much trouble.

After a Thanksgiving spent picking up people who followed a surfeit of turkey and wine and family by clambering behind the wheel of a car, Death came home. He emptied out his pockets and set the laundry basket into the empty fireplace. Saying nothing, he watched as it fffftthwipp disappeared.

He took a look through his men's magazines, but after a desultory line across his torso, tossed both obsidian blade and magazine across the room.

Death's laundry basket was not empty when it fell back. In it was a piece of pale celadon papyrus folded into a hedgehog.

He cradled the hedgehog in his palm and looked up to the other missives he'd received lately: the chrysanthemum, the cluster of oyster mushrooms, the tiny cyclostephanos diatom all painstakingly folded from the same pale celadon papyrus. They were getting increasingly complicated which was, he knew, a bad sign. The more sternly worded the missive, the more intricate the folding. A rock fish meant more trouble than a flounder.

They were also notoriously difficult to unfold.

He bet Abdiel liked imagining him sitting on the floor desperately trying to untangle a note that in the end would reiterate what a fuck-up he was.

Slowly, he untwisted each quill and unfolded each tiny paw and opened up the little ears and finally smoothed it out in front of him.

Beneath the usual letterhead were three words.

CUSTODES RECTORUM
INDIVISIBILIS AETERNA ET IMMUTABILIS

Tomorrow was yesterday.

Abdiel

HE STARED at it for seconds. When he screamed Molly's name, a shockwave pushed Metis into Jupiter's fluctuating girth.

"MOLLY!" he yelled, louder this time, and flares scorched the outer atmosphere.

"That was *way* too close," Bea thought, as she hurried from the clinic in Yemen.

She found him on Grand Street outside Molly's apartment, swamped in an oversized T-shirt that averred NEVER MIND

THE BOLLOCKS, HERE'S THE SEX PISTOLS. He hadn't bothered with shoes.

"Stop that!" she shouted as he opened his mouth again. "You're going to break something."

"Bea," he said, distraught. "Look."

She extracted the crumpled celadon papyrus from Death's trembling hand and felt around her numerous pockets before finding her reading glasses on top of her head.

"Why do they have to make these things so small?" Flicking her wrist, she settled the glasses on her nose. "Ah," she said, "so he's on to you."

"I don't know where she is, Bea. I can't find her. Supposing they already—"

"She's on the One," said Bea whose business was the living, "just south of 103rd St. But Neshama'le, you—"

It was too late, Death was gone and all that was left of his fury and fear were the ribbons of light dancing through the night.

"Beautiful, aren't they?" she said, exchanging glances with the young man who had bent legs and two crutches. Together they sat on a bench that hadn't been there a moment before and watched the once-in-a-lifetime auroras play out in the skies above Manhattan.

* * *

MOLLY WAS INDEED in the subway just south of 103rd, when the lights flickered and the train stopped.

She didn't let go of the pole because trains that came to a stop often lurched forward unexpectedly. Then she noticed the tall man next to her who had started cursing when he lost his connection was frozen, his face twisted and grotesque. And the father of a little boy doing Sudoku had stopped, his hand midair, about to remind him there were children present.

Death banged at the door of the northbound Seventh Avenue local.

Molly let go of the pole and leaned over the boy and his father. She pulled open the narrow window at the top. "What do you want?"

"I have to talk to you," he said.

"Fuck you," Molly countered and slammed the window in his face, as though Death hadn't had a million things slammed in his face before and found a way around all of them.

"Sorry," she said to the father and son who couldn't hear her. When she turned around, Death was there. He needed to feel the thrum of her soul, needed to know that it was inside her, secure and uninjured, but all Molly saw was his fingers twitching toward her belly button. She slapped his hand.

"Get away from me!"

"Please Molly, please, please. It's an emergency. Look," he said, Abdiel's quondam hedgehog shaking in his hand.

"What does it mean? 'Tomorrow is yesterday'?"

"I can't explain everything. They kept telling me I need to fix my mistake—which is you—because I didn't retrieve you when I was supposed to and I got your grandmother—"

"Yes, I already know that part."

"Butbutbut... I was told to fix that and then I said I would. That I'd fix it tomorrow. That's what I said, I said, 'tomorrow.'" But when you live forever, tomorrow doesn't really mean anything? I thought maybe they'd never figure it out? You know, what 'tomorrow' means. But they did."

"Is that why you were reaching for my belly button? To fix your mistake?"

"No, not me!" he said, waggling his hands frantically. "I just...I just wanted to feel that it was all right. Your Rag. That it was safe. That it was still inside you."

"Yeah, well, thanks for your concern. Now you know." She

turned her back on him and held the pole tight against her navel. "So *now* you can get the *fuck* away from me."

"Molly, please, you have to—"

"I don't *have* to do anything." She whipped back around and shoved her finger into his chest. "I never wanted you in my life and yet... you kept coming back. Then I when I actually *do* want..." The lining of the upper part of her nose started to itch and she gritted her teeth against the quavering of her voice. "Why?" she whispered. *"What did I do?"*

He put his hand to her cheek and his thumb to the corner of her eye where a tear had gathered for everyone who had ever disappeared from Molly Molloy's life without saying why. He sighed and stared at the little boy with his Sudoku and the angry man with his phone and the woman sleeping in the corner and all he wanted to do was lay his cheek to Molly's hair, listening to the minute creakings and pushings and flowings of her continued life.

"You're dying, Molly."

Then the tear that had been at the corner of her eye for everyone else was followed by another one for herself.

"What is it? Cancer?"

"What? No, not that. I mean you're aging."

"Yes, and?"

"You don't understand. You see her?" He pointed to a woman frozen in the act of putting on lip balm. "At this moment, she's not aging. She's stuck at"—he checked his list—"11:47:19 and change. Same with them." This time he pointed to the man and his Sudoku-playing son. "Same with all of them. Except you.

"None of them are dying, because at this moment, none of them are living. But you are. Every hour you spend with me passes. And when I leave, you're older."

"And?"

"It's not fair to you. If I keep this up, you'll be twenty-eight

171

and have a severe case of bifocals and liver dots." He worried a button on his coat, twisting it back and forth.

"Is that all?" Molly snorted. "Look"—she pointed to the bend of her jaw—"I eat fried food. I serve fried food. I sweat in one job and wear makeup in the other. I have breakouts. And when I came to you that first time, after IHOP? I had one right here. I covered it up and tried to keep it hidden by my hair but it was there. Except when I left you, it was almost gone. The guy playing music on the corner hadn't played the next note. Nothing had changed in the rest of the world, but I knew immediately that I had. I had changed. Grown older. I understand that," she said, pulling him closer. "It may be a stupid decision but it is mine to make, not yours."

The button he had been worrying came off and he stared at it, a spot of something in the middle of the nothing of his hand.

He threw himself at her, gathering her to him, hiding his face in her neck and mouthing silent Hosannas in praise of that jerk Salaphiel who volunteered him all those millennia ago and gave him this single true miracle.

Molly Molloy.

And love, because in the end he knew they were the same thing.

WHEN THE TRAIN STARTED, Molly held a much-folded piece of celadon paper in her hand. Having lost his pencil in a hurricane, Death had borrowed one from the Sudoku boy. He'd found a spot as far from the spilled Coke as possible, pulled out his Pikachu eraser, then drew and erased and drew and erased. Molly tried to see what he was doing but he drew like she wrote, his arm curved around the page, and she found herself oddly pleased to find that Death was also a lefty.

In the end, he gave her a picture of a grotesque centipede: Its head was an egg with a tiny upturned bump of a nose and pinprick eyes, settled on top of a dress. Sticking out from under the dress were two little appendages shaped like the blades of a hockey stick. After it was another egg in a dress on hockey sticks and another and another. He had erased the earlier attempts, so that they faded toward the end.

"If you see this"—he pulled out the obsidian blade that he'd used to loosen her grandmother's truculent soul—"Call me and slice. Start with the front. And don't poke, you might not get them. Sliiiiice." He slashed the blade diagonally through the air then pushed both the drawing and the blade into Molly's hand and promised that if she called he wouldn't be long away.

"*Far* away. You won't be far away."

"I may be far, but I won't be long."

* * *

"Dad?" Tori Green said to his father who was still contemplating whether he should point out to the cursing man that there were children present. "Did you take my pencil?"

CHAPTER 21

*H*aving a guardian angel—at least her guardian angel—was not all it was cracked up to be. Dee had a habit of popping in while she was taking tests and taking orders, making her lose track of both. She'd had to explain more than once that while TaaTaas! was public and he didn't have to knock thusly, the tiny bathroom stall at TaaTaas! was not and he did.

At night, he'd taken to lying with his head atop her belly button, putting uncomfortable pressure on her bladder.

Despite her promise that she would, she did not carry the obsidian blade with her at all times, partly because it did not fit comfortably in her pocket and partly because she didn't quite believe that she would be threatened by an egg in a dress on hockey sticks and certainly not while she was doing chores.

She'd just crossed off ~~CLEAN BATHTUB~~, ~~CLEAN REFRIG-ERATOR~~, ~~UNPACK OTHER BOOKS~~ and had clambered through her window onto the roof of Palmyra to tackle DEAL WITH CHRYSANTHEMUMS when the usual smell of onion and za'atar was cut with an overwhelming stench as pungent as a freshly unwrapped taxi freshener, if taxi fresheners came in frankincense and pineapple.

Something shimmered in the corner of her roof.

It was, Molly saw to her horror, an egg in a dress on hockey sticks and as it slid toward her, it left fading iterations of itself behind.

Its pinprick eyes above a piggy nose were steadily focused on Molly.

Shocked both by the thing itself and by how perfectly Dee had captured its likeness, she patted her apron absently before remembering that the obsidian blade was in her backpack.

"Dee?" she finally remembered to whisper. She cleared her throat and took a deep breath, but before she could actually yell, there was a fwwwwippp and a flap of canvas and Death stood in front of Molly.

"RAGPICKER!" the egg in the dress said, patting its robes until it found a pierced ball of pale blue chalcedony. It held it in front of its flattened nose. "What," the thing intoned, "is that smelling?"

"Go back inside," Death whispered to Molly.

"Yeah, I don't think so," she whispered back.

"We are being sent to rectify."

Cassiel stepped toward them with more copies joining the first, merging together like a time lapse movie of a centipede. Except the tail segments of this centipede were continuously chittering RAGPICKER! even as the newer parts reached into its robe with its free hand and brought out a large cube.

The centipede tossed it to Death.

"A new Book of Admonishments, since you are remembering none."

A piece of celadon papyrus folded in the shape of a flatworm bookmarked Admonishments I.

"You think I don't know Admonishments I?" Death said testily. "'Obedience above all?' I took Righteousness four—"

"I? I? You are forgetting who we are? We are the Custodes: Indivisibilis Aeternalis et Immutabilis—indivisible, eternal, unchanging?" As the centipede's voice grew, he poked the air in front of Death with an imperious hand. "There is no place for *I* in Indivisible."

If he had known Molly even a little, Cassiel would have avoided that bullying, poking, self-righteousness and saved himself from what was to come.

Death, who did know Molly, shoved his fingers in his ears as she stepped in front of the towering egg-in-a-dress.

"I got news for you, *bub*. There're *four i*'s in Indivisible."

The centipede froze looking down at her, though she could still hear the nattering of its earlier manifestations.

"What is that being?" Cassiel asked, waving the air in front of its piggy nostrils with its pomander. "Is that being your mistake?"

"Who the fuck are you calling a mistake, you cunt-less, ball-less, asshat? If you don't get off my roof, shit for brains, I will tear you a new—" From the third word, the blue pomander dropped from the front Cassiel's hands and he shoved them over his ears, babbling "**Non profanate nec linguam nec auriculam, non profanate nec linguam nec auriculam, non profanate nec linguam nec auriculam**" over and over like a horrified toddler.

Molly's eyes narrowed and her lips tightened and she reached out a hand covered in chrysanthemum dirt and the caked remains of yogurt from the bottom of the refrigerator.

"Touch," she said and poked him.

With a screech, Cassiel stumbled back among his still-jabbering past selves.

"Touch. Touch. Touch. Touch. Touch."

"Gaaaaaaaaaaaaagggggggghhhhhh," Cassiel wailed and with a pop, disappeared. In quick succession, all of the other Cassiels disappeared as well, taking their hectoring, intoning, tight-faced disapproval with them.

Finally, there was only that first Cassiel who yelled one final RAGPICKER! before—pop—it was gone, too.

She stared at the blank space, then turned back to Dee, whose hands had slipped from his ears to his mouth. His face contorted and he jackknifed forward, a rusty gurgle bubbling up from his insides.

Molly handed him the dead chrysanthemum then pulled his hair back and told him if he was going to vomit, aim for the pot.

He gurgled and jerked and gurgled some more and it wasn't until he stood up with an enormous cracked smile on his face that Molly realized that it must've been a long time since Death had laughed.

When he finally pulled himself together, Death picked up Molly's planters while she retrieved the chalcedony pomander from under her window. As soon as she got closer, she sneezed.

"Whatever this is, I think I—[a...choo]—I think I may be allergic." She sneezed again, then scooped up the pierced orb with a trowel and carried it to the edge of the roof before dropping it unceremoniously into a shopping cart filled with garbage bags.

"Ragpicker?" she asked, wiping her hands on a paper towel.

"It's not what you would call a high-status job. What I do. It's not like Choir or Intoning or Veneration."

As soon as the pomander was gone, Death took a deep breath of onion and cumin and earth and the Forest Berry shampoo Molly bought at the dollar store for over a dollar.

Death knew it was just a matter of time before other of the Custodes came, someone tougher than Cassiel, but because they had such a piss-poor grasp of time, he told her it would take years and years.

Molly nodded at his reassuring words, but now she kept the obsidian knife with her.

CHAPTER 22

*I*t was exactly two weeks later, while laying on Death's futon, her hands tangled in his hair, his mouth coaxing her tendrils, that Molly started to sneeze again.

"Are you okay?" he asked, wiping his mouth on the back of his wrist.

Molly swung her legs around, touching the floor, her palms clutching the edge of the bed, every breath followed by sneezing.

"What are you doing here?" Death hissed at Jophiel. He pulled the sheet out and tried to wrap it around Molly, but she pushed it away, her arms wrapped around her stomach as she sneezed once more.

"Oh, fu—" she said and vomited on the floor.

She bent over, her eyes tightly closed while Death pulled a handful of tissues from the box on the bedside table and began wiping her mouth. "Keep your eyes closed, Molly."

"What are you doing to your form?"

"Keep your hands to yourself!" Death shouted, slapping the multiple hands reaching for his lower parts.

"Please," Molly mewled. "Please. The smell is making me—" and she heaved again.

"He's leaving," said Death.

"We are delivering our message. Abdiel—"

"I really need the bathroom."

Death guided Molly, her hand shielding her nose and mouth, her eyes tightly closed against the endless roiling movement. He stood at the door, watching the curve of her back and the tiny indentations at her hip bones, while she crouched over the toilet.

Then Death grabbed Jophiel's arm and dragged him away.

"What message?" he whispered sharply.

"You are purifying and attending to Abdiel."

"No."

Jophiel stopped, his earlier selves still whipping around the tiny apartment behind him. "By what doctrinal authority are you refusing?"

"You want doctrinal authority? Here it is: I. DON'T. WANT. TO."

"But...but... **Obedentia super omnes**?" Jophiel intoned worriedly.

"OUT!"

Dee stood in front of the bathroom until he was sure Jophiel had left and then he knocked.

"Is it still out there?" Molly asked.

"Gone now."

While Molly brushed her teeth, Death opened all of his windows and taking a breath that had once served to set the universe expanding, gently blew out the scent of heaven and replaced it with the scent of Popeye's. The gauzy butterfly she'd wrapped around the chandelier fluttered.

After the glubglub of the gallon jug of water she kept in the bathroom, Molly emerged, standing at the doorway.

"What did he want?" Molly asked.

"Nothing to worry about. Just a messenger."

"What was the message?" Her lips tasted of mint and euca-lyptus and her bottom was full and round and a ruin of tendrils stood on end, covering his soul like fur and—

"RAGPICKER!"

With a muffled groan, Molly twirled around and bent back over the toilet.

"Oh, for the love of…WHAT!" Death yelled at the swirling, susurrating mass that would eventually be the Chief Adminis-trator of the Keepers of Righteousness, once he remembered how to recreate his body in the gravity of Down.

Abdiel hadn't been Down since…Well, since a very long time. Not since that disastrous wrong turn when he listened to those who thought choice and knowing were more important than obedience. He'd learned his lesson and had crawled back up, his metaphorical tail between his metaphorical legs, deter-mined *never* to make a mistake again.

The first thing he noticed was that the stench of corruption had not gotten any better in the intervening millennia and what's more, the smell emanating from the Ragpicker's naked and deformed body was almost as strong as that coming from the woman.

Abdiel paced the room, covering his nose with his pomander while Molly vomited.

Death closed the door gently and turned toward the Chief Administrator. "What do you want, Abdiel?"

"Do you remember Admonishments XXVII?"

"XXVII?"

"XXVII."

"Not offhand," Death admitted.

"You used it before when arguing against retrieving its Rag."

"I have pickups to make," he lied, "so why don't you tell me already."

Abdiel cleared his throat and let a small hum vibrate through the bit of empyrean that was his head, before intoning, "**Ad nobis neque initium neque finem vitae.**"

It is not for us to begin or end life.

"Molly?" he asked, his ear pressed to the door. "You okay in there?"

"Blurrragh," she responded.

"What are you trying to tell me?" Death whispered, standing right next Abdiel. "That she's sick? Because *I'm* telling *you* that if you come near her omphalos, I will—"

"The ending of life is not at issue," Abdiel said, removing the pomander from his nose and watching Death's face coolly.

"Then what?"

"It is with child."

Death stared unseeing at the bilious puddle on the floor.

He felt the thing that he'd carved between his legs. It was soft now and lay shriveled, like a slug on a salt lick. It was supposed to be just an ornament. He'd promised Molly it was just an ornament. He'd eaten her condom and promised her that there would be no consequences.

When would he ever learn. There were always consequences.

* * *

THE AIR TURNED sharp against Abdiel's outer limits and the dangerous fullness of Death's true form began to consume him. It was the kind of density that, when it happened last time, spelled the end of the Time Before. When the Custodes were not the Custodes but were the Everything resting peacefully at the center of the great Nothing. Until one part of that Everything developed will and self-knowledge and curiosity and broke away and in so doing, took on a power greater than all of them. A power that could not be destroyed but must be contained, controlled, quashed, if they were ever to return to the peace that was the Nothing of the Time Before.

There was a sudden bang. It wasn't big like that first one—the one when Everything and Nothing were crushed together until Change erupted from its ruin like egg from a clenched fist—just a bathroom door hitting wallboard but it made Abdiel jump anyway. Then Molly ran out, vomit on her breath and obsidian in her hand and Abdiel took a panicky step back as she sliiiiiiiicccccced across his present, past and soon to be future self, cutting away his robes and revealing the featureless pillar atop two hockey stick feet.

After a screech, several pops, and a fading complaint about damage done to his third best gown, Abdiel disappeared.

* * *

DEATH USED the swathe of empyrean Molly had carved from Abdiel's third best robe to dab at her mouth. While she brushed her teeth again, he finished wiping up the puddle on the floor then dropped the stained robe in the toilet and pushed the handle hard so that when time came, the water would flush the material woven from fine strands picked from the firmament and send it down the pipes to the submains and into the mains where it would join with the other floaters.

Molly put the obsidian blade on the narrow glass shelf next to the toothbrush holder. Death stood behind her, staring at her naked body with an anxious expression.

"Don't look so worried," she said to his reflection. "Clearly something about that smell sets me off."

He reached around, cupping her breast in his hand, feeling the new heaviness there. His thumb brushed lightly against the nipple that was larger and darker than before. He touched her belly which had always been softly rounded and now felt a little tauter. He reached his fingers into the portal through which life would come into the world.

It was only later that he considered whether it had been the optimal time to ask Molly if she'd lain with another man.

"*What?*" she whipped around. "What did that thing tell you?"

"Think hard," he said, sucking the lovely brackish sour taste from his fingers. "Dave the Manager or Edwin from class or—"

"I don't have to think hard." Her eyes narrowed. "I haven't 'lain with' anybody since I 'laid' you."

"So here's something funny." Death dried his fingers on the towel. "You remember how I told you that the Book of Admonishments says '**Ad nobis neque initium neque finem vitae**'?"

"Was that the one where you ate my condom?"

"Exactly, when I ate your condom. "

"And how *exactly* is that funny?"

"Come on, I'm going to make you some cereal. Settle your stomach." He herded her out of the bathroom into the kitchenette. He laid out a bowl and spoon and shook a box. "Don't want your blood sugar level to go down. I read that it makes people grumpy."

"Don't you fucking patronize me. Just tell me already."

He opened the box and stared inside. Molly liked Mini Wheats, but he'd forgotten to get more.

"Well, the funny thing is…You're with child." He shook the box again. "How about Bran Crispies?"

"What?"

"Bran Crispies?"

"Nooo. The other part."

"You're with child."

She stared silently.

"Molly?"

Still nothing.

"Maaaaahhhleeeeee," he wheedled. "Let's see, I, of course, also have Peanut—"

A serving spoon came down on the back of his head.

"You goddamn son of a bitch!" she yelled, reaching for him across the little table. He stumbled against a chair and then hopped back, trying to keep the table between them.

"What? You didn't want to wear a condom? You lying piece of shit!"

"I didn't lie! There must have been somebody else, but you just forgot?"

He dodged the plastic bowl.

"I did not forget that you, Asshole, are the only person I've slept with for months."

"But you don't understand. We're not allowed to create anything. And life above all..." He shook his head, his hand raised as he tried to think how to make her understand the enormity of it all. "To create life that would be hubris and I would absolutely, totally be forced back into Group for like *ever*."

Molly stopped, her mouth frozen open, her eyes burning. "What did you just say?"

"I'd be forced back into Group?" he repeated, suddenly unsure if it was the right thing to say.

Molly pulled on her pants and shirt, grabbed her shoes, slung her backpack over one shoulder and started to open the door, until he leaned against it.

"Where are we going?" He jiggled his leg the way he did when he was nervous.

"Get.Out.Of.My.Way," she said and shoved him hard enough to send him off balance and by the time he had his balance again, she'd unlocked the door and thrown it open, banging him in the forehead.

"If you ever knock on my door again, you better pray that I'm dead, because I will slaughter you."

. . .

THE DOOR HADN'T FINISHED VIBRATING in the doorframe before Death pulled on jeans. He was about to put on a clean T-shirt, but he was starting to panic and fished out his Echo and the Bunnymen T-shirt from the laundry, because it was Molly's favorite and it smelled like her still. He pulled the collar over his nose and knocked on her door.

There was a long pause and then he heard a door, the bathroom door, slam.

He caught a glimpse of light through the peephole.

"Go away. I want to take a shower so I need you to go away."

"Molly, Molly. I'm so, so, sorry. There's got to be something I can do."

"Make me not pregnant. Like you promised."

Death stood in the hallway outside of Molly's apartment, his forehead against her door.

"I can't do that yet. Not until she's born. Then I can take her soul back out as soon—"

"Not that! My whole life you've always managed to mess things up. Every time. Every time I start to feel like I'm in control, you come along and fuck things up. *You promised.* No children, you said. You—"

Then Molly stopped. There was something awfully familiar about those words, just the voice was different and she remembered the soft purple fuzz of the elephant who would protect her from the fury of deferred hopes and thwarted desires.

She put her hand on her stomach and wept and apologized.

"Her?" she asked, sniffling through the door. "How do you know?"

"I don't know a lot of things, but some things I do." There was silence on the other side, but his fingers traced the outline of her cheek against the door. He knew her cheek was there, just, in the way he knew that she was crying.

"Molly?" he called again. "You remember you asked me long

time ago if I ever transitioned anywhere else? I mean not on Earth?"

She didn't answer, but he didn't need her to.

"I said no, but I didn't tell you why. I don't go anywhere else, because there's no need. There isn't life anywhere else. This is it. And it's because of accidents. One thing hits another thing hits another thing and then you have a planet that's the right distance from a star the right size with an iron core sitting in magma that gives it a magnetic shield. It has the right combination of elements and a comet that ignites life, without blowing the whole thing to smithereens. There are billions of accidents that went into creating this. It doesn't make it any less of a miracle.

"Then by mistake, I hit you on the back, and everything changed. And that's what a miracle is. It's change. I can stay here forever. I will stay here forever, because you are my mistake and my miracle and I can't let you walk away."

She was slumping down to the floor and he knelt, his forehead against the door, his hand tracing the outline of her body on the other side of it.

Finally, the door opened and through the narrow slit and he saw Molly's swollen eye and her reddened nose.

"Molly?" The space in the center of his chest shattered. He needed to touch her, tell her everything was going to be okay. He started to reach his fingers tentatively through the gap and then pulled back.

"You going to slam the door on my hand?"

* * *

HE SAT beside her on the sofa, his clasped hands dangling between his knees, softly humming *Filliae Sion currite*, Run, Daughters of Zion.

He stretched his legs open wider, tentatively brushing his knee against hers.

"Don't."

Molly needed to hold on to her anger, because she knew the moment she stopped being angry with him, she would be angry with herself. She was pregnant by a man with fewer life skills than a jazz oboist, but it had been her decision; he certainly hadn't forced her. Once again, she would have to start over, this time with a child. With a tiny, vulnerable package of variables she couldn't control.

She needed to find a job. Now. TaaTaas! was not known for patience with pregnant entertainers. Nor was any ambulance service going to be anxious to hire an EMT who couldn't even fit behind a stair chair.

In eighteen years, she thought, she would be forty-three. That wasn't too old, was it? To begin living life for real? This time, she thought bitterly, without all of the mistakes.

"Molly? Talk to me?"

She shook her head.

"Please. You're not alone—"

"Yes, I am. I have no family, no real friends. No—"

"You have me. I'll be there."

"It's one thing for you to pop in and out of time like you do with me. I—god help me—agreed to it. She can't. I am not going to let you do this to her. She is not going to graduate from preschool with zits and her period."

Molly kicked the coffee table in front of her and then toppled over, burying her head in her sofa. Death held his empty hands in front of him and he saw the fingers, *his* fingers, insinuating themselves into the omphalos of a girl, a woman, his daughter who he would not know except at the end when the varied richness of the time before death that is called life, was over.

He spread his legs again, very slowly, until his thigh brushed hers and Molly didn't move away and then he stretched his arms wide until his arm touched hers and she didn't move away and he felt his chest collapse and something started to feel cool in the corners of his eyes.

All he wanted was this one short lifetime, but he couldn't because he was Death and he had a job and it had to be done or—

Or what?

He could almost hear Molly saying it, except that Molly was curled up in a ball, her arms bent over her head. What would the Custodes do if he just stopped? Put him in Group?

Then he just wouldn't go. They couldn't force him. The worst they could really do was ostracize him and if he never, ever heard someone yell "Ragpicker!" from behind a pomander again, it'd be a damn sight too soon.

CHAPTER 23

*M*olly sat at a bench with a slim woman in an unremarkable suit and unexceptionable shirt. As Molly peeled the tin foil from her chicken sandwich, she imagined the woman was a couple of years out of law school and had something to do with the courts. Public defender or prosecutor. Clerk, maybe.

When a man approached their bench, the woman took her phone from the outer pocket of her chic briefcase—a graduation present, Molly thought, too elegant for the rest of her ensemble—and started talking like she was in the middle of a long and complicated conversation.

The man's shoes split in the front with the tattered remains of plastic bags spilling out. One hand clasped the back of his jeans, holding them up. The other was jammed into a front pocket. He wore a heavy itchy-looking wool sweater over his bare skin.

He pulled out his hand, saying nothing, expecting nothing. It was an utterly hopeless gesture.

The woman next to her waved vaguely toward the phone, her shield from having to acknowledge despair.

Molly rummaged into her pocket and pulled out what change she had from the Halal cart.

"Good luck," she said to the man, who ambled off looking through the 84¢ in his hand.

"Hmmph," snorted a voice from a small, broad woman in a long, pleated chambray skirt and Liberty print blouse who was now on the bench next to her. Molly hadn't noticed the lawyer leave and as she peered around the plaza and sidewalks, saw her nowhere.

"You know he's just going to drink it away."

Molly ignored the little woman. Maybe he'd get something to eat, maybe he'd get something to drink. Either way, Molly knew enough about life to know how hard it could be and that she wasn't in a position to judge what someone needed to get through it.

"You may be right about it, but are you sure that's what is really best for him?"

Molly didn't think she'd said anything, but answered anyway. "Of course I'm not sure. But if I had to wait until I was sure, I'd never do anything."

The little woman frowned and started poking around in a bright yellow messenger bag. Molly moved over as subtly as possible just in case the lady in the Liberty print came packing a soup ladle, as they sometimes did.

"Oh for heaven's sake, Molly. You don't have to worry about me."

Now Molly *knew* she hadn't introduced herself. "How do you know my name?"

"Here it is. Do you want some? It's Concord Grape." She held out a piece of gum. Molly hesitated for a second, but then took it. There was something about the little woman with warm dark-brown eyes that made Molly think she was supposed to trust her.

"See," the woman started before popping the gum in her

mouth, "your name's been bandied about quite a bit, at least by Azrael, and I wanted to see if you were worth all the fuss."

"Azrael?" Molly was starting to feel a little zippy. Like that time she smoked pot and breathed in ammonia at the same time.

"Your friend, the Ragpicker," the woman said.

Molly stopped chewing. "Hunh. I call him Dee. And I don't like that name. Ragpicker. I don't think he does either."

"Neither do I, which is why I called him Azrael. I'm a friend. I should have introduced myself," the woman said, pulling her tight curls back into a length of elastic. "Name's Miriam, but my friends—well, Azrael—call me Bea. You should, too."

"You're not one of the..." Molly pushed her nose up with one finger and screwed up her eyes until they almost disappeared.

"The Custodes?" The little woman pulled herself upright and smoothed down her shirt. "I'm not *that* old." She sounded genuinely offended. "I'm taking it from your description that you've met them?"

"I wouldn't say 'met', exactly," said Molly. "They drop by every once in a while, stinking up the place and admonishing Dee about his mistakes, by which they mean me."

"Ahhh," Bea said with a mischievous smile. "So you've been introduced to the Book of Admonishments. What did you think of the Custodes' great contribution to arts and letters?"

"It's Latin," said Molly.

"True."

"It's crap."

A warm, throaty laugh rippled from the air. "Also true. Latin crap is probably the tersest and best characterization of the Book of Admonishments I've ever heard."

"Why have it, then?"

"The funny thing is the Custodes are so unimaginably old. They were when nothing else was and they miss that. They mistake absence for peace. But however old they are, they're like babies; they lack the imagination to see beyond themselves. Fortunately, like babies, they like to be tightly swaddled, so they're never happier than when they're bound by rules and ranks and ceremonies and Admonishments. Which is a good thing because we could never control them."

"Why do they pick on him?"

The woman held up a finger and started to blow an enormous purple bubble that finally burst in a fug of concord grape.

"On Azrael?" She started to rub remnants of bubblegum from her cheek. "You know what he is?"

"Death, you mean?"

"No, that's too one-dimensional. He's—you don't speak Aramaic, do you?"

Molly shook her head.

"Pity. Such a lovely language. A sensible combination of earthiness and divinity. So where was I? Right, he's not Death, really, he's Chalaf. Which means to pass on. But it also means to transgress. And to send out shoots and to become new. In short, it's to change. And if there is anything the Custodes hate, it's change."

"There's still a bit of gum…" Molly pointed to a purple spot on the woman's lower jaw. Bea peeled at it with her short nails.

"Did I get it?" she asked and Molly nodded.

"Neshama'le!" Bea's voice rang through the sky like a mother calling a child home for dinner, but one who knows that she won't have to call a second time.

The man pushing the stroller stopped and the baby screaming in the stroller stopped and the pigeon swooping down to follow the crumbs from the stroller and the old man watching the pigeon all stopped.

Molly couldn't help but smile broadly at the slim man with the big coat and the anxious expression.

"Bea? What are you doing here?" He turned nervously to Molly. "Are you okay? Why didn't you call me?"

"She didn't call, because I just wanted to meet her and she's her own woman, not a polyp on the side of your boat. So, what are you thinking?"

"Sixty-five years, maybe?"

"I'd ask for more," Bea said. "Go for an even century. Custodes'll never know the difference and that way you'll have some wiggle room in case of medical advances."

"What are we talking about exactly?" Molly asked

"Azrael wants a sabbatical. Just for a while. Just until you're, well…"

"Dead?"

"Dead, yes, couldn't have said it better myself. He's asked me to intercede on his behalf. Now, Neshama'le, have you given any thought to how you're going to contribute to the household income if you're no longer able to indulge in petty thievery?"

"I have a nest egg."

"A nest egg? Hmm. Molly, have you seen this 'nest egg'?"

"I haven't seen it, but he has mentioned it before. When we were talking about moving in together. Maybe getting something with a little extra space for the baby."

"I'm not sure I would trust his acumen when it comes to New York City real estate. So Azrael, let's see it."

"Now?"

"Yes," Bea said, threading her arm around Molly's elbow. "Now."

Death hesitated and looked at Bea then started rummaging through the Cake Taker, while Molly blinked several times trying to figure out how they'd arrived so suddenly and with no Whooshing of Winds or Curling of Colors at the little apartment above the Popeye's on 135th Street. Bea watched Death expectantly while he searched for the little keys that said "Yale" on them and opened the padlocks on the top and bottom doors of the ancient chest he'd been schlepping around since the Second Babylonian Captivity.

Bea peered in and then, with a quirk of her eyebrow and sweep of her arm, indicated the contents. Molly looked and wrinkled her nose.

"What *is* that?"

"My guess? Peppercorns, salt, ambergris, and...?" said Bea.

"Myrrh." Death smiled proudly. Then he opened up the bottom two doors, unleashing a tiny cyclone of fur and dust.

"Ermine?" asked Bea.

"Squirrel?" he said, suddenly feeling nervous and unsure. And trying to remember anything, anything at all, that might allow him to estimate the net present value of squirrel pelts and ambergris.

Bea sighed with the almost compulsory *Tchk* of disappointment. He knew he'd done something wrong and looked worriedly toward the table where Molly sat, her head bent over a flattened piece of celadon papyrus.

He squatted down trying to gauge the level of her dismay through the fall of brown hair hiding her face. He cocked his head to the side until his cheek was nearly flush with the table and saw that she had drawn a mockup of her apartment and magically fit his chest, his bed, and his pine table into her little apartment without imposing at all on the tiny room labeled Baby's Room, because from that moment on she knew that there was going to be hard work, but she liked the people in her life and that was miracle enough for one existence.

Death put his arms around her and leaned his chin against her shoulder. She rubbed her cheek against his.

Bea smiled to herself at the ancient boy and the girl who was too old for her years, because she knew that high-strung mystics made for terrible Chosen Ones. When things got weird —and things always got weird—they had fretful discussions about the Nature of the Soul, when what was needed was someone who knew how to pack light and run.

Bea closed the cabinet doors against the smell of myrrh,

which she had always abhorred. "Well," she said, "I really should get going." Death walked her to the door and she laid her hands on either side of his face. "I will do the best I can for you," she said fondly. "You've done well for yourself, little soul."

She took one step and then was gone, though her voice still rumbled in Molly's head.

"It's been a long, a long time comin'/But I know a change gon' come, oh yes it will."

CHAPTER 24

*O*nce upon a time, something nestled in the middle of a vast nothing. It was not unlike the jelly in Mr. Steinhauer's donut that started this whole mess in the first place. When after many eons that something nestled inside became the Custodes, they still tended to throng tightly packed like sardines. Or maybe it was like Saltines? Death couldn't quite remember which.

Anyway, Saltines or sardines, they descended on him accompanied by the entourage of past manifestations that wove in and out, clotting the air. They all of them talked at the same time; Death fingered the gauze butterfly that Molly had given him for luck.

"Is the Ragpicker making one of time's children thick with life? The Custodes are not allowed to make life. Hubris. Hubris. Hubris. Change is hubris. We are finding our pomander? The Ragpicker is having the attributes of man. Ragpicker, we are wanting to acknowledge the attributes."

Death reached his arms out to the side, while the shimmering coil surrounded him. Countless hands plucked at his body and chirped as they lifted his robes.

"These attributes. What are they for doing?"

"They're called legs and they're for getting around. These," he said lifting his foot, "at the bottom? These are called feet."

"Are they for locomoting? Are we seeing time's children use them for moving? Feet. Feet. Feet. Legs. Legs. What is the short leg with no foot?

"That is not a leg, it's like a handle. One holds on to it and pulls oneself along."

"Ahhhh. Hmmmm. Ahhhh. No. No. Hmmm? Are we seeing time's children pull themselves by their handles? Yes they are pulling the handle but they are not locomoting when they do so. What is the short leg with no foot for doing, Ragpicker?"

"Okay," he said. "It's not a leg or a handle. It's a toy. Stop it! It's my toy. I made it and it took me a long time to figure out how to get it to work."

"We see the woman who is thick with child, playing with Azrael's toy. Children like toys. Does the toy summon the child? Does the child summon the toy?"

Without any sense of before or after, cause and effect was necessarily a difficult concept for the Custodes. Back when Abdiel had forced Death to go to Choir, Death sang a little ditty about chickens and eggs called *Pullum Aut Ovum: Primum quod Venit?* A couple of Kyries later, Death said his Salves and skedaddled. Choir remained tied up for two hundred years.

"The Ragpicker is becoming other. Change? Change is hubris."

Some of the storm of parts picking at his body stopped.

"Dear, dear," said a voice that gradually congealed into Bea, still dressed for Council. "As I will be reading the sentence of the Council, perhaps, Azrael, you would like to pull down your robes?"

Death shook until the robes fell back down, catching on the past hands that were still feeling his legs and knees and ornament, even though the current semblances of the Custodes waited attentively.

"The Council"—Sanctus, Sanctus, murmured the Custodes— "yes, well, anyway, they [Sanctus, Sanctus] have passed judgment on Azrael. For his hubris, he is to be taught Time's dominion. He will feel the harshness that comes with life, so that he may understand why creation is reserved for those who die. The sentence shall end with the span accorded to the woman who led him into disobedience. This is the Council's [Sanctus, Sanctus] will."

New shuffling and new murmuring was added to the old until Abdiel took his spot at the head of the Custodes and cleared his throat.

"Beata Regina Caeli, Domina Nostra, the Custodes gratefully accepts the Council's [Sanctus, Sanctus] wisdom in upholding the Admonishments; however, we must point out that this leaves us without a Ragpicker."

"I did say this, but the Council [Sanctus, Sanctus] believes that whatever one such as Azrael has managed to do for nearly 200,000 years, should be an easy task for the legions of capable Custodes you have at your command, Abdiel."

"But—"

"What is that thing you're always quoting. Obedience something something?"

"Obedentia super omnes?"

"I do believe that's it."

"Yes, Beata Regina Caeli, Domina Nostra," said the dejected Abdiel. "The Custodes accepts the judgment of the Council. [Sanctus, Sanctus]."

"THAT WAS BRILLIANT," Death said, swinging Bea around once the Saltines or Sardines had gone. "I thought you were just going to ask if I could have a vacation, but this was so much better. I especially like the 'Dominion' part."

Even as he swung her around, her blue robes shrank back to chambray coveralls.

"Time's a bitch, Azrael. I wouldn't crow quite yet. How is Molly holding up?"

"I think okay?" he said worriedly. "She says she's okay." He began picking distractedly at the fabric of his robes.

"But something's bothering you. Out with it, Neshama'le."

Death sniffled. "She says she's okay but she's never had a baby before and women"—his voice dropped to a whisper—"they die." He stopped because he saw, as he always did, Molly's face drenched in sweat. Molly's skin coated with blood. Molly's body ripped open. Molly's throat raw with screaming. Molly's soul made ready for death by the insuperability of life.

"You mean in childbirth?"

He wiped at his long nose with his celestial sleeve.

"Molly is a healthy woman in a rich country. Others will die because they are too young or too poor or too despised. But not Molly."

"You don't know that. What if they have to break her open? What if they—?"

"Stop it, Azrael. Look, she's due in March?"

"The seventeenth."

"Why don't I come by and sit with you. When the time comes, just call me."

"But you're so busy."

"Pishposh. Call me."

THIS TIME, when he let go and fluttered through the ether, he landed in a very different world.

PART II
THE BOOK OF MOLLY

CHAPTER 25

*M*olly waited anxiously at the kitchen window. Dee had said he wouldn't be long but she wished now that she'd been more exact as to what "not long" actually meant for someone who knew no beginning and no end.

Then just like that, he was there, wearing an ecstatic expression and a mass of white robes floating high above his waist.

In the time it took her to write "Briefs" on the notepad stuck to her fridge, Death stepped into Grand Street and was hit by a taxi.

Molly raced out of her apartment but even in the stairwell she could make out the sound of wheels screeching and the jarring thunk of a skull.

She arrived just as the driver, a little man, sweating into a knit cap with the New Jersey Devils on it, leaned over Dee.

"Hello?" Death said experimentally. He watched with wonder as the man swayed above him. Then his eyes focused beyond him to the thick clouds moving over the pale blue sky. And finally on Molly's worried face and the curtain of hair gusting across her face.

"What the fuck do you think you're doing, you crazy fucking freak?"

"Hunh," he said, looking delightedly at the New Jersey Devil, who could not only see him, but yell at him.

"How are you?" Dee said, stretching out his hand with an enormous smile.

"He's fine," Molly said, who understood that the New Jersey Devil was afraid that he'd killed someone and even if that someone was only a lunatic, his papers weren't perhaps all they should be.

She understood that he was terrified that he and his family would be sent back to one of those war-torn countries that Death knew so well. So she did her best to reassure him that she was a paramedic (lie) and that Dee was fine (true) and that he shouldn't worry (true).

Then she put her arm under Dee's shoulders and helped him up, retrieving the Van he hadn't even realized he'd lost. He put it on, unsure in his walking until Molly took his hand in hers and pointed out the sign with the flashing palm and told him to wait until the palm was replaced by a striding man.

"Hunh," he said again, stunned by what time had wrought, the constant motion of people and cars and trees and light through the trees and clouds and smells and noise and a plastic bottle that had once held water but was now being pushed along the ground by a wind he could feel on his skin until a car drove over it with a thrilling crinch-crunch.

Molly, who had been the only thing in this world that moved, was now the only thing in this world that anchored him.

"What happened?" Molly asked, pulling him inside what passed for a foyer in her building.

"I got hit by a car," he trilled.

"I know that part. Before, when you were..." The door closed and she pointed up.

"They decided to give me a leave?"

They headed up the stairs to the second floor and after Molly had unlocked the door, Death tossed the dirt- and oil-smudged gown toward the repurposed laundry basket that held socks instead of souls.

"Oh, Jesus!"

Death yeeped, his hands flying to cover his ornament.

"What happened to your chest?"

Death raised one arm and peered at the tire-sized indentation in the side of his torso. He took a deep breath, held tight onto his nose and after a few seconds of straining, the indentation righted itself with a slight pop.

"Alrighty then," Molly said, squaring her shoulders, a thing she found herself doing more often now. "That was also weird."

She picked up the tire-marked puddle of firmament on the floor next the basket. "Do you know how long you've got?"

"I didn't ask."

"But for a while?" she asked hopefully.

"I didn't ask, Molly, because..." he said again and in two steps, he was next to Molly, his arms tight around her waist. "Because I don't want to know. I couldn't know. I—"

"You're right, I don't want to know either," she said, fingering the material that was heavy and smooth and strangely fluid. "Can this be machine washed?"

ON GRAND STREET, a woman dropped her hat in the street. She twirled back to get it just as the light turned and a driver leaned on his horn. A bird flew overhead, its shadow racing across the floor. A gust through the window blew Molly's perfect medium brown hair around her perfect medium brown eyes, so seductively ensorcelled by dark circles, and Death held her to him, feeling her heartbeat.

CHAPTER 26

The last time Death had stood in the River of Time it had been a sludgy, slow-moving rivulet. He'd had a list, but there were sometimes hours between pickups. Even on an exciting evening, when he'd sat unseen around the campfire eating dates and boiled roots, the cast of characters was largely the same and very little happened. A toothless grandmother alternated between scraping a hide with a stone and gumming it. A man hit at one stone with another stone. A woman picked bugs from her child's head, crushing them on yet another stone.

Very little was said, largely because no matter which fire Death was sitting around, the only words were food, fire, fuck and flee.

Then the big cats came, taking with them the possibility of even that rollicking conversation.

Now the River of Time was a torrent, filled with talk and activity. He used to be able to weave through a still forest of bodies, but now those still trees moved, danced, even. Death would move left, his partner moved right. Then they would repeat the whole thing.

Dee thought it was wonderful, though his partner in the

pavement pavane was inevitably less enthusiastic and would address him with a question that started jovially enough ("what are you smiling about...") and then ended with something that made Dee stick his fingers in his ears.

He was delighted to be able to interact, to show off his familiarity with the human condition, no matter often Molly tried to dissuade him.

Gesundheit. Is it cremains? They're really hard to get out of your nose.

Is that a lollipop or a condom? Lollipops are much tastier than condoms.

Generally, his attempts were met with either silence or an answering gambit that started with the friendly "Hey, buddy," or "Hey, pal," followed by Molly offering up an apology.

It started with that very first day when they went to the diner and Dee helped himself to a fistful of bacon from a large plate of it at the big circular table in the corner of the diner that was occupied, as it always was, with police officers just finishing their shift.

The police stared in disbelief after the young man in the huge, thick coat that flapped around his calves, the kind of thing that in their experience was worn primarily by people who had things that wanted hiding in their linings and their psyches.

"Sorry," Molly said and in a flash of inspiration added, "he's French."

By the time she'd finished apologizing, maligning the French and promising to send over another side of bacon, Death was standing at the wait station, a scalding hot coffee pot lifted to his lips.

Molly apologized to the waitress, blamed the French and when their meal was done, left a 100% tip and decided that the first lesson Death needed was patience.

. . .

HE DIDN'T WANT to be patient. There was so much that needed to be experienced. That needed to be watched and touched and heard and, if possible, tasted. He could not understand, given this infinitesimal blip of wonder, how people were willing to spend so much of it waiting. Waiting for bacon, waiting for coffee, waiting in the line at the halal cart for chicken shawarma. Waiting for change.

MOLLY SOON GAVE up apologizing or trying to make him blend in. She wasn't even sure she wanted him to. She didn't give a rat's ass if people thought he was weird because when she saw her face in the mirror, the one that had so recently been tired and cynical and calculating, it was still tired but the cynicism was being sanded away by a daily diet of amazements. The twirling of pizza dough through yeast-scented air. The sparkling coruscation of the Hudson River. The blinking of fireflies as someone butchered "Yesterday" at Strawberry Fields. The novelty plastic frogs swimming in a bin of water on Mott Street. Showers. The smell of paint. The feel of a droplet of cool condensation from the window air conditioner.

The way ice progressed across a shallow tray of water on a hot July evening until Molly yelled for him to "Shut the freezer now."

That evening, they went outside to find Irma, who usually parked her shaved ices cart somewhere south of Delancey. Molly got grape; Death got a little bit of everything while the line formed behind them.

An ambulance had stopped across Delancey and Molly waited at the stoplight to cross. It was one of the private ambulances that usually worked events but must be picking up slack for hospitals because of the heat.

"Grape is better," Death said.

"Yeah, it's usually the safest flavor," Molly responded.

Death then intoned **Grape is the safest flavor**, as he did when she'd told him something he felt was important and must be remembered.

Then the EMTs brought out a cot with a body enveloped in a roiling tangle of celadon-colored centipedes.

"What is that?"

"My replacements," Death said. "Do you want to swap again?"

"No, I don't. Why are they doing that?"

He tried to explain to Molly what it was like to have no time and no sequence. Unable to grasp before and after, the Custodes were simply piling on to the body, searching for a soul that had been there before, but no longer was.

Molly watched for a long time, long after both the grape and the everything cones were finished and the ambulance had left and the sun had gone down, gilding the roofs and corners of buildings.

An old man with a sheet-covered cage walked past on his way home from the bird garden.

"Dee?" she whispered. "Don't let them do that to me."

MR. AND MRS. GALINDO, who had been married for forty-five years, watched the young couple cling to each other as though they were old enough to understand that one of them would inevitably be left behind.

CHAPTER 27

The first thing Dave had said when she told him she was pregnant was "Congratulations!"

The second thing he'd told her was "You're fired."

Molly ignored him and went on to ask him for Thursday, Friday and Saturday nights. She would leave, she said, when she started to show.

Manager Dave leaned back in his chair and laced his fingers behind his head and told her she was pretty ballsy demanding the prime slots. He wasn't even giving Sienna—who was his current girlfriend—Thursday, Friday and Saturday.

Dave had never understood who Molly was, only what he wanted her to be. Having stood up to heaven's hosts, she was not going to be cowed by the manager of the TaaTaas! at 34th Street. She held up her phone and replayed their conversation and while he leaned forward, his expression less smug, she appended it to an email addressed to HR and to a reporter at the Daily News who seemed to have appointed himself to the breastaurant beat. She pressed send and told him that her emails were on a one minute delay and he had thirty-four seconds to change his mind.

So Thursday, Friday and Saturday, Molly worked the night shifts. During the days, she rushed to complete her EMT-Basic coursework, and took the civil service exam. Then she went to the EMS Academy in Fort Totten, near the Throgs Neck Bridge. By the time she was finished, she was visibly pregnant. While there was some concern in the NYFD about hiring a pregnant woman, there was more concern about *not* hiring a pregnant woman who was top of her class and top of the test.

True to her word, she quit her job at TaaTaas! There was no party in the staff room to wish her well. Instead, she and the other entertainers had a giggly Sunday brunch at Junior's. Sienna hesitated at the door with her daughter, until Molly ran to her, hugged her tight and thanked her profusely.

Dee tried to contribute to the household but was discouraged to find that the present value of molting squirrel pelts and superannuated myrrh was zero.

After looking at photos, two antiquarians pronounced the chest he'd been schlepping around for 2,500 years a fake. He wasn't surprised: he'd always suspected Tetep the Alamite ran a dodgy shop.

So they put the chest in the corner of Molly's—now their—apartment with a matchbook under one leg and the TV on top and filled it with the puzzles that Molly liked and the Trivial Pursuit they played to try to plug the vast holes in Death's grasp of the Canon.

To further his grasp of the Canon and hopefully spend a couple of hours without defaming the French, they went to the matinee of a very insignificant anniversary of *Star Wars* on a very large screen in the topmost theater of the nearest multiplex.

Death panicked as the stairs up to Theater Six moved on their own and started to clamber awkwardly back down but his hands stuck to the rubbery sugar-coated handrails and he fell head over heels *bop bop bop* down the escalator. Molly had seen him hit by a taxi and dragged by a bus, but still looked at him worriedly until he turned over on his back and waved. She switched for the down escalator and by the time she made it to him, he was surrounded by concerned people asking solicitous questions about his health and well-being. Once he found her in the crowd, he beamed.

Look! his face said. *They like me.*

Molly smiled back and decided he really didn't need to know the difference between *likability* and *liability.*

He was so taken with the experience that once they were up on the escalator to the mezzanine level, he smiled and lifted both hands, but before he could lean back, Molly grabbed the lapel of his greatcoat and told him to cut it out.

"One fall down the escalator is enough," she said.

"**One fall down the escalator is enough,**" he repeated.

Buying a giant popcorn and a single giant seltzer, they settled in. Death commented on the size of the spacecraft and then wondered about the white armor which afforded absolutely no protection and but made it very hard to distinguish one soldier from another.

"It doesn't matter," Molly whispered back. "They're clones."

After a long hushed conversation about the differences between clones and clowns, during which the woman beside them moved and Molly apologized, Death asked, "did clones have omphaloi?" And why did it matter that they were clones since their experiences were different, having survived the loss of friends and brothers and other selves who were gunned down while wearing cardboard armor.

SHHHHHH, said a man in the row behind them.

"So sorry," Molly whispered. "He's French."

She shoved the buttery bucket to Dee. "Popcorn now. Eschatology later."

Then came the moment when a green light hit a tiny blue ball and Obi Wan said, "I felt a great disturbance in the Force, as if millions of voices suddenly cried out in terror and were suddenly silenced" and Death thought about all of the disturbances he had attended and all the many voices that had cried out in terror and were suddenly silenced.

Then he thought about how he had moseyed along plucking Rags from ravaged omphaloi while humming Aramaic counting ditties and searching for uncontaminated food. Every one of them, he realized as he looked at Molly, her lips slicked with fake butter and her face illuminated by the flickering of light sabers on the screen, every one of them, every voice that that had cried out in terror only to be silenced, had been a different story.

Each one had been a little miracle.

Like Molly.

Death bent his head to Molly's shoulder and wept for the waste of it all.

"Jesus, get a grip," said the man behind them and kicked Molly's seat.

Molly led Dee out of Theater Six, fishing a tissue from her backpack. He dabbed at his eyes and nose stained by leaking stardust.

"Go to the bathroom. Run some cold water on your face," she said. "It'll make you feel better."

He didn't think the cold water on his face would make him feel better for the billions who cried out; he went anyway, then looked back to see if she was following.

"First of all, that's the men's room, I can't come in with you," she said. "Second, I can only be home for a few weeks when the baby's born, then you're going to have to take care of her. You need to learn to blend in, okay?"

Alone in the bathroom, Death washed his face and dried it with a paper towel. Another movie let out and two men joined him, quoting from a movie he hadn't seen. Death did as Molly had urged and followed them to the urinals and unzipped like they did, pulled out his ornament and then he, too, quoted from the movie he'd just seen.

"*I felt a great disturbance in the Force, as if millions of voices suddenly cried out in terror and were suddenly silenced.*"

Then he peed, but because he did not have a bladder, he let loose with a thin stream of liquid metallic hydrogen from Jupiter's interior, and the porcelain cracked with a loud pop.

The men sniffed the air, raised their eyebrows, zipped, flushed and left.

Death flushed too, only when he flushed, water flooded the floor.

Molly stood anxiously watching the door. She'd heard the crack and seen the two men race out. Not long after, Death followed, his footprints damp on the stained red carpet.

CHAPTER 28

*A*na Popich looked over the six couples who had gathered together in her windowless room made bright by yellow paint and pictures of smiling babies born to the previous inmates of what she liked to call her "Sunshine Room."

They were, as they usually were now, older, some quite a bit older, confident that with money and training, they were prepared for anything that life threw them. That, Ana knew, was a lie, the result of living lives that had never known a single curve ball. She also knew that the calm expression of mastery would be utterly gone at the moment of blood and placenta.

There was one younger couple. Molly Molloy who was—Ana ruffled through her papers—twenty-five. Her partner looked, god help them, even younger, and sat engulfed in a big old coat, clutching the pillow that was supposed to provide extra cushioning for Molly.

Ana talked about the important role played by partners and while Death looked on, she played a video in which the partner massaged a woman's shoulders and held her hand and told her to breathe before switching to a manikin who gave birth to a doll that was placed lovingly into the partner's waiting arms.

There was, Death noted, no blood and no shit and no pain and no screaming and no foul-smelling pus. No part of the manikin tore open and no organ hemorrhaged to a place it should not be and no one ripped through the manikin's belly with a rusted hunting knife or broke open its pubic bone. In other words, it had nothing to do with any of the pregnancies Death had attended and Molly held his hand and rubbed his back and reminded him to breathe.

The other mothers looked at each other and patted the hands of their partners, grateful that they'd been wise enough to wait until they were mature enough to have a child.

On the way out, the moms complained happily about how their little sluggers, their soccer players, their kickboxers kept them up all night and bruised their insides, laughing and boasting about their babies' antics before they were even born.

Molly jiggled up and down, trying to wake her somnolent little girl until everyone screamed YOU'RE GOING TO SEND THE ELEVATOR INTO FREEFALL AND KILL US ALL.

They finally made it out of the lobby and into the cooling night air.

"I hate Group," said Death.

The Birthing Class looked after the laughing woman and clucked, fearing for the future of her child.

"So what happened in there," she asked once they were safely in the subway. Death explained about the rips and the hemorrhages and the foul-smelling pus, until Molly told him to shut the fuck up or he wasn't going to be allowed to come to the birth of her daughter.

"She's *yours* now?"

"When you talk like that, she most certainly is."

* * *

DEATH DISCOVERED that when he put the TV on top of the Book of Admonishments, they could watch it at night without having to point their toes down. He never looked at Admonishments now that he had found this other book, one that held his interest more completely and which he quoted with the kind of relentless zeal that Abdiel could have only wished he'd brought to Righteousness.

"**Too many pounds and you increase your chances of gestational diabetes, hypertension and complications during labor and delivery,**" he announced as Molly started on the box of Do-Si-Dos.

"**The following houseplants are poisonous, some in very small doses: dumb cane, English ivy, foxglove, hyacinth bulbs (and leaves and flowers in quantity), hydrangea, iris rootstalk and rhizome, lily of the valley, philodendron, Jerusalem cherry,**" he intoned when Molly brought home a Christmas cactus that someone had left to die.

"**Eat sitting in a comfortable upright position. Lying down will put pressure on your esophageal sphincter,**" he pontificated, as Molly ate her egg noodles and hot dog circles with her feet propped up on the sofa arm.

A pillow came flying toward him but he snatched it out of the air before it hit the teakettle and he sat down to massage Molly's ankles.

One night late in her pregnancy, just two weeks before she was due for maternity leave, Molly woke up, her huge abdomen tender. No matter how she moved, she found it impossible to get comfortable; then as she lay in bed, hot fluids rushed down her thighs. She poked Death, who didn't sleep, but was trying to blend in by going still and closing his eyes. He yelped and leaped out of bed, turned on the light and grabbed the shapeless black dress draped over the chair back for her trip to the hospital. Then he turned to her and whimpered.

Blood drenched the nightgown and the sheets and her belly

and thighs. Molly leaned against the arm of the futon, but the movement caused a tearing pain in her abdomen.

Death grabbed The Book and ran his finger up and down the index looking for answers, every admonishment he'd ever learned, gone. Molly picked up her phone and dialed 911. She hoisted her backpack and began to hobble painfully toward the stairs.

"You going to keep looking at that book or are you coming with me?"

He threw the book on the floor, took her backpack and put it over his own shoulders, then carried her the rest of the way to the front stoop.

At that moment, Time moved faster than even he had thought possible. Doors slammed open and paramedics asked questions. What's your name? Who should we call? Molly's voice gave out and Death was at a loss for words. Breathe, Darlin, Breathe, they said and Molly's manila-colored face struggled under a clear mask with a bag hanging down as the gurney clanged down and someone said *severe maternal hemorrhage* then someone else counted down and four hands turned Molly on her side and the gurney clanged up and there were calls of *hypovolemic shock* and *fetal distress* and *abruptio placentae* and Death fell to his knees until the doors slammed open again and the gurney moved fast and a half dozen scrub-clad bodies took her away, leaving only a bloody footprint on the gurney. Someone whipped out scissors and started to cut away her nightgown. "She likes that one," he whispered. "She wants to wear it when she gets to the hospital," he said, though she was already there.

It was only when the sharp blade began to saw through the thick orange-painted skin of Molly's abdomen, only when a security guard reached under the operating table for his foot, that Death sobbed for Bea.

Didn't anybody tell you/Love had another side, Bea hummed and squatted down.

"Thank you, Officer Albenez, for taking such good care of my friend. His Molly is in surgery"—she pointed to the operating table above them—"and he's very—"

"He can't be in here. I have to file a—"

"No, you don't. By the way, Officer Lufton needs you in Psychiatry immediately."

"Yes, ma'am," he said after the briefest of pauses. Then he crawled backward and out of the room. When he got to the elevators, he thought how lovely the rain was in the streetlights.

"Neshama'le." She sat on the floor beside him. "Why didn't you call me earlier?"

"Mah jong dang," he wailed.

"Hold on a sec." Bea popped up. "Excuse me," she said to the befuddled OR nurse and touched Molly's forehead. "No, she's not going to die," she called under the operating table. "If you'd get out from under there, you could see for yourself."

Even after everything he'd been witness to, this he could not bear to watch.

"Give me your hand," Bea said gently and when he did, she put that hand to Molly's neck and he could feel for himself that though she was unconscious, her life was still thrumming in her marrow and there was another littler life that had also started thrumming on its own. Death popped his head up just in time to see the tiny blood-smeared thing pulled from the horizontal incision in Molly's abdomen before he passed out.

Bea apologized and dragged him out by the armpits, careful to avoid bumping into the legs of any of the urgent care team, telling them to go about their business and they did, though later Dr. Khatri had a funny feeling that something truly lovely had happened that she should be remembering but couldn't.

* * *

A COUPLE OF DAYS LATER, Dr. Khatri stopped by to check in on Molly. That was when she met the boyfriend, a tragically young man with dark hair, an enormous grin and a face that seemed off-kilter in ways the doctor found hard to pinpoint.

He cooed over the placid baby they'd named Miriam but called Miri, "because," he'd said, "she is a miracle."

Now, thought Dr. Khatri. *Now* he thinks she's a miracle. Wait until the diapers and sleepless nights piled up, then the young man would start to wonder whether anything that emitted nothing but shit and curdled milk and midnight screams, could truly be called a miracle.

As men got older, they were tired enough and had accumulated enough stuff to make them consider long and hard the problems of dividing assets against the problems of infancy. This meant that they hesitated just a fraction until shit and screams and curdled milk could be joined by a smile and then a laugh and then a mangled word.

This young man looked like he had nothing that couldn't be fit in a backpack and as soon as the novelty wore off, would leave Molly to take care of the miracle herself.

That wasn't her problem, though. Her problem was far more pressing.

"You mean I can't get pregnant?" Molly asked.

"You may well be *able* to," Dr. Khatri clarified, "but you mustn't. Your body would not be able to handle it."

She waited, eyeing the boyfriend, who continued to coo over Miri. Dr. Khatri wanted to shake him into understanding the subtext without being told.

Before she could tell the boy to pay attention, Molly piped up.

"When will I be well enough to have a ligation," she asked. "And do you know if it's covered by my insurance?"

"I would advise strenuously against it," Dr. Khatri said, glaring again at the boyfriend. "Your body has already been through too much and even with a tubal, you run the risk of ectopic pregnancy."

Now the boy looked at Molly.

"Amrita, it's so lovely to see you again," said a heavy-set woman with a halo of black and gray curls and a blue French workman's jacket who Dr. Khatri was quite sure hadn't been in the room when she'd entered and knew she had never met.

Later that afternoon, Dr. Khatri filed away Molly's chart, remembering nothing but that it had been a lovely day filled with many good things. She'd found a marble in her pocket that was blue and brown and green and white like a tiny earth. It was, she decided, the most perfect marble that could ever be.

* * *

THAT NIGHT back in their apartment while both Molly and Miri were still in the hospital, Death sharpened his obsidian blade, duct-taped his ornament to his torso, held a mirror between his knees and sliced off the bits of empyrean dangling down below and because those bits of empyrean couldn't simply be discarded, he took Bea's advice and slapped them, one each, on either side of his waist.

Which is how Death came to have love handles.

CHAPTER 29

*D*uring those first days when Molly was tired and hurting, Bea stopped by whenever she had time. She was there when Molly had to change the dressing because Death couldn't bear to see the broad stapled gash across Molly's belly and he hid in the corner of the living room.

Bea stormed out of the bedroom after him.

"Owwww," he said when she slapped him upside his head. "What was that for?"

"That's for being a coward. What are you afraid of? It's not like you haven't seen people cut up before."

"But she's Molly. She's Molly. She's *my* Molly. Supposing I do something wrong. Supposing her stitches come undone or she gets an infection or—"

"In other words, for the first time, you might actually feel responsible? How about this? How about you stop worrying about what might be and go deal with what is, you immortal wuss."

"Am not a wuss."

"Are so." Bea stopped as Molly hobbled slowly toward the bathroom. "Molly, dear, what are you doing up?"

"Getting scissors so I can change my own damn dressing."

Bea escorted Molly back to bed and helped her with her dressing while Death dissubstantiated and resubstantiated carrying a sofrito burrito, a keto lifestyle bowl and a large order of guac and chips that had been ordered by someone named Calvin.

Molly should have sent him back, but cooking required a sense of time that Dee simply didn't have. After a steady diet of oatmeal the consistency of mucilage and eggs the consistency of vulcanized rubber, Molly settled for giving him the stink eye and ate her pilfered meal with guilt and tabasco.

If Molly healed slowly, Miri started changing the second they got her home. Death loved her splotchy, greasy squishy-squash face with her lizard eyes; then a few days later it filled out and moved around as though someone had suddenly noticed that she'd never been properly inflated.

He loved her new face just as much, but now he was aware that every moment might be the last of something: The last time her head would wobble so loosely against his hand. The last time he'd be able to bathe her in the kitchen sink. The last time he would clean her little umbilical cord.

It was a hot day and Miri was fussy. Remembering what Bea had said about understanding touch in the beginning when there's nothing else, he picked Miri up and stroked her little wobbly head until she calmed down. When he went to put her down again, the shriveled umbilical cord caught on his shirt and came off. He put his thumb over her exposed omphalos and raced her to Molly.

"It came off," he said, shoving the withered brown remains in front of her nose.

Molly took the little twig from his fingers and the warm squirmy Miri from his arms. He left his thumb over her navel.

"They're supposed to come off, Dee," Molly said.

"But I can see her omphalos."

"I know," Molly said, seeing the terror in his face. She pulled his hand away, kissed his palm and settled her daughter to her breast. "Remember if you're with other parents, you need to call it a belly button. Omphalos is not a blending-in kind of word."

Omphalos is not a blending-in kind of word, Dee intoned to himself.

Later, when Miri's belly button was fully healed, Molly showed Death how to fit his mouth against her tummy and blow light breaths that made her skin sound like farts and made her soul and her laughter bubble. Then Death would rest his cheek against her tummy and try not to think of the day he would put his fingers to Miri's belly button.

CHAPTER 30

*B*ea was at a loss. That strange prickling in the arch of her foot had been niggling at her ever since Azrael first made his mistake. Once she'd known Molly was pregnant, she nodded, certain that the daughter would be the niggling's fulfillment. Bea adored Miri but there was absolutely nothing miraculous about her.

Miri walked at twelve months, butchered both English and Aramaic and steadfastly refused to poop on the toilet. Molly surmised that Death's habit of whiling away the hours spent waiting for the blessed event with stories about the Siege of Baghdad, the wars of the Three Kingdoms and the Black Plague might be making Miri constipated. She suggested that Frog and Toad would be more conducive.

Frog and toad are more conducive, he repeated.

It wasn't so long after, when Bea was babysitting, that Death and Molly returned from a movie to find Miri proudly repeating "I poop," in Aramaic.

And she had.

Molly was overjoyed.

Death wept.

CHAPTER 31

$\mathcal{M}$olly insisted on going back to work despite everything Dee had told her about the many ways people could and had died: crushed by a cow falling through a thatched roof; getting sepsis from the tooth of a beheaded enemy; falling down the Spanish Steps on a Segway; having a femoral artery pierced by the snapped wood shaft of a niblick and bleeding out on the 12th hole; stepping on an over-long beard while running from a fire and hitting one's head on the pedestal of a statue of St. Wilgefortis, the patron saint of beards.

Molly tried to reassure him that she would be careful not to drive a Segway or impale herself on a golf club or grow a beard, but her savings were low and even a diet of oatmeal and eggs required some money.

"Not necessarily," Death said, shuffling from foot to foot and wiggling his fingers in the air.

"No more stealing," she said.

Death did not think that having Mrs. Kelly do his laundry really constituted stealing. So he continued to dissubstantiate, stuff their clothes into the huge top-loader in the garage of her house in Bayside then resubstantiate back home. Except one day he miscalculated and Molly went to work before he could get his clothes from the dryer. Miri was not made of empyrean: She was made of blood and flesh and bones so could not dissubstantiate or resubstantiate and instead they had to take the B train to the F train to the Q30. When they arrived at Mrs. Kelly's, they were an hour and a half late and both the washer and dryer in the garage were empty, except for a pink apron stuck under the top ridge of the washer drum.

After changing Miri's diaper, Death slid her into her tummy pack, attached her passy holder to his collar and slung the backpack that served as a diaper bag over his shoulders. Thus girded, he hummed a little *"Pange lingua gloriosi prelim certaminis"* (Sing, my tongue, the glorious battle) and snuck around to the windows at the side of the house where Mrs. Kelly sat surrounded by clothes.

Some laundry, like her sheets or Mr. Kelly's shirts, were white or pale blue. Mrs. Kelly's own dresses were a tasteful combination of brights and neutrals. But most of the clothes belonged to the twins and all of those were black. His own Siouxsie and the Banshees T-shirt was there, the heavily mascaraed eyes peering from the folded pile.

Death watched as Mrs. Kelly stared unseeing at the stairs, rubbing her cheek with a small piece of cloth. It was blue and yellow and white and he recognized it as Miri's onesie, the one with a white petals around a yellow smiling face doing a somersault in a sky blue background on leaf arms.

Oopsie Daisy, it said.

Then Mrs. Kelly lay the Oopsie Daisy on the sofa cushion and did what she always did with life's wrinkles. She smoothed it out and began folding it.

"Ma, the fucking ice maker's on the fritz again," one of the twins yelled from the kitchen. Mrs. Kelly opened her mouth, but then her lip trembled and she plucked up the tiny blue and yellow white scrap of fabric from the sofa cushion and collapsed.

The girl twin came in, a sandwich in one hand and a glass of something without ice in the other. Whatever she'd been about to say froze as she saw her mother sobbing, her eyes swollen and nose red, clutching a dancing daisy to her heart.

Unsure what to do, the girl twin yelled out for the boy twin. The two of them looked warily at each other trying to figure out which one of them was responsible this time. Worried when they couldn't apportion blame, they approached their mother, taking positions on either side of her. One patted her back, the other tapped at her arm. They were awkward and bad at it, but even Death understood they were trying.

Soon Mrs. Kelly righted herself. The boy twin ran to get tissues, while the girl twin took her mom's hand, smiling her closed, weird, reticent love. Mrs. Kelly dropped the Oopsie Daisy on the floor and held her daughter who, though she looked so different from the baby she'd been, would always be her Oopsie Daisy.

He waited, trying to figure out how to get his laundry back from Mrs. Kelly, but then she gave everything that was black to the twins, having long ago given up distinguishing whose was whose. They fought between them over who got the Siouxsie and the Banshees T-shirt and the Echo and the Bunnymen T-shirt. They even fought over the one that said I Had a Whale of a Time at Buffy's Bat Mitzvah.

After, Mrs. Kelly tucked Miri's tiny clothes into a big Ziploc bag, clasping it in front of her while she stood in front of the diagonal wall beneath the staircase that was covered with photographs: school pictures, pictures of family trips to the Grand Canyon and Disney World, the Christmas card photos that she paid for every year at the JCPenney's Studio until the twins became teens and JCPenney's folded.

Then Mrs. Kelly put the bag containing Miri's tiny clothes

into a cupboard under the stairs, holding the door closed behind her as though afraid it might all get away.

Death and Miri took the Q30 bus to the F train to the B train and walked the rest of the way home carrying nothing but a damp pink apron.

When Molly came home, he made her a dinner of oatmeal the consistency of mucilage and eggs the consistency of vulcanized rubber. Molly pronounced them delicious and doused everything in hot sauce.

"That's new," she said, as he stood in front of her nervously smoothing his pink apron with the frills at the shoulders that said, "IF KARMA DOESN'T KILL YOU, MY COOKING WILL." Then he explained how their clothes had gone missing.

Molly sighed, and stared at the plate. She got her computer and searched through eBay until she found a lot of used baby clothes in the right size for Miri and another for her immortal lover who was, at least, trying.

Next week when the new clothes came, Molly took her little family to the Suds 'n' Stuff near the Episcopal church and showed Death how to load up the clothes and the soap and told him to stay when his clothes were in the dryer, lest things went missing.

"It's really not so bad, watching the laundry," Molly had said.

He and Miri spent many hours watching the clothes, crowing with glee when they saw her favorite shirt tumble by and he wondered how he could have ever deprived himself of this joy.

It's really not so bad, watching the laundry, he repeated.

CHAPTER 32

t work, Molly was partnered with a man whose name was Samuel Jones, but whom everyone called Zamboni on account of his size and gruffness. When it was announced that the new woman would be his partner, Zamboni did not hide his disapproval.

"The only woman I would trust to have my back will be naked and holding a bottle of massage oil," he said to a roar of laughter and much arm punching.

Their first two calls were routine enough. A boy with purplish fingernails and clammy skin and a terrified mother, required a dose of Narcan. A delivery guy who'd hit a pothole and then the curb. His pupils were uneven and sluggishly responsive, but he'd had a helmet and would survive.

The third call came from the 28th Street Station. A woman reported a man who "might be sleeping or might be dead" but should be gotten off the platform. Unfortunately, the good Samaritan had to take a meeting before 911 could find out more details. Once they got there, Molly and Zamboni split up, Zamboni taking the downtown platform, Molly the uptown.

As soon as she made it down the stairs, she was hit by the stench of frankincense and pineapple.

"You smell that?" Molly asked the station manager as she buzzed open the emergency gate.

"They don't pay me enough to smell what there is to smell down here," the manager said from the safety of her plexiglass box.

Once past the turnstile, Molly looked around until she saw the tangle of silvery centipedes with little piggy noses and pinpoint eyes, with hockey stick feet and floating robes and querulous Latin, plucking relentlessly at the man's torso. Their pomanders were no longer held in the pockets of their robes, but rather suspended around their necks on tight greenish-gray ribbons, rocking beneath their chins like censers, suffusing the air with the stench of heaven.

When Molly tried to yell for Zamboni it came out as a sneeze. Not a delicate sneeze that could be accommodated by single ply tissue, nor even the more manly triple-ply sneeze, but rather a giant, cerebellum-scrambling, "Krachow."

Still, it did what it was supposed to and got Zamboni's attention and as soon as she thought his blurry image was looking at her across the tracks, she pointed him frantically toward the tangle, then began feeling her way along the tiled wall, sneezing, sniffling and blinking back tears.

The emergency gate buzzed and then banged shut and Zamboni raced past her, smacking her with the longboard.

"Hey, Molloy, you coming or not?" Zamboni said.

Molly pushed her way through the throng of Custodes and began compressions, her nose dripping on the man's shirt. It was hard to keep up her rhythm surrounded by centipedes shrieking something about "**Contaminare**" and "**Profanate.**" Not that it really mattered; Molly knew the body was an empty shell, though she couldn't explain how she knew to Zamboni or why she'd started singing Ah, Ah, Ah, Ah like some complete noob.

Finally, she pushed one of the weird celadon colored paws away from the man's stomach and yelled "He'b did aweady. Don u hab sompace you godda be?" and wiped her nose on the robe of the nearest celestial centipede.

With a screech and a pop, the last of the Custodes disappeared, taking its frankincense, pineapple and admonishing with it.

Molly leaned back heavily onto her heels.

"That time of month?" Zamboni asked. Molly bit down hard on her back teeth.

That night, Zamboni went to The Fire House, which wasn't a fire house, but a place with hot wings and cheap beers. There he told New York's Bravest and New York's Finest and New York's Strongest about his partner who didn't have the balls.

They laughed.

That night, Molly went home to an apartment that smelled of burned kasha. She had dinner and played with Miri; then later, after showering and putting Miri to bed, she told Death about the knot of centipedes. He stroked Molly's hair and then her body and then he stroked the inside of her while his tendrils reached for her and hers—less visibly—reached for him. Though after she had stiffened and he had muted her heated sounds with whispered repetitions of *profanate* and *contaminare* so that they wouldn't wake Miri.

Molly giggled and cuddled and switched on *Law and Order*. Death put his long coat on over his naked body and took out the trash.

Two weeks later when Titus Torrence got his arm caught in machinery at a construction site, it was Molly who tied the tourniquet around the bones and muscles and skin shredded above his elbow while Zamboni vomited in the corner.

It was Molly who angled her body around the young man

and held his cheek with her hand and whispered to him not to look.

In the months that followed, Zamboni's grudging respect grew. Molly developed a reputation among those who inhabited the tight-knit community on the front lines of carnage. She was tough and capable and though they never told their supervisors, at any Mass Casualty Incident, they would look to Molly Molloy, the woman who was allergic to death, to tell them who actually had a chance at life.

The only day Zamboni had seen her waver was at a brownstone in Brooklyn. They had raced down the stairs into a basement cluttered with the piles of boxes labeled with grease pencil —Games. Christmas Village. Summer Clothes. Above them all hung a pair of damp denim-clad legs that smelled of piss. Anyone looking at the young man's swollen tongue and purple cheeks and bulging eye, knew they were long past too late. But Molly grabbed hold of his legs, tears streaming down her cheeks and yelled at Zamboni to cut him down. And Zamboni did. He kicked away a box that said Frank's Stuff and laid the young man reverently on the floor between paint cans and spackling buckets. Then he pushed on his chest singing ah, ah, ah, ah staying alive, even though he was cold.

Zamboni told New York's Finest, Bravest and Strongest that he'd even begged Molly to join them at The Fire House but Molly had thanked him and said her boyfriend would be picking her up.

The boyfriend hardly seemed old enough. He had an odd face, a long broken nose and his eyes were uneven. His body was lumpy under an outsized coat that looked like it belonged to some high school production of Sherlock Holmes.

Zamboni thought he was wearing a bright yellow knit ascot until the man unwrapped his coat and unsnapped a snap and Molly pulled out a sleepy baby wearing a fluffy hat with a chicken beak on the front.

He watched the young man hold Molly and whisper to her. Then Zamboni shook his head and walked away sorry that Molly had decided against joining them at The Fire House, because no civilian could ever know what death was really like.

That night Dee held the drained Molly nestled in the nook of one arm. In the nook of his other arm, the wide-awake Miri waited for her evening story. He couldn't reach Frog and Toad and Molly had put the kibosh on his stories of the Thirty Years War and the Taiping Rebellion, so he told her the other story. The only story before Molly that was really his.

"Long, long, long ago in a place far away and nearby," he said in the sing-song voice that had been deemed too quizzical for Veneration, "there were two things: The vast Nothing and Being. Being wasn't anything in particular, it just *was*. It existed as it had for billions and billions of eons. It might have been that way still except something happened and a Bit broke off.

"I'm afraid I can't tell you what it was or when it was, I can only tell you *that* it was. Some say it was an accident. Some say it was the Bit's fault. That Bit was curious and obstinate and tore himself free. Hard to say as it was long, long, long ago before there was any such thing as memory.

"Still, the result was the same. When Bit tore away, Being, which had always just Been, had become something else. It had become Smaller and it didn't like Becoming at all. It just wanted to Be. It divided itself into millions of pieces to find its lost Bit. It's like when we cut a loaf of bread: we get slices for Mommy's cheese and pickle sandwiches but we also get lots of crumbs that go all over the place.

"The curious, obstinate Bit had discovered that it liked Becoming and it searched around for something to become again. There weren't many models, just Being and Nothing and the Bit had been the one and couldn't become the other so it tried for something new and unique and singular and became I.

"I hid from Being, which wasn't hard because there was such

a lot of Nothing. I liked Nothing, but I especially liked those crumbs that were scattered throughout. The crumbs could be batted around, so I batted them.

"But then I batted one and it broke.

"Yuh-oh, I thought, that's going to be trouble."

Molly's body jerked as it sometimes did when she fell asleep. Death wrapped the edge of the fuzzy blanket over her and pulled her closer.

"And it was trouble. When it broke, it exploded into an enormous aster of light with nets of color inside. It was bright and searing and it was the first thing I ever saw and I knew it was beautiful.

"But Being saw it too and I was found. 'Time!' Being yelled, because that's what I was called then, 'cut it out!'"

"Being wanted to join back together and just Be. It was restful. But I wanted to Become again. It was fun Becoming. Things changed."

Death reached for the faded sippy cup with the stars and rainbows and moon on it.

"Miri, my Miri? Are you done with your water?"

"Mo!" the defiant little girl said and sucked hard with a sharp slurping sound.

"Where was I? Oh, yes, but Being did not give up so easily. I was forced into things like Venerating and Praising and Intoning, subjects so mind-numbingly dull, that I had no imagination left over for Becoming. Which, now that I think of it, was probably the point.

"But it was really too late, because things I had batted around had started to Become all on their own and could no longer be stopped. Then through a long chain of miracles I couldn't begin to imagine, some one of those things became a woman. Then I batted her and she was fixed.

"Yuh-oh, I thought again, that's going to be trouble.

"And it was. I became something else again, I became a man,

after a fashion, then a father, after a fashion, and for the first time, I truly understood not only the extraordinary wonder but also the excruciating price of Becoming."

Miri's lips gaped open and cold water leaked from her cup, soaking Death's shirt. He plucked the cup from her limp hand and set it gently on the side table. He turned off the light and draped his arms around Molly and Miri. He stared into the dark.

"I don't know how I will ever be able to bear it."

CHAPTER 33

*A*s soon as Miri turned three, Molly started the preschool application process.

Death was resolutely against it.

"What if she gets sick?" he asked.

"What if she falls?" he asked.

"What if there's a food shortage and the older kids eat the younger kids?"

At which point, Bea suggested that Miri would benefit from more time talking about Daniel Tiger's Neighborhood and less time talking about the Donner Party.

The first several days at school, Death stood by the news kiosk across the street, pretending to look through the stripped mass markets until one of the security guards told him he was making some of the mothers nervous.

Miri had only been in school for two months when they got an email saying that one of the third graders had lice and Death resubstantiated outside Ms. Ortega's class and knocked on the glass.

Ms. Ortega came to the door.

"Mr. Molloy?" she said and stared down the hall wondering how he'd managed to get past security.

"There's a plague. I've come to take Miri home."

"Abba?" Miri said.

"What are you talking about, Mr. Molloy? And Miri, back to the blue circle."

"But owange cicow is my cicow," Miri said.

"Go to the blue circle," Ms. Ortega repeated and called the front office.

Narisa Ortega had met Molly Molloy on the first day of school then again for Parents' Night. She was a sensible, funny young woman whom the children seemed to trust instinctually. She talked to Molly about being class parent, but Molly demurred, saying that her schedule was too erratic. She suggested that Miri's father would be delighted, but there was something about the man with his long oversized coat and the constant staring over his shoulder like he was waiting for the bail bondsman that made her think better of it.

Now it was the beginning of November and the Ladybugs still didn't have a class parent.

"Hey, Lisa?" she said, when the front office finally answered. "It's Narisa from Ladybugs? I've got Miri Molloy's dad here. He somehow got past security." There was a long pause followed by a "Hmmhumm. Anyway," she continued, "he wants to pick Miri up?" She cupped her hand over the phone. "Something about a plague?" She blocked the doorway with her body and checked to make sure that Miri was staying in the blue circle, which was the one farthest away from the door.

"What kind of plague, Mr. Molloy?"

"Lice," Death mouthed.

"Lice? Lice is a nuisance but it's hardly a plague and besides it's not in our class. Not even in our grade. I'm going to have to ask you to leave."

She looked down the hall, relieved to hear Sam in the dark

blue uniform that had gotten tighter over the past few years and made a whispered shuck shuck shuck noise as he walked.

"Sir, I'm going to have to ask you to leave," Sam repeated.

Then Death heard Lisa on the other end of the phone.

"Narisa? Do I need to lockdown?"

Death looked down the hallway to another teacher standing silently, one hand on the door with the Caterpillar on it, one hand raised behind her to warn back curious children. He looked at the Ladybugs frozen in circles on the brightly colored rubber floor. He looked at the guard reaching for his radio. He looked at Ms. Ortega's door, with the bright construction paper Ladybugs, each spot bearing the name of a child, taped to the new blue paint that must have been applied when they'd added a sturdy deadbolt to the inside.

He saw his own wrists buried in the pockets of his oversized coat and pulled them out.

Ms. Ortega flinched, then looked with relief at his smooth empty hands and at Molly Molloy coming quickly down the hall.

"Dee? I got your text. I didn't understand what…"

Death ran toward Molly, holding her tight whispering about the lice and the flies and the diseased livestock and the boils— not like the ingrown hair on your knee, do you remember? Yes, I remember. Well, they're not like that, they're huge and don't heal—and then there's hail and then…then the first born die. Even the littlest and Miri…Miri…

"It's just lice, Dee. Kids get lice. Miri is going to get lice, too. And you know what's going to happen when she does? Not boils on livestock or whatever. We're going to wash her hair with a special shampoo and comb it with a special comb and wash all of her sheets and blankets and clothes in hot, hot water and remind her not to share brushes and hats with friends but she will and we'll have to do it all over again."

She settled her hand over the placket of his greatcoat and undid one button. Then she looked into his eyes.

His hands fisted around the sleeves of this latest in a line of voluminous outerwear stretching back to the fringed shawl dyed Tyrian purple that he'd started wearing back in the time of Sargon of Akkad to disguise the many ways he was making himself human and that he wore now to disguise the many ways he had failed.

He moved her hand and undid another button and another until they were all undone. He shrugged off the worn greatcoat, revealing his thin, featureless torso and preternaturally smooth arms covered only by a T-shirt with a surfing Snoopy and the word Cowabunga! He put the worn greatcoat on top of the trash can. Molly considered it briefly, then draped it over her arm, smoothing the lining with its profusion of parti-colored pockets.

Death walked back to the Ms. Ortega's classroom. "Can I give Miri a hug before I leave?"

Ms. Ortega watched the skinny man in his skinny jeans as he knelt down with his arms open wide, a look of love and sadness on Molly Molloy's face as he wrapped his daughter into his arms. Miri curled her little arms around his neck and gave him a big kiss.

"Mr. Molloy?" Ms. Ortega said on an odd impulse. "The Ladybugs still needs a class parent, if you'd be interested."

She would never regret it.

Death wanted—as children do but adults too often do not— to be happy. He touched things that even the Ladybugs suspected shouldn't be touched and tasted things they knew shouldn't be tasted. And while Ms. Ortega tried to figure out what had happened to the bus, he found bubble wrap for the Ladybugs to pop. On a trip to the Museum of Natural History, he stopped in front of a lingerie shop and gathered the children to the broad window, his long nose touching the glass. Even as she hissed at him to get moving, she realized that neither he nor the children were looking at the bras or swimsuits on the mannequins. They were all looking at the wall of brightly colored pinwheels on the back wall that were kept turning by a fan in the corner.

When she thought back over her long career teaching Ladybugs and Sprouts and Tadpoles, she would always remember Mr. Molloy as the best class parent ever.

He even took Hammy the Hamster home for the summer.

CHAPTER 34

Seconds later, Miri was in kindergarten for the whole day and Death started looking for a job. He'd always suspected that Intoning and Veneration were busywork and not truly marketable skills and in New York City, at least, that proved to be true. Employers didn't even seem to know what Intoning or Veneration were. What they wanted was Experience, Education and Recommendations.

Molly was in the playground of the building complex sharing snacks without peanut butter and drinks without sugar, when the super's daughter, who had been clambering where she shouldn't have, fell down. Molly checked the little girl's eyes and her reflexes and watched her for an hour, then told the super's wife she would be just fine. As a gesture of thanks, when the super cleared out the bicycle storage room, he offered her the pick of the unclaimed bikes.

Which was how Death got a job. Being an under-the-table bicycle messenger paid poorly, but it did have flexibility, so he could be available whenever any of several classes that followed the Ladybugs needed him.

The minutes flew by unconscionably fast and Miri no longer

wanted to walk home with her father. She wanted to walk home with her friends and talk about how weird and awful boys were, girls were, teachers were. Parents—

"You've got to stop this, little soul."

Death bounced back from the edge of the latest rooftop in the series of them he used to follow Miri's progress.

"She needs to be able to complain; shared misery binds friends together. You, meanwhile…"

"What about me?"

"You have eternity to skulk around like the sneak thief you are, you have only this one life to get out. Meet people. Make the most of it."

* * *

THAT NIGHT when he was snuggled next to Molly, he told her what Bea had said.

"But I've met a gajillion people already," he said. "You were the only one who liked me."

"When you say met…did you talk to them or just pull their souls out of their belly buttons?"

He pushed the tip of his nose down, thinking of Farlan Dorch. Farlan had been conscious and hadn't yelled or cried or turned away when he saw who was poking around his belly button and Death had thought that perhaps by holding the Rag half in and half out of his body, he might be suspended in time, while leaving him cognizant enough to chat.

After several seconds of inchoate babbling and uncontrollable flatulence, Death pulled harder and put an end to it all.

Molly threw her leg across his and smoothed the furrows between his brows.

"I try when I make deliveries—to talk?—but they just grab their sushi and slam the door."

"Yeah, well." She pulled out a pretzel stick from a bag of

them and waved it. "All their lives have they looked away...to the future, to the horizon. Never their minds on where they were. What they were doing."

"Your voice is weird."

Molly pointed her pretzel stick at Yoda on the TV.

"Look, I'm not making fun. There are always people like that. But there are also people who've lived enough to know the future isn't guaranteed and that the present deserves attention, too. You just have to find them."

* * *

THEN ONE DAY after he'd dropped off a Fancy Delancey (smoked tuna with horseradish dill cream cheese and wasabi flying fish roe on a pumpernickel bagel) at a building on Tompkins Square Park, he saw his old friend—the bald one with the bloodshot eyes, mottled skin, and sagging body who most certainly did not have an infinity of future—head into the 10th Street Baths where Death hadn't been since his sabbatical had begun and he'd discovered running water.

He signed out of the delivery app, locked up his bike, went inside, paid the fee, took a short bathrobe and odd rubber slippers and met the man in the changing room.

"How's Masha?" Death said, grateful for the familiar tattoo.

"Do I know you?" the man asked.

"I used to come a lot but not so much now that I have a wife and a daughter and a shower," Death said brightly.

The man, whose name was Gennady, though most people called him Gene, said nothing. The past few years had taken their toll and he was no longer as certain about what he knew or who.

Though he couldn't imagine himself speaking to such a young man.

He didn't like the new people taking over the baths. The new people were the reason Gene, though he was retired, and could come any time he wanted, no longer came in the evening or on weekends or the days on either side of the weekends. He came on Wednesdays, when he could avoid the young men who had too much hair and too few disappointments. Then he could eat his borscht in peace without someone squeezing next to him, phone in outstretched hand. Borrowing his backstory because old people made their photographs seem more authentic when they posted them online.

Gene escaped into the super-hot Russian Room. He wasn't surprised when the young man followed him. They usually did, marching in then oozing out five minutes later unless they were in a group and then they would try to outdo each other, opening the door minute by minute until Gene yelled at them to stop letting the heat out.

This young man lay on the bench utterly still until Gene got up to check on him, afraid he had burst something.

"Hey, kid," he said and Death opened his eyes.

Gene liked the young man's eyes. They were misshapen in a way that made him look both startled and quizzical and were filled with an odd combination of the hope of youth and an ancient knowledge that the light at the end of the tunnel was a train. He even smelled old. Not like buckwheat and cabbage and poverty and lost countries. He smelled old like books that hadn't been checked out of the library for a long time and were in danger of being deaccessioned.

"I'm going to go cool down. You should, too," he said and when the man dove straight in to the icy plunge pool, he came out baptized by Gene's respect.

They went upstairs and enjoyed a bowl of borscht and some herring in companionable silence before Dee went off to make sure his daughter did her homework and Gene headed to the grocery store to pick up radishes for his wife.

Over subsequent baths and borscht, Death made a friend.

They did what friends did and talked about jobs they'd retired from. Gene had spent thirty-five years at a tool and die shop in a place that was now called SoHo, though the last time he'd been by the old shop, young people were lined up outside waiting to buy skateboard-themed T-shirts at unconscionable markups.

Death had taken to heart Bea's dictum that friends bonded over shared misery and it turned out that they had a lot in common, and could spend hours complaining about martinet bosses and pointless rules.

When Gene would complain about his wife, Masha, a harridan nag who was always forcing him to eat radish salad, Death joined in, just to be agreeable.

After he'd made more drop offs for more busy workers, Death would head home, desperate for Molly to come back so he could love her and put lie to the tales he'd told in the name of friendship, all the while knowing that unlike Masha, she was the greatest, the most beautiful, the most intelligent, most perfect woman who ever created herself and that she would never, ever make him eat radish salad.

One day, Gene stopped coming to the baths. Death asked Boris what had happened and Boris said he'd heard from Frank that Masha had died. Nobody seemed to have a phone number or an address or even a last name. Molly suggested they look through the obituaries, but the obituaries were reserved for celebrities who'd made art or money and not for harridans who made radish salad.

A few months later, while on a delivery, Death found Gene sitting on a park bench with a Tupperware bowl on his lap. Death sat next to him and said he was sorry to hear about Masha.

"Did you know her?" Gene asked, unsure who this young man was. He didn't much care for young people.

Death said he hadn't had that chance and Gene proceeded to tell him that she'd been the greatest, most beautiful, most intelli-

CHAPTER 35

*J*t seemed to Death that he had just put snickerdoodles into the oven for the Teacher Appreciation Bake Sale and when he took them out again, Miri had gotten a scholarship for college in St. Louis.

Molly wasn't quite as shocked. After eighteen years, she was ancient for an EMT. Her back hurt, her knees were stiff and there were times when her soul felt just as stiff and pained. Several of her colleagues had retired, burned out less by the physical pain than by the despair of loading another gurney into another ambulance.

"We have a saying," Death had told her once after a long day of cleaning up the aftermath of guns and drugs and doing something stupid in an attempt to get likes on Instagram. "'Humanity is doing the same thing over and over again and expecting different results.'"

"It's *our* saying, Dee, and it's 'Insanity is doing the same thing over and over again and expecting different results.'"

"You sure?" he asked.

She thought about it a little and admitted that she wasn't.

* * *

THEN ZAMBONI RETIRED, leaving his wife with the house and the car while he joined a cruise line as a paramedic. It allowed him to travel the world, which he'd always wanted, and not spend money, which he'd never wanted. At his retirement party, three guys were embarrassed to find that they'd all gone to the same stationery store around the corner and bought the same spiral-bound notebook decorated with the same bright red sand bucket emblazoned with the word FIRE.

Printed underneath were the words, Bucket List.

Zamboni joked that three wouldn't be enough to handle everything he intended to do but secretly he gave one to Molly, the only person he was truly going to miss. "Miri's been in college for two years," he said, "it's time for you to start living your life for real."

It was raining when the party ended, so Molly took the crosstown bus, even though it was slow. She opened up the book and tapped at it with the end of the pen while staring out the window at the way the streetlights sparkled in the rain. The bus reached her stop without Molly having thought up a single thing that would mark the beginning of living her life "for real." At first, she'd thought it was cheapness or lack of imagination but then she decided it wasn't.

"What's a Bucket List?" Death asked when Molly came home.

"It's supposed to be for big events that you imagine will have more meaning than the small, everyday stuff."

He watched her put the kettle on to boil and loose tea into the pot. "I like everyday stuff," he said.

"I know you do," she answered.

The teakettle rattled, the steam billowing into the air. Molly poured the water into the pot, swirled it around a few times and covered it with a kitchen towel. He waited for the clink of the metal tea strainer on the mug and the tannin-scented air and cherished this everyday stuff that would not be everyday always.

* * *

THAT NIGHT MIRI called and said she was pregnant.

Molly took a plane out to Missouri.

"Where's Dad?" Miri asked and closed the door to the bedroom, keeping hold of the knob behind her back.

Molly got on the phone. "Where are you?" she asked.

"He's parking the car," she told her daughter, while Death resubstantiated in front of Miri's door. He closed his eyes, put his fingers in his ears and blew hard. Bits of silvery tendrils sprouted from his chin.

Molly shifted from foot to foot, trying to relieve the pain in her lower back that had flared up over the flight, without exacerbating the pain in her knees. She would have to get another cortisone shot soon.

"Mom? Are you okay?"

"Yeah. I'm just wondering where your dad is."

"You called him two seconds ago."

"I know," Molly said. "Is the doorbell working?"

"No. That's why there's a piece of tape on it. He'll have to knock."

"Oh," Molly yelled toward the door. "So your dad has to knock?"

And Death knocked thusly.

Miri clenched her teeth though not hard enough to make her molars crack. She peeked in to the bedroom. "I just need a couple more minutes," she said through the gap in the door.

And while she was dealing with the room's occupant, Molly kissed Death and the silvery tendrils on his chin and upper lip and cheek strained toward her. She stroked them back into place, then Death furrowed his brow, because when he did it in the mirror, he thought it gave him gravitas.

"So he's here," Miri said, closing the door behind her again.

"Who?" Molly asked.

"Alex. My boyfriend?"

Molly looked to the hollow-core bedroom door. "Can't we just talk somewhere in private first?" she asked quietly. "Take you out for lunch or—"

"I need him here. But there is something..." She nodded to the tiny bathroom that Molly had at first thought was the hall closet. Once they were all crammed inside, Miri closed the door and blocked it with her body as though she expected them to flee.

"I...his parents are like, I don't know. They're really nice."

Molly could feel the pain in her daughter's voice and the pain in her own heart because ever since high school, "really nice" had stopped meaning kind or patient and started meaning slim and well-groomed and well-educated, with interesting jobs that paid well.

People whose joints didn't freeze up in those seconds before the pain stopped.

"What did you tell him?" Molly asked.

"I didn't lie, Mom, I was just vague. Told him you were in medicine and that Dad, you were an independent contractor," Miri said, ashamed of her parents but so much more ashamed of herself.

"What's a contractor?" Death asked cheerfully, so Molly wouldn't have to speak through the itching of her nose and the watering of her eyes.

"Oh god, Abba. And *please*, try not to be weird."

Molly took over the conversation with Alex. He was older than Miri and nice enough but, she thought, rather full of himself. When he talked about his background—his father had a job in "finance" that sounded at least as vague as "independent contractor" while his mother was a writer—Alex tried to make clear that he understood his privilege, which was why he'd taken several gap years during which he'd travelled and done Good Works before returning to school for Landscape Architecture.

"Do you want something to drink?" he'd asked. He came back passing around glasses of seltzer and as he sat down, he rotated his ankle stiffly.

Molly was a connoisseur of aches and stiffnesses and asked him about it.

"Oh, I forgot. You're a doctor."

"In the medical field," Molly said tersely.

After a second's hesitation, he said he was from New York, too, which was what brought the two of them together at first. On his seventh birthday, he'd gotten a skateboard and had ridden ahead of his parents.

He wasn't very good at it, though, and had bumped into a lady then a cop yelled at him and when he put his foot down, he stepped on something and lost his footing and his skateboard and he fell forward, shattering his ankle on the curb.

"Oh," Molly said, "I'm so sorry."

"No, I'm good. I've got a stiff ankle, but if I hadn't fallen? There was a guy who got killed at the intersection right in front of me. He was killed by a kid who'd just learned to drive. I wonder sometimes, if I hadn't fallen, maybe that would've been me, you know?"

Molly clutched at Dee's hand, pulling it away from the nonexistent coat and the nonexistent pocket and the memory of the man Molly had tried to save but couldn't.

So, Alex and Miri were married and six months later, they had a daughter named Lucille, after Molly's grandmother and Suzanna after Alex's mother, Susannah, but with a "z" and without an "h" so that no one would confuse the two.

CHAPTER 36

When Miri was tiny, her yellow bucket had been used to slosh water in the tub. When she was small, it was used to mold sand. When she was older it was used to hold change. She and her mother would sort the pennies, nickels and dimes and wrap them for the bank.

The quarters, they kept for the Suds 'n' Stuff.

Then the Suds 'n' Stuff switched to cards and Miri got a job that paid better than stuffing pennies into wrappers and the change accumulated until Molly took the bucket to a bank with a machine that sorted coins for an 8% fee.

It was overflowing by the time Molly headed out into the raking light of an autumn evening. There was a van double-parked in the bike lane. She'd started to peer around it just as the plastic handle of the bucket broke and coins flew into the air and an SUV made a sharp turn from the blind corner.

One thing hits another thing hits another thing...

There was a bump and wheels squealed and coins rained down on asphalt. Molly heard them wobbling on the street beside her, then she heard sirens, then she heard nothing.

The first thing Molly thought was that none of her usual bits hurt: not her neck, her back, her shoulders or her knees.

The second thing she thought was: *Yuh-oh. This is going to be trouble.*

She felt trapped, like she had at that motel in Seaside Heights where the sheets and blankets were tucked too tight and she'd fought against them, finally yanking them loose in the middle of the night.

Now, though, she was the one who had to be yanked loose. She twisted and pulled, gradually peeling away her legs and arms. Freeing her head. When her torso came unstuck, she found she could move around a little, bumping into dead ends. Some ends were teenier and tinier than others, but no less dead for all that. She'd read once that if you touched the wall with one hand and followed it using that hand only, you would eventually get out of any maze. So she clung to the wall and felt her way around, going up and down and in and out of small spaces and smaller spaces but she never stopped because she knew that beyond these walls, someone needed her.

* * *

BEA HAD RUSHED UP AS SOON as the universe began its wobble. Death sat just inside heaven's gate, one arm cradling Molly's body, the other hand grasping his obsidian knife.

Behind him, the Custodes stood in a tangled, apprehensive mass while bits of empyrean that had once been attached to legs or arms or robes swirled about like cherry blossom petals on a windy day in April.

"Are you going to use that on me, too?" she asked.

Death's blade fell noiselessly to the firmament and he snaked his other arm around Molly's broken body, his face buried into her graying hair. He began to rock back and forth, voicelessly pleading with her not to go, though she was already gone.

Bea knelt in front of him, setting her fingers to Molly's collarbone, feeling simultaneously the lack of a pulse and the presence of her soul. Even after two millennia of comforting people for their losses, she wasn't sure how to comfort Death as he learned the price of his bookkeeping.

Where, Bea thought, *was her miracle?* She'd done what she could. Now where was the promise that would make this sacrifice bearable?

She steadied herself as another shudder ripped through the cosmos. The surface of Azrael's skin had started to shimmer like water just before boiling. His hair writhed, the color of space beyond the last light of the last star. Bea touched his frigid skin and when he raised his eyes, she saw in them the final perimeter of existence slowing its expansion from 82.4 kilometers per second per megaparsec to 80 and she felt a chill through her back.

"Azrael," she said anxiously, "what are you doing?"

His lips didn't move but a voice with the timbre of absolute zero vibrated everywhere.

"I made a mistake," it echoed. "There will be no more."

The Custodes who had run from Death's fury started forward. It was only when she heard the repeated *Hallelujah, -lleluja, -luja, -ja,* of the assembled Custodes that she understood what he was doing.

"You can't, Azrael. You ca—"

"I. AM. THE. ONE. WHO. *CAN.*"

"If you do what I think you're doing, if you erase everything, Miri will die. I will die. You will—"

"She will not die, she will never have existed. *You* will never have existed. *Molly* will never have existed. And I," the voice dropped to a whisper, "will remember *nothing.*"

"Please, Neshama'le. Please."

Somewhere beyond the dark despair that clung to her, Molly had felt Bea's pleading warmth, she could almost feel her, arms outstretched, trying to hold back an abyss. Molly moved faster, sliding and gliding across cold dank walls, until she came to a tiny oculus that felt like blue. If she'd been able to see, she'd have recognized the color of a hospital gown, but she couldn't. Instead, she felt the millions of tendrils, all of them reaching out from a soul screaming for oblivion.

Death sucked in a deep breath as Molly surged toward him. She swirled around his skin, trying to touch him without hands, talk to him without words, comfort him without a heart and Death's tendrils reached for her like an anemone for a clown fish.

Then something touched her that did not love her.

* * *

FOR COUNTLESS EONS, Abdiel had been fighting for a return to the time before Azrael's first becoming. It had been calm then. No differences meant no decisions and without decisions there could be no mistakes either.

That had been real peace—not the momentary lulls that passed for peace now—and it was so close that the Chief Administrator could almost taste it. Like he could almost taste the bitterness of Azrael's regret for that first becoming and his need to take it all back.

Until the Rag of that second mistake reached out to him.

That, Abdiel decided, was enough.

The Chief Administrator grabbed one of the Rag's edges and yanked it after him as he marched toward the Mangles. All he needed to do was to feed a single tattered edge between the rollers and the Mangles in their relentlessness would take care of the rest, sucking it in and plopping it back out squeezed dry of all of the beginnings and endings and mistakes and consequences.

It would no longer recognize itself as any different from of the millions of other souls trundling through the troughs toward the Sea of Tranquility. It would no longer know Azrael and more to the point, Azrael would no longer be able to distinguish it. He would be angry but he would stop dawdling and put an end to the whole sorry fiasco.

Except Azrael's hold on the Rag was joined by another as the Queen of Heaven's arm shot out impossibly long.

Held tight between three celestial beings—two who loved her and the other who didn't—Molly began to stretch. She didn't like the stretching. Didn't like the way she unfurled, a sail loosed from the mast, buffeted by heaven's currents, with every moment that had gone into the making of her suddenly exposed.

There were a gajillion of them, moments big and small: The sleepiness of the back seat of the car while her parents whispered in the front. The broken basalt porch step where she wiggled tiny toes sticking out from a blanket with satiny edging that felt cool between her fingers. The joy of running across newly cut grass in flip-flops followed by the embarrassment of being reprimanded by a woman in a straw hat with the word Aruba in yellow. Grandpa Dan teaching her how to play cribbage while sipping on a gin rickey, the smell of lime still on his fingers. Jacqueline Thibaut cranking up her AC and her Satchmo so that Molly would know what it felt like to be cold enough for hot chocolate. The certainty that letting Dylan Henrickson feel her breasts had somehow given Grandma Lucy a heart attack.

Arguing with Zach over soapy red-sauce stained water in the kitchen at Odd Fellows and over a handful of black-eyed Susans and daisies on the sleeping porch. Zach naked and alive and Zach clothed and dead.

Miri's delight in sledding down Frog Hill by herself followed by a dog that was not hers. The worried look over her shoulder as she left home for her first date. Her thinly disguised embarrassment at introducing her parents to Alex's "nice" family.

On the gossamer screen was Death, too: the eater of Atomic wings, the stealer of Pinkies and Diet Cokes, the guardian of sleep, the drunk would-be hula-hoopist and reverent reciter of names, the believer in her, the chewer of condoms, the lover and finally, as a partner in a partnership that needed and deserved tending, loved.

The Chief Administrator looked at the battered, striving Rag in his hand. It was a mess, a disaster. A soul in a storm that didn't have enough sense to stay down when a tornado blew in.

And what was the point of it all?

Azrael didn't look at his Chief Administrator, but Abdiel heard him anyway.

These stories, the real stories, have a beginning you have no say in, a middle made up of a crapton of stupid decisions, an end you can't prepare for and no moral to make sense of it all.

But she did the best she could, Azrael said, his voice no longer cold and limitless, but broken and immediate.

And it was enough.

As the Chief Administrator watched his Ragpicker drop his lips to the body's closed eyes, Abdiel had an idea that did not sit well with him.

What if he'd been wrong?

What if this wreckage, this messy, excruciating *something* was better than nothing?

He shook his head, trying to clear the thought away. After all, he'd led in righteousness. He'd written the book of righteousness. He had to be—

Do not make the mistake, the Queen of Heaven's voice brushed against the limits of his mind, *of thinking that being righteous is the same as being right.*

There was a problem she didn't understand. If he'd been

wrong about even one thing, it would cast doubt on the right-ness of everything else.

Or what? This time it wasn't the Queen of Heaven's voice but the memory of the Ragpicker in that earlier moment when he smelled so earthly and questioned so openly.

What happens if we choose some other path?

Abdiel let go of the Rag and stared at the opalescent blobs in the trough behind the Mangles. He picked one up. It weebled for a moment, as they did, then went still and when he stretched it out, there was nothing in it but the distorted reflection of his own small eye.

"Well, *just darn it*," Abdiel said.

The Custodes gasped as their Chief Administrator let the soul fall back into the trough. When he stood up, he held instead the opalite pomander that Phanuel had lost in the confusion. He tossed it into the air once then twice, feeling its heft as it fell.

Then he threw it at the lead Mangle on the left which rico-cheted, hitting the lead Mangle on the right. A second later, those two first Mangles creaked and groaned and toppled, announcing their own destruction and the destruction of every Mangle hereafter.

A sea of faces looked at Abdiel, waiting for him to mark the narrow path of righteousness that would lead back to peace. With a sigh, he cracked his knuckles and stretched his neck from side to side.

"Listen up, boychicks." Styluses and parchment appeared from the folds of every robe. "I said **listen**," Abdiel intoned. "There are going to be some changes."

Bea scratched furiously at her instep with the toe of her other foot.

She hadn't seen *that* one coming. She'd been so sure that her miracle would be Miri or Azrael or Molly. But that was the thing about mistakes and miracles. You could never know what they led to. You didn't even know which was which.

The only thing she could say with any certainty about miracles was that they always came with casualties.

She sat down and wrapped her arms around Death, casualty of miracles, and began to sing him those songs she'd accumulated over centuries but that he was only now able to understand.

"I need to go," she eventually whispered. "Return her body. When I come back, you're going to have to let her go." She felt the tremor of worlds breaking inside him but the worlds outside held. "What do you want to do, little soul? Keep her with you? Shrink her universe down to a pocket the size of a half dollar?"

She stroked his hair and put her lips to his forehead, rocking him.

"Let her go, Neshama'le. When the time comes, you will find her again. They all come to you in the end."

CHAPTER 37

*I*n the end, Death had let Molly go, following her as best he could. He darted back and forth along ethereal winds until with a sudden gust, he lost track of her somewhere above the Florida Keys.

Tomorrow he would find an apartment in Havana, hoping that she had landed somewhere nearby. For now, he packed the chest he'd been schlepping since the Second Babylonian Captivity, only now it was filled not with ambergris and squirrel, but with five boxes of photographs, a faded red T-shirt, a crumpled green gauze butterfly and seven vases and no TEMPORARY CONTAINER because whatever she had been in life Mary Molloy's death had given him his one true miracle.

Death sat, the spiral-bound book with the red bucket that said FIRE dangling loose in his hands. Around him, in that millisecond when nobody else would die, the dust motes stayed suspended in the late autumn sun. Molly's clock, the one that looked like an old schoolhouse clock with a pendulum but was made from particles and plastic, took two AA batteries and said Montgomery Ward in flowing antique script, was silent.

Instead of recording big future events in her Bucket List,

Molly had filled it with page after page of the everyday: doctors' appointments, groceries, wedding venues, diaper services, groceries, insurance, pain relievers, groceries, chrysanthemums, birthday cake, milk. At the very end, she'd written in her rushed handwriting:

Deal with change.

The Bucket List would be placed reverently into his old chest. The Book of Admonishments went to Junk Luggers.

Death unzipped the dark green plastic suit bag containing the greatcoat that Molly had gotten Martinized back on that day when he'd texted her about the plague at PS42. He took it out, feeling the familiar weight of it. He unbuttoned the front, letting his fingers run over the stitching of the little pockets that Molly had reinforced so no soul would fall out when she wasn't there to help him find it.

Deal with change.

He found Miri sitting on a bench staring numbly at Lucy and her friend playing catch-the-leaves under a tree in the park's corner and he began to tell her everything. Miri listen to him silently, hit him twice and when he wrapped her in his arms, she cried and he cried.

Deal with change.

Then he went back to work.

Abdiel had said there would be change but Death no longer had the patience to wait for an official report folded like a young fiddlehead fern or a leafy sea dragon that would tell him that change had begun for real.

Instead, he did what Molly would have done and dealt with it himself. Holding that first basket filled with souls nestled under one arm, he climbed halfway Up, held on to a rung, and shook them out, dispersing them through the ether like dandelion seeds on a summer wind.

It took time but eventually and without the benefit of Veneration or Contemplation or fiddlehead ferns, things began to change.

The Rag of a girl who had been married off at eleven and died in childbirth at twelve, found itself reborn as the eldest son of the Headman in a village and when his time came, he stood against tradition and refused his blessing to the marriage of girls younger than sixteen.

A man whose country had been disdained and poisoned by the plunderings of richer nations returned as a journalist, an implacable exposer of those plunderings.

And a boy who had moved from foster home to foster home until he could bear it no longer, would, in his next life, care for forgotten child after forgotten child because it turned out to be nearly impossible to ignore other people's stories when they lived inside you.

As for Azrael himself, aside from visits to Miri that were often enough to give her love and support, but not so often as to give her osteoporosis, he worked tirelessly, searching the environs of every death for Molly.

Then one beautiful day in Antigua, he picked up a couple of American college kids from the bobbling wreckage of jet skis, alcohol and presumptions of immortality.

As he waded back to shore, a thin woman dressed in khakis and a pink polo shirt with a trident and seaweed and a hotel name embroidered in gold thread turned to watch him.

"Do I know you?"

ACKNOWLEDGMENTS

I started this journey out late in life and knowing nothing. The writers and readers who believed in my previous books gave me the courage to strike out on my own with this odd little book that fit nowhere.

If I acknowledged everyone I should, Molly would be double its current size, so let me start with the bare minimum. With Mel Sterling, editor extraordinaire, who made this better in every way. To Reina of Rickrack Books who through judicious copy-editing and proofreading, blocked my worst impulses.

To my friends and Beta readers--Adriana Anders, Marielle Brown, Ro Merrill, R.L. Davennor, and anyone else I forgot— I'm beyond grateful for your help and generosity.

To Victoria Heath Silk who took me by the hand when I was drowning and with the utmost patience and creative genius arrived at Molly's cover.

Finally, to the people at Sungrazer Publishing, who took a chance.

ABOUT THE AUTHOR

Maria Vale is a double-Rita finalist whose books have been listed by Amazon, Library Journal, Publishers Weekly, ALA Booklist, Kirkus, BookPage and others among their Best Books of the Year. Trained as a medievalist, she persists in trying to shoehorn dead languages into things that don't really need it. She lives in New York City with her husband and two kids.

ALSO BY MARIA VALE